Stay Away

By Anthony Stamp

Copyright 2025 Anthony Stamp
All rights reserved.
ISBN: 9798307687598

Cover Art © Max Goodyear

This is a work of fiction. Names, characters, businesses, places, events and incidents are either products of the author's imagination or used in a fictitious manner. Any resemblance to actual persons, living or dead, or actual events is purely coincidental.

No part of this publication may be reproduced, stored in a retrieval system or transmitted in any form or by any means without the prior permission in writing of the author nor be otherwise circulated in any form or binding or cover than that in which it is published and without a similar condition including this condition being imposed on the subsequent purchaser.

Prologue

Sitting on the cold, damp ground with her back up against the trunk of a large tree she wept. Tears rolled down her cheeks and dripped into her upturned hands; hands that were covered in blood. She closed her eyes tight, but her mind replayed every slash she had taken with her razor sharp claws. She hated what she was, what she had become.

The screams of her attackers as they realised their mistake echoed round her head. Her inner wolf remained alert and forever watchful, but Sally sat crying and ashamed.

Why had they followed her? She hadn't wanted to hurt them, but they'd pushed and taunted her, safe in the belief she was a defenseless girl. She'd tried to escape but they surrounded her, cornering, blocking off any escape route she'd had. That's not something you should do to a werewolf. Had they known what she really was they'd have stayed away. Thankfully she hadn't killed them. Their screams had drawn people to the alley to see what was going on. She had to flee before she was seen. Would the inevitable crowd that gathered believe the four guys when they heard their story? A young girl with claws and elongated canines would surely sound like a tall tale, wouldn't it?

She just wanted to be left alone to live in peace and to keep secret the truth of the monster she saw herself as.

The sound of police sirens getting closer brought her to her senses. It was time for her to go. She didn't have much time to get out of the area before the hunt would start and she would become the prey. She wiped her eyes with the back of her hand. She felt the blood smear across her cheek. Getting up on her feet she sniffed the air, then with a last look back over her shoulder towards the alley she made her way quickly through a nearby park and headed towards home.

She hadn't lived in the area for very long, a matter of weeks, but she knew she had to move on again. She seemed destined to continue the hunt for a place where she could feel safe, a place where she didn't have to fight to survive, a place where nobody knew what she was and wouldn't hunt her down like an animal, a place where she could finally settle down and make a friend, a real friend.

Chapter 1

The bushes to her left rustled as she ran along the footpath. She looked around, the rustling stopped. Probably a rabbit. She dismissed the thought. She continued on her way and the rustling started again, this time closer, the sound was following her. She ran faster, the noise from the bushes matched her pace and became more forceful. This was no rabbit. Clearly something substantially larger was moving through the shrubs. She ran at full speed away from the path and across the common. Suddenly, the animal burst from the hedge line and came racing towards her. She wasn't usually frightened of dogs, but this one was particularly large. She could hear the pounding of its paws on the ground getting closer. She glanced quickly back over her shoulder. She couldn't believe her eyes. If she didn't know any better, she would have sworn it was a wolf, but even then, an unusually big one. The wolf didn't slow or change its course. She felt fear starting to build inside and she froze. She stood and watched as the wolf closed in and her fear turned to panic. She turned and tried to flee but her legs felt like she was running through water.

The chase was no contest, and the wolf caught his prey easily. He closed his mouth around her arm and sharp elongated teeth pierced her tender flesh then continued into the bone. She cried out through gritted teeth as the immense pain shot through her arm. It took her breath away and her legs gave way underneath her. She tried to curl up in a ball, an automatic reaction to the agony and the attack.

The wolf continued to bite and rip at her flesh. She lashed out with her hands in panic, desperate to get the animal off her. In the struggle they both rolled down the grassy embankment. The wolf lost his grip, but no sooner had she reached the gulley at the bottom the wolf was on top of her again, biting her arms as she tried to protect her face, slashing its razor sharp claws through her clothing and across her stomach. Each slash felt like a hot knife, the sting of the claws opening her skin was nothing she had ever felt before. More pain shot through her body, along every nerve and through every muscle. There was blood everywhere now and the wolf slipped into a feeding frenzy, growling and snapping his jaws, biting anything he could get at, ripping off chunks of flesh. In horror, the girl realized the wolf wasn't attacking, it was eating. She screamed and the wolf howled at the moon.

Sally was woken by her own scream. She sat up quickly, breathless and panting. Her skin was cold and sticky with sweat, her hair clung to her head as if she had just stepped out of the shower, her heart racing inside her chest.

The nightmares had never gone away and they were always the same, always about the night when she stopped being a human, the night when her life changed forever and she was turned into a monster, a creature which often frequented other people's nightmares, the night she became a werewolf.

The memory of the wolf attack was as clear now as the night it happened. Sometimes she wished the local werewolf pack had let the rogue wolf finish her off instead of running him out of town. The pack saw it as saving her life, Sally didn't. To her they'd simply sentenced her to a life of nightmares and rejection. The rejection by people had stopped when she came to Popwood, but then again, the residents here didn't know what she was. The nightmares, on the other hand, continued.

She sat in bed, the sheets twisted and tangled around her body and legs where she had tossed and turned in her sleep, trying desperately to get free of the wolf's jaws. She disentangled herself from the bed clothes and made her way to the bathroom where she splashed water on her face. There was no going back to sleep now. She stepped into the shower and turned on the less than powerful jet. After that she felt more awake and padded bare foot into the kitchen.

Sitting at the kitchen table she ate the breakfast she had prepared the night before; a nice healthy mix of cereal, fruit and natural yoghurt. Her wolf wanted meat and grumbled inside but her human side couldn't face anything more than her healthy option this early in the morning.

Her desk in the living room was covered in papers, notes

she'd made, cuttings from newspapers and ideas for magazine and news articles. She flicked through each pile waiting for something to shout, 'write about me' but nothing seemed to spark her interest. One of the drawbacks of living in a sleepy little village like Popwood was nothing newsworthy for a freelance journalist to write about ever happened. Working in The Black Bull behind the bar and as a waitress may pay the bills but it was never going to satisfy her need to investigate and write interesting stories; stories of life and living, of fears and adventures, of politics and corruption.

The cereal had used up the last of the milk in her fridge. Luckily, living above the village post office, which also doubled as a one stop shop for the locals meant she didn't have to go far for fresh supplies. Dressing quickly in an old Classic Rock tee shirt and a pair of jeans, she headed downstairs, appearing in the shop from behind the counter.

"Mind you don't stand on anything sharp, Sally," shouted Joyce the shopkeeper. Popping down into the shop in her bare feet was a regular occurrence for Sally. "Becky was in earlier and knocked over a box of drawing pins when she was getting some coloured pens from the stationary shelf."

"Okay Joyce, cheers," replied Sally.

"Oh, and she said when you eventually roll out of bed, to tell you to meet her in The Black Bull before it opens. I told her you work very hard on your newspaper articles on a night so not to be so cheeky. You deserve a sleep in now and again."

Sally looked at her watch, it read 07:08. What sort of time did these people get up if they considered this time of the morning to be a sleep in?

She spent the next couple of hours trying to make a story about mountain bikes damaging the foot paths through the north woods sound interesting and newsworthy. It wasn't going well so she gave up and headed off to The Black Bull to meet Becky.

"Morning sleepy head," laughed Becky as Sally walked through the door. "Lovely day, isn't it?"

Becky's hair was immaculately done as always. How she found the time to coax her mass of black hair into those beautiful, flowing curls every day Sally had no idea. Running a brush quickly through her own blonde hair each morning was about all Sally could manage. Thankfully her hair was straight as sticks and only about shoulder length.

"I've been up hours writing thank you very much," Sally replied. "Anyway, why are you so cheerful this morning?" Sally knew quite well that Becky was never anything but cheerful.

Becky smiled and patted Sally on the cheek.

"I guess it's just seeing your happy smiling face."

Handing Sally a poster, she had obviously just finished making, Becky added, "Here, make yourself useful and stick this up on the notice board out the back."

"What is it?"

"A poster."

"I can see that," said Sally, rolling her eyes. "What's it for?"

"Well read it and find out."

Becky headed off to the noticeboard at the front of the pub and with the drawing pins she hadn't managed to spread over the floor in the village shop she attached her colourful and cheery poster.

Sally disappeared in the other direction down the corridor behind the bar which led to the kitchen. She walked slowly as she read the poster.

The Black Bull
10 Year Anniversary BBQ & Camp
South Woods Clearing

All Staff Invited
Saturday 16th July

(Bring Your Own Tent – Food & Drink Provided)

"A barbeque and camp!" she shouted.

"Yes," replied Becky, popping her head through the door from the bar again. She continued before Sally had a chance to reply, "isn't it exciting? You can share my tent. Tim's providing all the food and drink. He's even letting Regular

Dave run the bar for the night so everybody can go. It's going to be a great night."

Regular Dave was The Black Bull's pet name for Dave Kennedy, who was their oldest regular customer and rarely missed a night. Tim Shepperd, the Black Bull's landlord had never let anybody take over the pub, Sally wasn't even sure if Tim had ever been on holiday. She certainly wasn't sure letting Regular Dave run the pub for the night was one of the best ideas Tim had ever had.

Sally made a quick mental calculation and was a bit happier when she realized the date of the barbeque wasn't a full moon night. However, it was close enough for her to be starting to get a little bit edgy.

"I've never been camping," said Sally.

"You'll love it," Becky replied, in her usual enthusiastic way. "I can't wait. I've been to see Bill up at the farm and he is going to let us borrow the big half barrels they use for the summer fete barbeques, and then there's the generator of course. I thought me and you could make bunting to decorate the clearing, so it looks a bit more colourful and-"

"Bunting?" said Sally, interrupting Becky who was in full flow. "You want me to make bunting?"

"Yeah, it'll be fun. I've nearly got everything we need."

"Can't we just buy some off the internet?"

"No," said Becky. "Making it will be much more enjoyable and a lot cheaper."

Becky was a true villager and had lived in Popwood all her life. Her family had been the local organizers of every event happening in the village. When her mother and father moved to the Lake District to take over her Gran's guest house, Becky had remained in Popwood and continued her family's tradition. Sally had heard stories from Becky about the summer fetes, steam rallies, horse shows and agricultural shows to name just a few. It seemed somebody from the Millar family had always played a large part in organizing each of them and Becky Millar wasn't ready to let that particular tradition slip just yet.

Sally fixed the poster to the noticeboard and tried to think of a suitable excuse to get her out of having to go camping, where she would undoubtedly catch the scent of rabbits and trees and the fresh evening breeze; all the things that stirred the wolf inside her.

"Are you sure people will want me there?" Sally asked. "After all, I've not lived here very long."

"Of course they will. You may not have lived here very long but you work in The Black Bull, and this is a party for us, not just the village."

Sally just screwed up her face. She had always tried to keep away from large groups of people. Her inner wolf got agitated if she felt crowded, and if her wolf was edgy then so was Sally.

"Aww, come on, Sal. It'll be fun."

Sally didn't answer, she just stared at the poster, trying to find a way out of going but coming up with nothing. She felt Becky's arm slip around her waist.

"What's up, Sal?"

Sally paused. "I'm just not very good around people."

"Sally. You work in a pub. You're around people all the time."

"That's different," Sally replied. "I'm working when I'm in here. I don't have to worry about whether people like me or what they're thinking."

"Well, on the 16th of July you'll be partying instead of working," said Becky and gave Sally a little hug before making her way back through to the bar. "I don't know what you're worried about. Everybody likes you." She shouted as she disappeared through the door. "You always get the most tips so you must be doing something right."

***

Over the next two weeks Becky rushed around making sure everything was organized so there would be no last-minute surprises. Most days Sally spent at least some time at Becky's house, helping her make enough bunting to circumnavigate the earth and trying to convince her inner wolf that being surrounded by a large group of partying humans wouldn't be as bad as it sounded. Her wolf wasn't convinced.

As the day grew nearer, Sally started to feel a little more comfortable about it. Popwood was the only place she'd been able to fit in, maybe it was time to start getting to know the rest of the village a little better and try to become one of them.

The morning of the barbeque and camping celebrations was the start of a lovely sunny day, and the weather forecast suggested the whole weekend was going to be the same, hot sunny days and warm summer nights. They couldn't have planned it better if they tried.

Becky came calling early and dragged Sally out to help set up the camping area. The first thing they did was to put up their own tent. Sally managed to persuade Becky that their tent should be located near the edge of the clearing. She didn't want to be in the middle of the God knows how many other tents, her wolf was already wanting to pace and the best way Sally could think of to calm her down was to select a spot with an easy escape route to the surrounding woods.

As the area took shape and the decorations were looped from tree to tree, Sally actually started to feel happy about being there. She had to admit, Becky had a real knack for creating the best atmosphere possible. The small clearing looked beautiful and peaceful with sunlight beaming through the tops of the trees, and there was the sound of birds singing all around them.

By midafternoon more of The Black Bull staff started to arrive, pitching their tents and visiting the recently erected beer tent. Somebody had brought a small but powerful music system and Sally's idea of a beautiful and peaceful place in the natural world was shattered.

The two half barrels on legs, serving as a barbeque grill, were lit and once the shout, 'grubs up', went out everybody descended upon them, each coming away with plates full with steak, sausages, beef burgers, chicken, skewers, jacket potatoes, salad and sweet corn. In fact, Sally couldn't think of any traditional barbeque fare not on offer. The food and drink didn't look like it would run out any time soon and the more people consumed the happier and louder the party became.

When darkness eventually did come and the temperature started to cool a little, Becky supervised the positioning and lighting of a large metal fire pit in the centre of the clearing. This girl seems to have thought of everything, thought Sally. Camping chairs were then pulled up around the fire and from somewhere a couple of guitars appeared. Sally's biggest surprise of the whole day was when Becky got up and, accompanied by Tim the landlord on guitar, she sang a stunning version of Purple Rain by Prince. Sally didn't know Becky had such a beautiful voice and she just sat back and let the feeling and emotion in Becky's performance wash over her. Even her inner wolf curled up and dozed. At the end everybody clapped and cheered, Sally got to her feet in appreciation of her best friend's talent.

"That was beautiful, Bex," said Sally when Becky

returned to the seat next to hers. "I had no idea you could sing like that."

"She's the pride of the village and no mistake," shouted Tim.

For once Becky was a little speechless and just smiled while her cheeks flushed red.

"So, what other hidden talents do you have you haven't told me about?" Sally asked.

"Me?" said Becky with a laugh and took a long cool drink. "It's you who has the secrets."

Sally suddenly started to feel uneasy and wondered what, if anything, Becky had heard. Did she suspect that Sally was a werewolf after all? She felt the fear start deep in her stomach; the fear she would be called out for what she really was in front of everybody; the fear that her peaceful stay in a quiet little village would soon be over.

"What do you mean?"

"Well," Becky sat forward, "I've just realized I've been your friend for about a year now and I don't even know where you come from. All I know is you're a Northern Lass, as you put it." Becky emphasized the words, 'Northern Lass', by holding up her hands and miming some inverted commas with her fingers.

"Oh, I'm just from a little place in the northeast that you won't have heard of."

Becky gave Sally a look, which clearly meant 'You're

keeping secrets' but before Becky could press the point the music stopped, and people were shouting for Becky to give them another song.

"Come on!" said Becky, standing and holding out her hand to Sally. "You can help me with this one."

Despite Sally's protests, Becky dragged her up out of her chair and told Tim to start playing, Crazy Little Thing Called Love. Sally joined in rather quietly but did her best to distract Becky from thinking anymore about any secrets.

As the evening went on, the fire in the metal fire pit died down and people started to slip away to their tents. Sally and Becky were the last to turn in, because Becky insisted on making sure the fire was out, and the lights and generator were tuned off. The woods suddenly returned to its normal peaceful old self. The kind of woods Sally enjoyed the most.

Once they were in the tent and tucked up two surprisingly warm sleeping bags, Becky took no time dropping off to sleep. She hadn't mentioned secrets anymore, but Sally still couldn't settle, her mind kept repeating over and over Becky's comment from earlier – "It's you who has the secrets." She lay there for a couple of hours, but the words wouldn't go away, they just echoed around inside her head. Eventually she gave up trying to sleep and crept out of the tent, hoping some fresh air would clear her mind.

She noticed the scent immediately, it was unmistakable, and her wolf shot to attention at once, her hackles beginning to rise. Sally froze and looked around the area for the source of the scent, seeing easily through the darkness with her enhanced werewolf sight. She suppressed a growl when she saw a large black wolf with its paws up on the barbeque table eating what was left of the sausages and beef burgers. Anybody could have seen this was larger than a wolf should normally be, but the scent told Sally exactly what it was, a werewolf.

She hadn't had any trouble from other werewolves since coming to Popwood, so seeing one now was something she wasn't ready for. Sally was downwind so if she just kept still maybe the werewolf would eat it's fill from the table then slip back into the woods. She watched as the wolf did just that, slipping silently between some bushes and into the tress. But now what? Sally now knew there was a werewolf prowling the area and would soon get sick of leftover sausages and possibly come back looking for fresh meat and live prey.

There was nothing else for it, she would have to track him and make sure he stayed away from the camp, but she would have to do it in her human form, which wasn't ideal. *Change, let me out, he's in our territory.* Her inner wolf was agitated. Not now, Sally thought to herself and to her wolf, I can't change while there are people around. Somebody may get hurt. *There's danger, let me out.*

Once the werewolf was out of the clearing Sally made her way to the trees where he had disappeared and she crouched just inside the cover of the bushes, sniffing, testing the air, searching for the werewolf. She found a trail leading away from the camp. She followed it slowly and silently. He seemed to be just walking normally and not hunting like a wolf would ordinarily be doing. This was extraordinarily strange behavior for a werewolf in his wolf form. Why would he have shifted fully if he wasn't hunting? She continued to follow and left the camp further and further behind. Maybe he was genuinely just passing through and was now making his way out of the area and away from Popwood.

She was about to abandon her tracking and return to the others when she saw him. A huge black male werewolf with a powerful body and large paws, he looked even bigger from here. He turned slowly but didn't attack, he just stood there watching as if he was studying her.

Sally could feel her hackles rising again under her skin and a warning growl came instinctively from deep within her throat. She was no real match for a fully shifted werewolf while she was still in human form, but shifting now wasn't an option, he would be on her before she could complete the change and would probably kill her straight away. Her inner wolf, however, wouldn't back down. Showing a sign of weakness now could be suicide.

She started to slowly back up hoping to get a tree or two between her and the wolf. It was then Sally caught the second scent. This wasn't a lone wolf. The second scent seemed to be heading in the direction of the camp. She had been tricked and let the wolf lead her away from the humans she was trying to protect. She knew the male wolf could move faster than her in his wolf form, but she retained a lot of her wolf speed while she was human. She had to try to warn the others so she turned and set off as fast as she could. Her werewolf speed and strength, mixed with her human agility, helped her stay ahead of the advancing predator for the moment but she wasn't sure for how long. He seemed to slow as Sally got closer to the camp then, to her surprise, he just gave up. She never slowed to find out why. She continued straight to the camp as fast as she could.

She could still smell the other werewolf inside the camp when she got back to the clearing but what she saw sent a stab of fear deep into her heart. The second werewolf, a slightly smaller dark brown female, was stalking up to a tree ready to pounce. Standing with her back to the tree, a look of terror on her face and unable to move was Becky. She was trying to scream but no sound was coming out and her knees were starting to give way. The female werewolf was moving slowly towards her, teeth bared, and her powerful legs flexed ready to lunge.

Sally ran at full speed across the open camp area and slammed into the side of the female werewolf. In a flurry of limbs, claws, growls and snarls they both rolled into the bushes to the side of Becky and disappeared from view.

Stay Away

She got her arms around the wolf's neck and squeezed. It was like holding onto a bucking bronco. The werewolf worked herself free and Sally felt a claw slash across her face then teeth bury into her upper arm. Sally's fingers grew claws of her own and she sank them into the wolf's shoulder, the pain forcing it to let go. Before Sally could recover, the wolf was on her again slashing and biting. Both her hands had grown claws by this time and Sally put all her force behind a flurry of punches and slashes, forcing the wolf away. Sally's teeth elongated and she sank them into fur and flesh then with a twist of her body she managed to throw the wolf off of her and it rolled down the bank. Sally was up in an instant and ready for the wolf to renew her attack. The werewolf didn't attack however, she just got to her feet and stared at Sally, who returned the challenge with her own stare. The supernatural female intruder then turned and continued down the hill, disappearing into some more bushes and away.

Sally calmed herself and her inner wolf the best she could. Her claws slowly disappeared and her teeth returned to their normal size and shape. She then made her way back through the bushes at the top of the hill to Becky, who was still frozen to the spot, the look of terror still on her face. As Sally emerged Beck dropped to her knees, tears streaming down her face. Sally held out a hand to her.

"Come on Bex," Sally whispered. "Let's get you back to our tent".

Becky couldn't speak, only stare at all the wounds on her friends' face and arms. Sally pushed her gently back into their tent.

"Oh my God, Sally. Look at you. That big dog."

"Listen," said Sally, "I'm alright. I just need to go. Okay?"

"You're hurt."

"I'm fine."

"But the blood."

"Bex, I have no time to explain," said Sally. She could hear some of the others venturing out of their tents to see what all the noise had been about. "I need to get away from the camp and I need you to stay in the tent."

"But you need to get to a hospital, Sally." Becky managed to splutter.

"I'll be fine honest. Just trust me on this. Please."

"Sally you're cut to ribbons."

Sally held out her bloody hands, palms up, "Shh, Becky. The others will hear. Just stay here and pretend you never heard anything. Tell them I went home poorly during the night. I'll explain everything tomorrow."

"Sally!"

"Please, Bex," panic starting to appear in her voice. "Promise me you'll stay in here. Don't tell them I'm hurt. Please. It's important. I'll explain, I promise. But not now. I have to go. Promise me, Bex."

Eventually Becky nodded. "Okay I promise," she said.

With that Sally was gone, using the darkness of the camp to slip quietly away into the night.

She wasn't about to abandon the camp and leave everybody at the mercy of two supernatural predators though. Ignoring the pain of her injuries, Sally prowled around the perimeter of the camp, searching for signs of the two werewolves. All she found was the scent from where they had entered and left the campsite. She decided to follow the trail of the female. It led away from bushes where they had fought until it joined with the male a short distance away. From there they both headed west, away from the camp. For the next hour Sally roamed the area in case the two werewolves returned. Once she was convinced they'd gone, she carefully made her way home so she wasn't seen and got cleaned up.

Why had the two wolves just given up and moved away from the camp? She couldn't understand their behavior at all. If they were intent on attacking humans, then even a full campsite would be no match for two fully shifted werewolves. It didn't make a lot of sense. She was only happy she'd managed to get back to the camp before the female had attacked Becky.

Tears filled her eyes when she thought of her friend. How was she going to explain this? When Becky found out what she was it would mean the end of their friendship. There was no way she was going to be able to hide it now. Becky had seen all her injuries, injuries which were already almost fully healed. By the time she met Becky tomorrow she wouldn't have a scratch, and Becky would guess what she was and only see the monster, not the girl she really was inside.

If the villagers found out as well, she would be driven out. No ordinary person would want a supernatural monster living next door. Everybody in Popwood had always been friendly and kind, but all that changes when the fear starts to build, and the rumours spread and grow. Farm animals that had been attacked by foxes would now all be blamed on her. Farmers protecting their livestock usually come hunting with shotguns and there's no telling who else would get hurt just because of her.

Sally didn't get any more sleep. She sat up in the dark trying desperately to come up with a story that would explain to Becky the events of the night and the lack of injuries in the morning. She drew a blank.

Chapter 2

It was early the next morning when Sally stood outside Becky's front door. She stared at the doorbell, not sure if she wanted to press it, now she was here. Her stomach was turning somersaults, and her hands were shaking and sweaty. She shifted her weight from one foot to the other. Her fingers fidgeted with the hem of her jacket. She tried to tell herself the conversation might go better than she expected. After all, Becky was her best friend, and best friends understand when the other has troubles on her mind don't they? Anything was possible. But she knew from bitter experience that it was much more likely to go badly. Heartbreakingly badly.

Her mind flooded with dozens of thoughts, each one a reason to turn round and go home yet she knew she couldn't. She had to knock; she had to face whatever judgement awaited her on the other side. Still, her hand wavered, hovering just inches from the doorbell, trembling with doubt. The familiar scent of blooming flowers from Becky's hanging baskets, along with the faint aroma of coffee and bacon sandwiches coming from inside the house filled her nostrils. The smell served as a reminder of the warmth and comfort she yearned but sensed was slipping away. She reached for the doorbell once more, only to hesitate again. What could she say when Becky asked where all her injuries were? What explanation can she possibly offer that wasn't going to cause her friend to freak out? The Lycanthropy had worked its magic and healed everything. The lacerations on her neck and face, once so visible, were now nowhere to be seen. There was no other way. She had to tell Becky the truth and hope her friend would understand then see there was a lot more to her than the stigma attached to the word, werewolf. It was a big ask. She took a deep breath and pressed Becky's doorbell.

The door had barely opened when Becky launched herself at Sally, flung her arms around her neck and hugged her tight.

"Thank, God you're alright," said Becky still holding on. She didn't seem to want to let go so, with a little trepidation, Sally wrapped her arms gently around her too, wondering if this was going to be the last time her touch would be welcome.

Eventually, Becky stepped back. Sally held her breath.

"I'm sorry Sal," she said. "I hope I didn't hurt you. I just-"

The look on Becky's face said it all, Sally knew what her friend was looking for, the cuts and bites she'd seen only eight hours before, but she wouldn't find any, not even a scratch. Sally stood there and let Becky look, not trying to hide anything. There was no point trying to pretend anymore.

"You… you're not hurt." Becky stammered. "She looked down Sally's arms and up on her neck. She put out her hand and touched the skin on Sally's face. "I thought… I thought that dog had savaged you all over. You were covered in blood, you had cuts everywhere, your face was… it was cut to ribbons."

Sally wasn't sure what to do next. Any vague plan she had for what to say, how to start this off, had vanished just like her injuries. She was sure the doorstep wasn't the place for whatever was going to happen next though.

"Can I come in?" said Sally. "There's something I need to tell you."

Becky just stared, her mouth open, a mixture of shock and confusion all over her face.

"Please." Sally almost begged when Becky didn't say anything.

"Err, yes of course," said Becky, snapping out of her trance and stepping back to let Sally walk in. The barking that usually greeted Sally whenever she visited Becky started at once. "I'll just put Penny out the back.

Sally stood in the middle of the room living feeling like she was waiting to take the long walk to the gallows. When Becky came back, she sat down slowly on the settee, waiting for Sally to say something, her eyes wide and her mouth open. She said nothing, just sat there, staring. Sally thought she looked like somebody waiting for an explanation; she was right, and Becky deserved one.

"This isn't easy." Sally started to pace back and forth across the carpet. "I don't know exactly how to say what I have to. I suppose I'd better just come right out with it." She paused again. Becky's eyes were still searching her face and arms where she'd seen cuts and blood the night before. "How can I put this?"

Sally continued to pace, wanting to say the words but frightened of the response she was going to get.

"Will you sit down and just tell me. I don't understand, Sally. Where're all the cuts?"

Sally continued to pace up and down. Becky patted the seat next to her.

"Sally, sit down and tell me. You're driving me crazy with all this wandering about."

Sally stopped pacing then sat at the opposite end of the three-seater settee, not wanting to get too close to Becky and still struggling to find the words. This wasn't the sort of thing she could just blurt out, but there was no easy or gentle way to put it.

"Sally, you're scaring me. What is it?"

Sally looked across at Becky, ready to gauge her reaction, then she took a breath. This was it, there was no going back now.

"There's a reason why I don't have any injuries from last night." Sally paused yet again, one last attempt at trying to find a different way to explain it. "I'm not what you think I am."

Becky looked confused. There was another silence

while Sally searched for the words again.

"What do you mean? That doesn't make sense," said Becky.

Sally paused again but there was no getting out of it. She just had to say it outright, so she closed her eyes and said the one sentence she had never wanted to say to anybody, but especially not to Becky.

"I'm a Werewolf."

The room went silent, and time seemed to slow down. Sally was sure even the clock on the mantelpiece stopped ticking for a second as its heart skipped a beat too. She was holding her breath and Becky was doing the same, still staring with ever widening eyes and her mouth wide open now.

"You're a what?" Becky finally managed to say.

"I'm a Werewolf." Sally repeated. "You know, the full moon and howling type of thing. A Werewolf."

There was another awkward silence before Becky carried on.

"Come on, Sal. Stop mucking about."

"I'm not. It's true. I'm a werewolf."

"A werewolf," Becky repeated slowly.

Sally just nodded. Becky's face went pale.

"Don't be silly. What's this all about, Sally?"

"Look I know it's not easy to believe but it's the truth. I was bitten by one when I was sixteen and now, I'm one too."

Becky got up off the settee, walked a few paces and

turned to face Sally.

"Sal, I'm not sure why you think this is a joke, but I can promise you, it's not funny."

She stared again at Sally's face and arms.

"It's not a joke, Bex."

Becky backed up until she was against the wall, saying nothing, just staring. The barking from Penny outside getting louder. Her trance breaking when Penny's barking reached more of a screech than a bark.

"Penny! Be quiet!" Becky yelled, and the barking stopped. "No, Sally. Stop this game. I want to know what's going on."

Sally got to her feet and Becky seemed to try and push herself into the wall.

"It's not a game, Bex," said Sally. "Look," and she showed Becky her arms once more. "You saw the cuts and bites I had last night. They wouldn't just heal overnight, would they. Not unless I wasn't quite normal, wasn't quite… human."

This was it. The moment Sally knew was coming. The moment Becky told her to get away from her, to get out of her house, the moment she lost her best friend.

Becky slowly reached out and touched Sally's face again then pulled her hand away quickly. Sally took Becky's hand and put it back to her cheek.

"See," said Sally, "The cuts really have gone."

"But how?" asked Becky.

"It's called Lycanthropy. As well as being a kind of half human, half wolf, it gives me the ability to heal quickly."

"But that's impossible. There's no such thing as werewolves."

Sally took Becky's small letter opener from the mantlepiece and made a little cut on her hand.

"Watch."

She held out her hand so Becky could see the cut. As Becky stared the blood stopped, the cut closed slowly then grew steadily smaller until it vanished.

"That's what happened to the cuts you seen me with last night."

"Then it's true. You really are a…"

Sally nodded.

"A werewolf. I didn't want you to find out like this. I didn't really want you to find out at all."

"Why?" asked Becky.

"Because I didn't want you to hate me."

"Why would I hate you?"

"Because that's what usually happens when people find out they have a monster living near them."

"You're not a monster."

"I am, Bex. When I change, that's what I become. A werewolf. A monster."

"Stop saying that. You're my best friend."

"I know," replied Sally, "and you're mine. But you've

never seen me as I really am."

"This is how you really are, Sal." Becky looked Sally up and down. "This! How you are now."

"Not when I change. You wouldn't like me then. You'd be scared of me."

"No, I wouldn't," said Becky far more calmly than Sally had expected. She obviously hadn't taken in the full meaning of what Sally was saying yet.

"Well, you're in a minority, Bex. Other people get scared. That's why I never tell anybody."

Who else knows?"

"Nobody. Well, other werewolves I've met know straight away. We have a very good sense of smell. I can't hide it from them, and they can't hide it from me."

"What about your family?"

Sally's eyes started to well up with tears.

"Yes, they know. I had to tell them."

"How did they take it?"

"Not well," said Sally, "Mam wouldn't believe it and thought I was going off my trolley. She still won't talk to me about it. She gets very upset whenever my, condition, as she calls it, is mentioned. I think she's a little frightened of me too."

"That's quite sad," said Becky. "What about your dad?"

"When I finally convinced him I was telling the truth, he went off it. I got a lecture about how I'd promised not to go on the common on my own and how I'd let him down.

Whenever the subject comes up he just gets angry and vows to get hold of the one who did it, string him up and kill him very slowly. He gets a little over dramatic sometimes."

"You can't really blame him for feeling like that."

"I don't," Sally agreed, "and if I ever meet the one who did this to me, I think I'd be happy to do dad's bidding for him."

Becky sat back a little at that comment. A concerned look came over her face.

"Don't worry," she added, "I'm not a killer. I just get a little over dramatic too. I've never killed anybody."

Becky relaxed again and smiled but if Sally was honest with herself, if she did ever meet her attacker she would make him pay dearly for what he'd done to her, what he'd made her into.

"So how did you get bitten by a werewolf?"

"I was out for a run on The Common. I heard it in the bushes and ran but I wasn't fast enough. The local werewolf pack found me half eaten and took me in."

"Jeez. That's awful," said Becky. A look of horror on her face.

"Yes, well as my dad had angrily explained, if I hadn't gone out on The Common alone while they were away like I'd promised, I wouldn't have been turned into this creature."

"Don't describe yourself like that," said Becky, a look of sorrow, almost pity on her face.

"Sorry."

There was a moment of stillness where the two girls just stood and looked at each other. Sally didn't know what else to say and was relieved when Becky eventually spoke.

"Do you have any brothers or sisters?" asked Becky?

"Yeah, I have a younger sister, Jasmine." Sally was happy to move on from the subject of killing, being bitten and wanting revenge on the werewolf responsible but went a little quiet at the mention of her sister's name. Thoughts of how much she missed Jasmine and what the werewolf attack had robbed her of flashed through her mind. The trips to the playground and theatre, the days spent in town shopping and the tradition of ending the day with Jasmine's favourite ice cream. These were all memories she wished she could forget because they hurt so much, but at the same time she needed to remember them. She missed Jasmine most of all.

"Were you and Jasmine very close?"

Becky reached out her hand and rested it on Sally's arm as if she sensed the feelings Sally was going through. It was a comforting touch which Sally appreciated. They both sat on the settee at Becky's coaxing. This time Sally didn't sit at the opposite end.

"Yeah," Sally nodded, "we still are. She isn't scared of me. She doesn't see me as a monster. She just wants me to be there. I wish I could be."

"You're not a monster."

Sally laughed, "I don't think everybody would agree with you there. The only time I've not felt like a monster since it happened is on the few occasions I've met up with Jasmine."

"You've been back home then."

"No," said Sally, "it would only cause trouble with the local pack there. I had a bit of trouble with them."

"Trouble?"

"There's certain pack etiquette which I didn't agree with. The alpha female decided to make an example of me and her and two of her Lieutenants jumped me once night on my way home. I made a bit of a mess of them."

"You beat them up?"

"Kind of. Anyway, after that they saw me as a threat and wanted me out of their territory. In return they promised to protect my family and make sure they remained safe as long as I never came back. I think it was a threat, but I took it as a guarantee of my family's safety. So, I left."

"So, you can't see your family?"

Sally shook her head.

"They've travelled to see me a few times, when it's been safe enough. I loved seeing them." A tear finally escaped from Sally's eye. "Jas always gets herself upset though when it's time for them to go. She threatened to run away a few times and come and live with me. That's why I've had to stop telling them where I am. After their last visit that's what she did and turned up on my doorstep. I took her home, or as close as I could anyway, but mam blamed me for encouraging her, which I hadn't, and there was a big argument. Mam made it clear that she didn't want Jas to turn into. 'a thing like you'. It was when she used the word 'thing' to describe me that I decided to move on again and not tell them where I was. I've not seen Jas since."

More tears escaped from Sally's eyes and trickled down her cheeks and she felt Becky's arms around her.

"I'm sure she didn't mean it like that," said Becky.

"She did. Don't worry, Bex. I'm fine. I just miss them, that's all. I don't like not being able to see them because I'm like this. I hate being a monster." She caught the look in Becky's eyes at the word and corrected herself for Becky's sake. "I mean a werewolf."

"It's really sad seeing you like this, Sal," said Becky. "I don't think I know you very well at all and I thought I did."

"You know me better than anybody, Bex. I've not told anybody about my family or my background, the real me."

"You've always dodged the subject when I've brought it up. I just thought there'd been a big family fight, and you would tell me about it when you were ready."

"Well, in a way that's the truth."

"You should tell them to come and visit you here," said Becky, "your family I mean. They must be missing you and your mum can see it's a nice place and everybody here likes you."

Sally could tell Becky was trying to lighten the mood.

"I can't bring them here. They aren't safe around me. It's better for them if I stay away. I don't think mam and dad like me anymore anyway."

"I don't believe that for one second, Sal. I think it's just an excuse." Becky paused, "Come on. What're you really afraid of?"

Sally thought for a few seconds. What was it that had her so determined to isolate herself from her family? She had always known the answer to that question really. She'd just never admitted it to herself.

"Just getting them hurt. I don't want them in any danger because I've turned into this… this thing."

Becky stroked her hand up and down Sally's arm again. "You're not a thing so stop talking like that. You're my best friend."

"Well, you're my only friend," said Sally. "I've searched for a place without a werewolf pack for a long time, somewhere I could settle and make a friend. Somewhere nobody had to know what I really was. I didn't think I'd ever find a place like that, until I came here."

"Well, there aren't any werewolves around here, are there." Becky said with a smile.

"No," Sally laughed, "Just me. The one you seen last night won't stay around now I've shown my face."

Sally realised what she'd said the moment the words

came out of her mouth. Becky froze, her mouth open and her eyes wide once more.

"Oh my God." She sat up straight and stared at Sally. "That big dog last night was a werewolf? I was about to be attacked by a werewolf? It was going to bite me and make me one too."

Sally reached out and took Becky's hand.

"No, she wasn't. She was just trying to keep you away from the food. She was hungry. That's all."

Sally thought it was best to make up something that wasn't as frightening as the truth and sounded almost feasible. It didn't work.

"Yeah, hungry for something a bit tastier than some overcooked, leftover burgers."

Becky's breathing got faster, and Sally could feel her starting to shake.

"Hey, don't worry," Sally spoke softly, trying to sound as calm and comforting as she could. "They've gone now. They were just passing through."

Becky seemed to calm a little for a moment until what Sally had said registered.

"They?" Becky gripped Sally's hand tighter, "You said 'they'. Oh my God how many of them are out there." Becky was starting to shake again.

"Hey, hey, it's okay," said Sally, trying her best to calm down a now hyperventilating Becky. "There was only two, but they're gone now. I was tracking the male when I caught the scent of the female coming from the direction of the camp. That's when I ran back and, well, you know the rest."

With a few deep breaths and some reassuring strokes on the arm from Sally, Becky managed to calm down.

"You came back and saved me," Becky smiled, "I can't believe you fought a werewolf for me."

"Becky," said Sally, looking her straight in the eyes, "I am a werewolf."

"Oh yeah," Becky started to laugh, "I bet you can kick some serious butt too."

"I sure can," said Sally with a smile and a squeeze of Becky's hand, "so don't worry. Nobody is going to hurt you while I'm around." She wiped away a tear from Becky's cheek.

"I think it could prove very useful having a werewolf as a friend."

They both laughed and gave each other a long loving hug.

"I can see a problem though," said Becky, looking up from the embrace, "If I get into any trouble it will have to be during a full moon." She started to laugh but stopped when Sally didn't. "Sorry, did I make a bad joke."

"Promise me you'll stay well away from me on full moon nights."

Becky nodded. "Okay."

"I mean it, Bex, stay away."

"Yeah, well away. I promise."

Sally paused and took a few deep breaths.

"Good," she said, calming down a little and smiling, "Besides, I don't need the full moon to shift. The full moon is just the time I can't stop the change, not for long anyway. I can hold it off for a few hours but eventually I have to shift under a full moon."

"You don't need the moon?" said Becky, "I thought when the full moon comes out werewolves change but were just people at other times."

"You watch too much television," Sally started to laugh, "Don't believe everything you see in the late-night horror films."

"So, I suppose the old silver bullet thing is wrong as well."

"No, that one's true. I can't go near silver at all, or it makes my skin burn and blister, it's very painful. If the silver gets into my bloodstream, well then, it's game over."

"Oh dear," said Becky sitting up straight again, "I gave you a silver necklace for your birthday, didn't I?"

"You did," Sally laughed again, "Which is why it's still in its box in my bedside drawer. Sorry."

Sally could see the inquisitive look on Becky's face she always got when there was about to be a barrage of questions heading her way.

"Does it hurt?" Becky asked.

"Does what hurt?"

"Changing into a..." Becky hesitated before she seemed to force the word from her lips, "werewolf."

Sally nodded. "Yes. It hurts like hell. Lots of my bones break and reset in different shapes. I'm used to it now though."

Becky winced. "I wish I hadn't asked that now. It sounds horrendous when I think of it like that."

Sally smiled. "Then don't think about it."

She hoped the questioning was coming to an end, but Becky pressed on.

"So, can you control the change at other times? Whenever you want? Like that werewolf last night?"

"Yes, I can change any time I need to."

"It must be pretty cool sometimes to be able to turn into an animal and disappear into the woods or somewhere."

"It isn't, Bex. I can't control my wolf when she comes out and I don't remember anything I've done, where I've been, if I've attacked anybody. That's why I don't shift when there're people around."

Sally wasn't really comfortable talking in detail about being a werewolf, but she wanted Becky to have all the facts and not just what she'd seen on television.

"I've woke up a few times and gone back into town to hear people talking about the big dog they'd had to run away from and the howls they'd heard during the night. I've always tried to find out if anybody had been hurt and then moved on to somewhere else before somebody did or they found out it was me."

"Have you changed into a wolf while you've been living here?"

"Yes. Every full moon. My wolf gets agitated being cooped up inside for a whole lunar cycle."

Sally could see more concern moving over Becky's face.

"It's okay. I've always gone way over the other side of the south woods, never near the village."

She squeezed Becky's hand.

"Now you know about me," said Sally, "keep yourself locked in on full moon nights. Stay safe."

"You wouldn't hurt me, Sal."

"I don't know what I'm doing on a full moon, Bex. Just stay away. Okay?"

Becky agreed and they gave each other another long hug.

The barking from Penny was once again getting to a height you could describe as hysterical.

"I'll go and let you calm Penny down."

Sally left Becky to let her little dog back in and crossed The Green again, this time with a little more of a bounce in her step and made her way up the side steps that led to her little flat above the village shop.

For the rest of the day, everywhere Sally went in the village there seemed to be a vague scent of werewolf. The two rogue werewolves had clearly been around the village while Sally had been healing or talking to Becky and that worried her. There should be no reason for them to hang about a quiet little village like Popwood, not now they knew there was another werewolf living here. She didn't like it. She was starting to get a strange feeling she was being watched. Outwardly, to the villagers, she was the same Sally Bowers going about her usual routine. Inwardly she was an unsettled mess, and her inner wolf couldn't rest, which made her even more fidgety. Sally's inner wolf was wanting to be let out to run, to check the area and hunt the two rogue werewolves. She had trouble convincing the animal inside things were alright, because Sally wasn't totally convinced herself.

She found it hard to concentrate on work in the Black Bull that evening. Questions rolled through her mind; questions like why the rogues hadn't moved on, what they wanted in Popwood and had they stayed because she was here. Sally had a horrible feeling she was the reason they were hanging around and she was endangering Becky and the rest of the village just by being there.

By the time it was Sally's turn for a coffee break she'd made up her mind it was time to move on again. The last thing she wanted was for the lovely people of this village to get hurt because of her, especially Becky.

"Come on," said Becky, sitting down in the chair at the opposite side of the table, "what's up?"

Sally looked up from the still full cup of coffee in front of her and smiled, trying to hide the worry she was feeling inside.

"What do you mean?" Sally replied.

"You've been pouring the wrong drinks, giving the wrong change, only taking half the meals out and you've sat staring at that coffee for fifteen minutes without taking so much as a sip. It's not hard to see there's something troubling you. You're never like this."

"There's nothing wrong. I'm just a little under the weather today."

"Rubbish," said Becky, "You're never under the weather. In all the time I've known you I've yet to hear you complain about even a headache. There's something wrong." Becky reached across and rubbed the back of Sally's hand. "You can tell me; I'm your best friend."

Sally twirled the coffee cup around on the table. She knew Becky could tell whenever there was something bothering her and there was no way she would let it drop until she found out what it was.

"Sally," Becky squeezed Sally's hand, "Tell me. It's not because I know your secret is it?"

Sally stopped twirling the cup and looked up. She hesitated and took a breath.

"No. It's not that. It's those two werewolves," Sally whispered, "They haven't gone."

Becky sat upright and looked around, checking there was nobody in earshot.

"Have you seen them? Where? In the village?"

"No," Sally shook her head, "I haven't seen them, but I know they're here. I've caught their scent all over the village. Old scents, places they've been. They've kept out of sight, but their scent is everywhere."

"Why've they stayed?" Becky asked. The worry now clear in her voice.

"I don't know. Rogues usually just pass through places like this."

Sally took a sip of the now cold coffee and screwed up her face. She could sense the anxiety rising within Becky and smell her fear. She wished now she hadn't told her about her worries. Telling Becky she was leaving was going to have to wait.

"I'm sure they'll move on soon," said Sally pushing the cup away from her, "Come on. We best get back to work."

They both left the table and headed for the bar again, but Sally could tell Becky wasn't totally convinced the rogues were simply going to move on.

The Black Bull started to fill up with the usual late evening crowd and Sally was kept busy, which helped put the thoughts of the rogue werewolves out of her mind. She was starting to enjoy the chatter and jokes again while she served drinks and delivered meals to tables when she caught the scent; a fresh scent this time; the scent of a werewolf, and it was in The Black Bull.

Chapter 3

Sally stopped dead in her tracks. She held onto the two meals she was carrying instead of placing them on the table in front of the waiting customers. Her hackles began to rise under her skin. The scent was strong and unmistakable. It was a male werewolf. She looked around the bar slowly, he was in here somewhere. A stranger should have stood out but all she could see were faces she knew, regular customers and other villagers.

"Mine is the steak and ale pie," she heard a voice say.

"Sorry?" she said.

"The steak and ale pie," said the customer sat at the table in front of her. He pointed at the meal in Sally's hand. "That's what I ordered."

"Of course," Sally grinned, "My head is a mess tonight. It's been one of those days."

She placed the meals down in front of two of the people at the table.

"No, the gammon is mine," said one of the others, holding up his hand as if he was at school and wanting to make a point.

"Oops," Sally put on a fake little laugh.

She swapped the meal to the other side of the table, knocking over a drink as she did so. The man in direct path of the tsunami of beer heading across the table jumped up quickly but wasn't fast enough to save his trousers from getting drenched.

"I'm so sorry," said Sally in a panic and whipping a cloth out of her apron to try and mop up as much of the liquid as she could before it could spread any further.

"Is everything okay?" asked Becky, appearing at the table as she always did whenever a crisis sprang up.

"It's just me being clumsy," said Sally.

Becky helped Sally clear the table of the mess after moving the customers to another and getting them a fresh round of drinks on the house. There was nothing either of them could do for the man's trousers, so he disappeared to the gents to hold his crotch under the hand dryer for a while. Sally kept scanning the room, still looking for the source of the werewolf scent.

"Are you okay, Sal?" asked Becky.

"What do you mean?"

"You haven't stopped looking around the room since you tried to drown poor Tom in beer."

Sally sniffed the air again trying to home in on the direction of the scent."

"There's a werewolf in here somewhere," she whispered, "but I can't see him."

Now it was Becky who started to look around the room in alarm.

"Shit! Really? Where?" Becky moved closer to Sally, using her like a shield.

"I'm not sure," Sally sniffed the air again.

She walked slowly between the tables, her senses alert and the wolf inside pacing. The werewolf had left his scent on chair backs, door frames and wooden pillars. He wasn't trying to disguise the fact he had been here, and Sally found it easy to follow the route he had taken from the front door, through the bar and towards the rear of the pub.

"I think he must have slipped out the backdoor to the car park." Sally handed Becky the empty glasses she was carrying, "Stay inside."

She made her way quickly to through the pub, her nose working overtime as she took in the scent of everybody she passed. The werewolf scent was leading her passed them all.

She headed down the passage, past the toilets and stepped out into the night. She sniffed the air again. The scent was heading across the carpark to the woods that lined the edge of the village.

The light of the late summer evening was starting to fade but Sally's wolf sight made it as easy for her to see as if it were daylight. She scanned the line of trees and bushes at the far end of the carpark and spotted the two human shapes standing just inside the tree line. Her inner wolf started to growl, and Sally could feel the rumble rise to the back of her own throat as the two figures stepped out from the cover of the trees.

She stared directly at them, a challenge to a wolf. The

two rogues walked forward side by side, away from the remaining bushes and headed towards her. This is it, she thought, now I'll find out what these two want.

The door behind her swung open and Sally recognised Becky's familiar scent.

"Are you okay out here, Sal?"

"I thought I told you to stay inside," said Sally, turning to see Becky, a concerned look on her friend's face.

"I was worried about you. I told Tim you were feeling unwell and just needed some air. He would have come out to find you if I hadn't."

"I'm fine," said Sally, "Now go back inside. I won't be long."

When she turned back towards the carpark, the two werewolves were gone. Sally scanned the tree line again but there was no sign of them.

"I think you scared them off, Bex."

Becky stepped out of the doorway, as she reached Sally she whispered.

"Was it the same ones that were at the barbeque the other night?"

Becky held on to Sally's arm, Sally could feel her friend shaking and sense Becky's fear.

"Yes. I don't know why they are still around, but I don't like it." She put her arm around Becky's shoulders. "Don't you worry about it. I'll have a look for them tomorrow and clear them out. We'd better get back inside."

Sally finished out her shift at The Black Bull without any further incidents but couldn't understand why the two werewolves had disappeared. Their visit to the pub was an obvious attempt to draw her out and they had managed it. Becky coming outside wouldn't have bothered them one bit, she was sure of that. So why the sudden change of plan and the disappearing act?

When she left the pub with Becky later, Sally could still smell the werewolves faintly, but she suspected this was just a left-over scent from earlier. All the same, she walked Becky home to make sure she got there safe and sound then walked back across The Green to her own flat above the village shop.

She had a restless night. She tossed and turned in her bed, trying to get to sleep but the two werewolves were playing on her mind. She couldn't work out why they had disappeared. They had her out in the open behind the Black Bull on her own. Leaving suddenly didn't make any sense. Eventually sleep did come and she wondered off into the usual nightmare.

The animal came out of nowhere. She knew it was coming but her legs wouldn't move. It was if she was trying to run through syrup. The wolf didn't seem to have the same problem and was soon upon her. It smashed into her knocking her to the ground then pinned her down with its paws. She lashed out but the wolf took no notice of her wildly flailing arms. She could feel its immense weight crushing her ribs and she tried to scream but no sound came out. The wolf bared its teeth, drool dripping onto her cheek as it looked into her eyes. The growl started deep within its throat then erupted into an angry snarl as it lunged open mouthed at her face.

Sally screamed and sat up in her bed, sweat running down her face and neck. She was panting as if she'd been on one of her training runs. After taking a few moments to wake fully and take a precautionary sniff of the air, confirming she was safe in her bed and it had only been another of her nightmares, she slid out from under the duvet and walked barefoot to the bathroom. She splashed some cold water on her face and stared at herself in the mirror.

"Pull yourself together, Sally," she said to the reflection in front of her.

For the next few days Sally sniffed around the village looking for scents and clues, trying to figure out what the two rogues were doing and why they were still here. They were good, all she discovered were old scents. Just enough to let her know they were still around but not enough for her to track them in any one direction. She was being stalked, watched, studied, she could feel it.

It was her day off so she decided to start at the south end of the village and do a full sweep. She made her way slowly through the village, looking up each little side street and track. She passed the main housing estate, carried on round The Black Bull and on toward the village church and graveyard. She made her way round The Green to the north end of the village checking behind the terrace of houses where Becky had the end house then over behind the shop below her own flat.

The scent of Popwood had changed. To Sally the rogue werewolves' scent had contaminated the clean smell of woods and fields, of wildflowers and crops. She felt a sadness inside. She had brought this sweet little village into her world and put it in danger.

She found the strongest scents at the northeastern end of the village so she walked out of Popwood where the main road passed an old disused industrial estate and made its way into the village. The derelict industrial units had been deserted for years and Sally thought they could have probably provided the rogues with shelter and an easy way for them to keep a close watch on her.

The rogues weren't easy to track and they had done their best to hide the direction of any route they were taking, but Sally's wolf senses were keen and she was determined. After some crisscrossing of the river the trail eventually led her to the old mill warehouse at the northernmost end of the industrial estate.

She stood at the fence, searching the building for signs

of entry. Her eyes easily catching details that a normal human would miss from that distance. Old oil drums that had recently been moved, dirt from the ground now up the side of the drums indicating they had been rolled, trampled grass, a forced window.

She was standing upwind so the rogues would probably know she was there and were maybe even watching her at this very moment. She wanted them to know she was looking and wanted them to know she'd found them. She waited to see if they'd come out and face her. With her scent being blown towards the warehouse she had virtually rang the doorbell. It was their move now.

Her phone started to vibrate in her back pocket. She took it out and looked at the caller display.

"Hiya, Bex."

"Sal, where are you? I've come to pick you up for the gym and Joyce said you haven't been in all morning. Is everything okay?"

Sally looked back up at the warehouse, she thought she'd caught a movement in one of the lower windows but there was nothing there now.

"Yeah, I'm fine," she replied, "I just came out for a morning walk and forgot the time." She wasn't sure she'd convinced Becky, but she stuck to the story. "I'm just up Northend. I'll see you in the shop in ten minutes."

Stay Away

She entered her flat from the side stairs, collected her gym gear and walked down the inner stairs and into the shop. Becky was talking to Joyce about a scarecrow competition the village held every summer.

"Me and Sally will make one to represent the shop," said Joyce. "We can sit it out the front on the bench opposite."

"Is it that time of year again, Joyce? I thought you were going to keep last year's and use it again. It won, didn't it?"

"That's cheating," said Becky, "All scarecrows have to be new each year."

"She knows that, Becky," said Joyce, "She's only winding you up."

Sally didn't know at all. She wasn't in the mood for making a giant stuffed toy either, not with two rogue werewolves prowling around. She just laughed it off though as she did with all the strange but quaint little customs the people of this village seemed to have.

"Shall we get going, Bex?" said Sally, changing the subject quickly.

They jumped into Becky's little Citroen C1 and headed off for their usual Wednesday morning gym session.

"Now I understand why I have trouble keeping up with you," said Becky as they both worked out side by side on the rowing machines. "This werewolf business explains a lot."

"Sally laughed, "You do okay."

"I look like I've been in the shower with my clothes on,"

Becky replied, "You look like you haven't started yet."

They did their usual workout going from the rowing machines to the cross trainers, onto the tread mills and finally the cycling machines. The rogue werewolves never left Sally's mind as she worked out. She trained harder and faster than usual as if she knew she had a fight ahead of her, a fight for Popwood, a fight for her home.

They got changed and slipped into the Jacuzzi to let the warm jets of water and bubbles relax the tension and sooth their muscles.

"You're still keeping something from me," said Becky, "You know I can tell."

Sally knew only too well there was very little she could hide successfully from Becky for any length of time. How she had hidden her lycanthropy from her for so long was still a mystery. Becky seemed to have a sixth sense about these things and could always tell when somebody in the village was worried about something or needed help or just simply a little company. No matter what it was she always knew just the right thing to say or do. Sally looked around to make sure there was nobody within earshot.

"I think I know why those two werewolves are still around."

Becky opened her eyes and lifted her head, looking at Sally and waiting for the answer. None came so she prompted a little.

"Is that a good thing or a bad thing?"

"It's good, I guess. It means I know what I have to do to get them to move on."

There was another pause. Becky waited for Sally to go on, but the pause continued.

"Well," said Becky, "are you going to tell me or am I going to have to beat it out of you?"

Sally just raised an eyebrow and looked sideways at her.

"It's because I'm here," Sally said, "I'm sure they think the pickings must be good here if I've stuck around."

"What pickings?" asked Becky, "Not people?"

"No. Rogues tend to hunt wild animals, so I'm told, but they don't mind taking farm animals too. When that happens then farmers usually get a little upset."

"I can understand why," said Becky.

"Well, if the rogues stay here and do take a farm animal or two then Ted is going to go looking for whatever is killing his sheep. If he does, then there's a good chance somebody will get hurt. I can't allow that."

Becky sat up in the water.

"You're not going after them, are you?"

"No," Sally smiled, "I don't want to draw any attention to myself from the villagers and if there's a fight that's what could happen. The best thing to do is for me to leave, you know, move on again. They will probably follow me or even carry on to where they were going in the first place."

"No," said Becky, "You can't."

"I have to. I don't know of another way to get rid of them."

"What about the Police?" Becky asked, "We could go to the Police."

"And tell them what?" laughed Sally. "Believe me, you don't want to be going to the Police and telling them you suspect two rogue werewolves have moved into the area. You'll be laughed at all the way to a padded cell."

"But why should you have to go? It's not fair." Tears welled up in Becky's eyes. "There must be some other way to make them go."

"This is the only way I can think of, Bex," said Sally, "Don't worry, I'm used to having to move on."

Becky started to cry properly.

"I'm not though, you're my best friend" she sobbed, "I don't want you to leave. Please, Sal, there must be another way."

Sally put her hand on Becky's arm and squeezed gently.

"If I stay then I put you all in danger. I won't do that. You mean too much to me."

"If I mean that much then stay, please."

"I can't, Bex. It's too dangerous for you. I'm sorry but I have to move on."

With that Sally stepped out of the jacuzzi and headed for the changing rooms. Wrapping herself in her towel as she went.

The drive back to Popwood in the car was a quiet one. Becky drove and sniffed but didn't speak. Sally couldn't think of anything to say so said nothing. When they reached Popwood, Becky drove past the shop and parked up at the back of the row of houses where she lived.

"You forgot to drop me off," said Sally.

"I'm not dropping you off," replied Becky. "You're coming in with me while I try and talk some sense into you."

Sally sighed, "I'll come in for a coffee, Bex but my mind is made up. I'm leaving tomorrow."

The two girls walked to Becky's back door in silence. Sally tried to think of something to say but nothing seemed to be appropriate for the occasion. She had never been very good at making small talk and made it a point to avoid goodbyes.

As soon as Becky opened the door Sally's hackles started to rise. She grabbed Becky and pulled her away, stepping between her and the opening.

"Hey, careful," said Becky, rubbing her arm.

Sally didn't reply, she just pushed Becky further behind her and sniffed the air.

"Go! Now!" said Sally, keeping herself between Becky and the door.

"What do you mean?"

"Go!" repeated Sally, "Get in your car and drive."

"Where to?"

Anthony Stamp

"Anywhere, just go. I can smell a werewolf in there."

Chapter 4

Becky backed away from the door slowly and stared at Sally, confusion all over her face.

"Run!" Sally shouted.

Becky turned and fled towards her car.

Once Becky had disappeared through her garden gate, Sally stepped through the back door, closing it quietly behind her. Standing in the kitchen she sniffed the air, gathering as much information about the intruder as possible before going any further. The scent of werewolf was fresh, minutes old at the most. She noticed the kitchen window was slightly ajar with marks at the edge where it had been forced open. Penny, Becky's little Shelty, was hiding under the kitchen table, shaking and growling.

"Stay there, Penny," said Sally, hoping the little dog would take her advice and keep out of the way.

Following the scent, she made her way into the front room. There were two distinct werewolf scents, one musky and strong, a male, and one slightly lighter and nervous, a female. There was a faint sense of fear coming from the female's scent. The perfume she also smelled was fresh but there wasn't a perfume yet capable of masking a scent from a werewolf's keen sense of smell. She recognised both scents immediately. These were the same two werewolves she'd been tracking all week, the ones who'd crashed the party in the woods.

The front room was empty but the front door, which led straight in off the street, was open slightly. Sally crept through the room, staying mindful of everything around her. The scent turned left towards the stairs. Why was the front door open if they had entered at the back then disappeared upstairs? This was a question for later she decided. She closed the door and dropped the latch before making her way to the foot of the stairs. The scent of both werewolves was still strong meaning they'd both gone up to the next floor. Sally's fingers grew long sharp claws on one hand which then grew into a large and powerful wolf paw. She could feel her inner wolf rising to the surface, the uneasiness of the situation putting it on alert. Her skin started to prickle.

Be careful, there's danger here. We're outnumbered. We need to get out.

Her inner wolf tried her best to persuade Sally to leave the house and get away.

Sally ignored the voice inside. Her wolf usually made all the right decisions, but this was Becky's house, and her friend was in danger. She wasn't leaving just yet.

As silently as she could, she took each stair and followed the scent to the first floor, constantly listening for any sound from the rooms above. Three doors faced her when she reached the top; all were open. The rogues had obviously searched each of these, she could smell them. The bathroom opposite was empty, she could see that from where she stood. That left the two bedrooms. The back bedroom was the closest, so she headed for that one first, all the while her senses monitored everything around her, ready to react to any movement from the other room. She scanned the room from the doorway, sniffing the air for any clue as to where a werewolf may be hiding. They had been in here but clearly weren't there now, there was nowhere they could hide in such a small room. The wardrobe was too small and the rest of the room was bare. That left the one remaining room, the front bedroom, Becky's room.

Sally's inner wolf started to snarl inside as she approached the door and the scent of both werewolves got stronger. She pushed the door wide open, so she knew nothing was hiding behind it, and stepped in. The room had been searched thoroughly, drawers were open, both wardrobe doors were wide. Judging by the raised valance they had even looked under the bed, which Sally also did just in case there was a werewolf hiding under there. The room was empty, and the windows were closed. The werewolves weren't in the house, but she could have only missed them by seconds. They must have made their way out the front way when they saw her and Becky approaching from the back, that's why the front door was open.

Panic suddenly rushed into Sally's chest and took her breath away. She realised she hadn't heard Becky's car pull away. The werewolves would have known she would enter the house without Becky as soon as she caught their scent.

"Oh no," said Sally, the feeling of dread squeezing her chest tighter, "they know Becky's out the back on her own."

She dashed from the room, jumped from the top of the stairs to the bottom and was running as she landed. She burst out the back door and saw Becky's car still parked in its usual spot. Still alert and looking for signs of the two rogues, she ran over to the car and to her relief found Becky just sitting there, a look of worry in her eyes and the unmistakable scent of fear teeming from the pores of her skin. Sally looked around the area quickly and sniffed the air again. There were no werewolves near that she could tell.

"I thought I told you to drive?" she said as she opened the car and got in next to Becky.

"I know you did," said Becky, "but I wanted to know you were okay. Anyway, I have nowhere to drive to." Then her eyes widened and her mouth dropped open. "Sally, what's happened to your eyes? They've turned a kind of orange colour." The look on Becky's face turned into one of terror. "Oh my God, you aren't going to change into a werewolf now, are you? Not while I'm here?"

Becky grasped clumsily at her seat belt, trying to unfasten it and move herself away from Sally but in her panic she couldn't seem to find the button. The longer it took the more Becky panicked and she started to pull at the belt, trying to wrench it free.

"No, Becky, it's okay, calm down" replied Sally, reaching out to her friend with hands that were now human. "It's okay I promise. I'm not going to shift. You're safe, Bex."

"But your eyes…" Becky seemed lost for words.

"I know but don't worry. Look."

Sally calmed herself down and Becky seemed to do the same as she stared at Sally's eyes, which Sally assumed were now changing back to her usual bright blue.

"There," said Sally, "they've changed back. See, there's nothing to worry about."

Becky noticeably calmed down, grinned, then changed the subject. "Are they in there?" she said.

"No, but they have been and very recently," Sally replied.

"But why? What would they want with me?"

"I don't know, Bex."

"What if you leave and they stay?" said Becky.

The situation had changed with the rogues targeting Becky's house. Sally couldn't move on now, not without the worry of Becky being in danger. She could feel her own anger starting to smolder inside. The rogues had stepped over a line involving her best friend.

"I'm going nowhere, Bex. Not now you're on their radar." Sally patted Becky's leg. "Don't worry, I'm not going to let them hurt you. But we need to get you out of here for a while. Come on, it's safe to go in now."

"Get me out of here?"

"Yes. You need to get out of the village for a little while."

"But I have nowhere to go."

"Go and visit your mam and dad in The Lakes for a few days," Sally suggested, "I'll get things sorted here and give you a ring when it's safe to come back. I know where these pieces of dirt are hiding out. They may have a problem with me, but they don't bring my best friend into the mix and get away it."

Once inside the house they went upstairs. Becky emptied her gym bag onto the bed and started to fill it with a few changes of clothes. Sally noticed Becky stealing little glances at her now and again. Every time Sally looked up, Becky looked away.

"What's the matter, Bex?"

"Nothing's the matter. Why?"

"You keep staring at me."

"I'm just keeping a check on your eyes, so I know when to run."

Sally stood and stared at her. The fear that Becky was feeling wasn't just limited to the two rogues. Becky was now frightened of her too. The truth hit Sally deep inside and almost took her breath away. She had always known Becky would eventually be too scared to be her friend, but she hadn't expected it to hurt so much.

Sitting down on the bed Sally patted the space next to her

and Becky eased herself down, keeping a little distance.

"There's no need to be frightened of me just because my eyes change colour, Bex. That doesn't mean I'm going to suddenly turn into a wild animal."

"What does it mean then?" asked Becky.

"I'm not always sure why they do that," replied Sally, "They change when I get strong 'wolfy' emotions for some reason. When I partly change, they go that colour or sometimes if I'm sad or angry, feelings like that can trigger the colour change."

She sensed Becky start to calm down and relax a little.

"Is that what colour they are when you're a wolf?"

Sally shrugged.

"I have no idea. I've never seen myself as a wolf."

"Never?"

"No. When I'm a wolf I don't know about anything I see or do. I have no control of what I do and no memory of being in my wolf form."

"That's so sad," said Becky. "I bet you're a beautiful wolf."

Sally had never been comfortable taking compliments. She felt her cheeks blush with embarrassment. Becky stiffened a little once again and she knew her eyes were changing again.

Moving closer she put her arm around Becky's shoulder. "Don't worry. While I still vaguely resemble a human I will never hurt you, Bex. I promise."

Sally could feel the tension in Becky's muscles easing and the smell of fear lessened.

"That explains why you wear sunglasses a lot," Becky laughed, "to hide your eyes. I thought you were just being a cool chick."

"I am a cool chick."

They both laughed out loud and gave each other a hug before they finished Becky's packing.

It didn't take long to fix the kitchen window and Becky's car was soon packed with her at the wheel, ready to go.

"You be careful, Sal."

"Hey, don't you be worrying about me," said Sally with a smile, "I'm a big bad werewolf remember."

"I know," said Becky, "But there's two of them and only one of you."

Sally reached through the car window and rubbed her hand over Becky's cheek.

"I'm sorry for putting you in danger, Bex," she said. "I didn't mean for all this to happen.

Becky just smiled. "Don't worry about it. It's all part of having a werewolf as a best friend I guess." She laughed then nodded towards the house next door. "I've asked a neighbor to watch Penny till I get back. Don't forget to tell Tim I've had to go and see my mam at short notice. He'll need to get my shifts covered at the pub. Oh and…"

Stay Away

Sally put her hand over Becky's mouth.

"Go. I'll sort everything out."

Becky smiled but the worry on her face was all too plain to see. She went to say something else but took a deep breath instead then started her car.

Sally watched and waved as the car moved off, trying to keep the happy smile on her face as long as she could. Once the car turned the corner Sally knew her eyes would once again be a golden orange as the anger started to grow inside.

"Now for those two pieces of dirt," she growled quietly to herself.

Not following the road, because that would take her up wind of the werewolves' den, but going cross country directly from the back of Becky's house, Sally headed straight for the Old Mill Warehouse.

When she got there the warehouse still looked deserted. She crept between the small outbuildings, quickly checking each one to make sure there was nothing and nobody hiding there. Then, as silently as her human form would allow, she approached the side of the warehouse where a small window was the easiest and most obvious way in. Carefully she crept to the window from the side and peered through the dirty glass, searching for any telltale signs that somebody had been living there. The whole ground floor was empty, apart from some old crates and oil drums that were stacked neatly at the back of the building. To her right she could see two small rucksacks tucked underneath some shelving with blankets stretched out on the floor in front of them. It looked like there had been two people sleeping there very recently. Other than that, the ground floor was empty. The floors higher up looked to have been either demolished or had simply rotted away in many places. Sally remembered seeing a sign on the gate that led in from the road saying, "Dangerous Building – Keep Out!"; the rusting metalwork was obviously why.

It was clear the werewolves weren't there. They must be still snooping around the village. She didn't want to leave her scent all over the place to alert the rogues she had come calling, so she left the way she had come and made her way back into Popwood.

For the next few hours Sally searched the village thoroughly from one end to the other. She even checked the holiday cottages to the south and the surrounding woods, but apart from old scents she could find no sign of the two werewolves. Instinct and the rucksacks at the old mill told her they hadn't left the area. Werewolves were very good at remaining unseen when they wanted to and these two seemed to be specialists at it.

It had been a few hours since Becky had set off on her journey to visit her mother and Sally figured she would be there by now and be desperate for an update. The Contacts list in her phone only contained the two numbers, Becky, and Home. She didn't use the 'Home' number anymore, not since her sister had run away to come and find her. Because of that, the last phone call she had taken from her mother hadn't gone well and, at her mother's request, Sally never called back. She knew it was all said in the heat of the moment, but she thought it was best, under the current circumstances, to break contact with her family for a short while. That had been before she settled in Popwood and as more time passed Sally found it harder to press the 'Home' quick dial on her phone. She pressed the quick dial link, 'Becky', and waited for the phone to ring. Her call went straight to Becky's voicemail and she listened to Becky's cheerful voice, almost singing the request to leave a name and number. When a beep sounded, Sally left a message.

"Hi," said Sally, "I just wanted to check you were okay and to let you know I'm fine. There's no news to report at this end yet. I'm still working on it. Give me a ring as soon as you can. Cheers."

Sally ended the call and set off for home, checking the woods behind The Black Bull on her way but still found no sign of the two rogues.

The total disappearance of the two werewolves bothered her a great deal. She knew they wouldn't just leave, and she felt anxious at being unable to track them down as easily as she'd expected.

She sat at her kitchen table, a cappuccino cupped in her hands sipping the hot drink wondering what the pair were up to. They wouldn't have left their bags at the old mill if they were moving on and there weren't that many places in the village to hide. Not from a nose as sensitive as Sally's anyway.

She looked down at her phone lying on the table in front of her. There was still no return call from Becky. She picked it up and dialed. Again, all she got was the voicemail greeting.

"Hi, Bex it's me again. Is everything okay? Give me a ring when you get the chance, pet."

It wasn't like Becky not to return a call at the earliest opportunity. Sally remembered Becky's parents lived somewhere remote in the Lake District and she thought that maybe there wasn't a very good mobile signal up there. She decided to drop Becky a text in the hope it would get delivered if she suddenly got a bit of a signal.

The sun eventually disappeared behind the hills west of the village and Sally got ready to head back to the Old Mill Warehouse. She put on some dark clothes and tied her hair back into a bunch, so it was out of the way. She was sure the wolves would return to the warehouse at night, so she was going to pay them another visit. If they weren't there this time, she was going to wait inside until they turned up.

"This ends tonight," she said quietly to herself.

She gave Becky one last call but still didn't have any luck reaching her friend.

Sally knew Becky called her mother regularly. There probably wasn't a day when she didn't call at some point, so maybe they had a landline. She decided to call in at Becky's house on the way to the old mill and see if she could find an address book containing a phone number for Becky's parents. She knew it was a long shot because Becky probably knew her parents phone number by heart. It would be saved in her phone anyway, but it was at least worth a try.

She had a spare key for the back door which Becky had left with her for emergencies so, slipping it into her pocket, she left her flat and headed off across the village green.

As soon as she went in through the gate she could see a small white envelope pinned above the handle. To Sally's surprise the name on the front of the envelope was hers. In a scruffy scrawl it read, '*Sally*'. She sniffed the envelope, it had the smell of the female werewolf all over it. Sally got an uneasy feeling in the pit of her stomach and her inner wolf started to pace. It felt the same unease as Sally. Anger started to flutter inside. A low quiet growl started deep in her throat. She pulled the envelope from the door and ripped it open. Inside she found a small, handwritten note.

'I think you may have lost something valuable. If you want it back unharmed then come to the old mill warehouse. We will be waiting.'

Chapter 5

Sally dropped to her knees, tears welling up in her eyes. What had she done? Somebody else she cared for was now in danger and it was all her fault. First her family, and now her best friend.

She looked at the handwritten note, staring again at the scruffy writing. No, this wasn't her fault. The rogues had done this. They'd brought Becky into the equation. She couldn't stop the growl that had started deep in her throat from now coming out through gritted teeth. She crumpled the note in her hand and dropped it on the floor.

She felt a sudden and ferocious rage building up inside. Her wolf was growling and pawing at the surface, she wanted to be out, and it took all of Sally's determination and self-control to stop herself shifting and becoming the monster she resented. Now, however, she had the strongest reason ever to become that monster, to go on the hunt and take care of the two rogues who had invaded her territory and taken one of her pack. If they hurt Becky in any way, those two werewolves were going to pay dearly for their serious lack of judgment.

She'd never faced two werewolves before and, if she was honest, she wasn't sure how she would fair against these two streetwise specimens, but she wasn't going to let that prevent her from getting Becky back safe and sound.

Making her way through the darkness, being sure to

approach downwind this time, she closed in on the old mill warehouse. They shouldn't have told her where they were holding Becky, that was their second mistake. Their first mistake was to bring one of her friends into the argument, her only friend, her best friend. Sally paid little attention to the light rain that had begun to fall, her focus was on finding the two werewolves who had kidnapped Becky, and making them pay for trying to force her hand; a hand that had now grown into a large paw with razor sharp werewolf claws. The rest of her may have looked human but, even ignoring the claws, Sally wasn't the same, pretty, trendy, nineteen-year-old blonde girl who the residents of Popwood knew so well. This girl was a hunter, a predator focused upon closing in on its prey, silent, deadly.

It was a constant struggle to stay in her human form as she made her way to the rogue's suggested meeting place. Her inner wolf was agitated, and Sally was angry. She had to resist her inner wolf's urge to change because she needed to be fully aware of everything to get Becky away from her captors safely.

Using the same route as she had earlier, Sally crept passed the outbuildings, checking each one again just in case. The two rogues knew she was coming this time and she didn't want any surprises they may have planned for her. She spotted the window on the side of the mill she had looked through on her previous visit. Now, there was a faint light flickering inside. The window had been opened; an easy access invitation that the werewolves on the inside would obviously be watching. Keeping low to the ground and in the shadows, she made her way towards it.

Crouching below the window she sniffed the air. Two very distinct scents filled her nostrils, each one she recognized instantly as werewolf. They were close by and probably waiting. The third scent was that of her friend, Becky. Sally guessed she would be further back from the window, putting the two rogues between her and the 'something valuable' they knew she would come and claim.

Sally could smell werewolf all over the window frame too. This was their way in and out. Because of the trouble she had had tracking them she knew these were smarter werewolves than any others she had faced. If they were in hiding, they wouldn't have left a window open and unguarded. This was a trap, and one Sally wasn't going to fall into. She moved slowly away to find another way in.

Above her, maybe twenty feet up, and further towards the back of the building, Sally spotted a small door with a beam sticking out above it. Probably a loading point for the mill back in its day, which meant that there must be a floor above. It was probably made a little more solid than the other areas if it was a loading platform. There was also a ladder leading down from the door, but it had been cut off halfway up the wall, probably to stop unwanted visitors using it to gain access. This deterrent was designed for unwanted human visitors and hadn't been made with a werewolf's strength and agility in mind. Sally leapt up quietly and caught hold of the bottom rung, pulling herself up the rest of the way until she stood on a small platform facing the door. Hoping the hinges wouldn't creak, she opened the door slowly and slipped quietly inside.

The floor in this area was still intact as Sally had guessed. She made her way to a good vantage point that gave her a view of the whole of the ground floor. She crouched down when she spotted the two human shaped figures watching the open window. Becky was tied to a chair in the far corner of the room. The male rogue was talking to her. Sally listened in.

"There's nothing for you to worry about. As long as your friend does what we want you won't get hurt."

"I'm not the one who should be worried," Becky replied.

"Meaning?" snapped the female.

"Meaning that when Sally gets here you two are in big trouble."

"We can handle your little friend," the female responded. The mocking tone a little too cocky for Sally's liking.

Becky started to laugh, "If my memory serves me correctly, you couldn't handle her when you were a wolf. What makes you think you can handle her as a human?"

Sally was impressed with the level of confidence Becky had in her ability, but she knew this wasn't going to be easy and if Becky inadvertently talked the female rogue into shifting into her wolf form things would get even harder. As

Becky had pointed out earlier, there were two of them and only one of her.

The female growled at Becky's last remark and moved towards her. Sally saw Becky tense up. Her outward show of courage nothing more than bravado but still impressive to Sally. She knew Becky would be terrified inside.

"Kiera!" said the male, "Leave it. She's only trying to wind you up and I need you to focus. Sally could be here soon."

Kiera stopped and stared down at Becky, a wolf challenge that Becky wouldn't understand. Becky stared straight back at her and Sally could see the agitation on the werewolf's face. Kiera huffed and stood in front of Becky with her arms folded.

"That's if she comes at all. The last I saw of her she was sitting in her flat drinking coffee. She didn't seem that bothered about you."

So, the female had been watching her in her flat. Sally felt a little uneasy learning she could be spied upon in her own kitchen and not even know it.

"Kiera!" shouted the male again. "I told you to leave it."

Kiera walked back towards the open window, but her eyes didn't leave Becky until the last moment.

Sally knew the situation below her could get out of control very quickly and the female seemed to be on a hair trigger. It was time to get down there.

There was a set of stairs leading down to the back of the

open area below, which seemed to be the only way to the ground floor. The rest of the floor looked to have been removed or simply rotted away. A little way further back beyond the bottom of the stairs she noticed a fire exit, the door of which had been chained closed on the inside. Sally decided that was their way out once she had Becky away from the rogues. Moving silently towards the back of the building she descended the stairway then headed towards the others, keeping to the darkness as much as she could.

"I can smell her," said Kiera, "Get ready, she'll be coming in any second."

Sally stepped forward into the light from behind them.

"She's already in," said Sally, unable to prevent an underlying growl as she spoke.

The two werewolves spun round in shock at the sudden announcement of Sally's unexpected arrival behind them.

"Impressive," said the male with a smile and a nod.

"Oh, I'm full of surprises," replied Sally. No smile, just a straight-faced stare.

The two werewolves parted, ready to defend themselves. Kiera hesitated and backed up a little when she looked down at Sally's partially changed hands and the claws that were all too visible protruding from powerful wolf paws.

Sally was outnumbered and needed to weigh up the two streetwise opponents facing her. She didn't attack, but kept very alert. Besides, all she wanted now she had seen Becky was unharmed, was to get her friend safely away from here. Putting Becky in the middle of a werewolf battle would only put her in danger and there was a chance that Becky could be pulled into the fight as a shield or even bitten if things got out of hand. If, on the other hand, the two rogue werewolves made it difficult and pushed their point, well, that was a different story.

Kiera moved slowly further to one side, keeping her eyes on Sally, especially on her claws, edging closer towards Becky.

"I wouldn't do that if I were you sister," Sally snapped, "You go near her and me and you are going to have a serious falling out."

Kiera stopped and looked from Sally to Becky, as if trying to gauge the distance and work out who would get there first. She must have decided that she could beat Sally to her hostage because she lunged forward suddenly. Sally spotted the move almost before Kiera made it and ran at her full werewolf enhanced speed.

They both reached Becky together and Sally rammed her shoulder into Kiera's chest sending her sprawling across the floor. Kiera rolled a couple of times and was back on her feet in an instant. She lunged again, this time directly at Sally. With a simple swerve of her body and sweep of her arm, Sally deflected her attacker easily and raked her claws down Kiera's back, slicing through clothing and flesh at the same time.

Kiera cried out at the pain then turned and launched herself at Sally again. Using Kiera's momentum, and a perfectly timed sweep of the foot, Sally sent Kiera sprawling across the floor in the opposite direction. Again, Kiera was back on her feet immediately but the pain from her injuries was showing on her face. The male rogue stepped between them just as Kiera was about to begin another attack.

"Let's all just calm down shall we," he said. "Your friend is in no danger."

Sally started solum faced and moved her gaze slowly and menacingly from Kiera to the male.

"Then why is she here?"

"It was the only way we could get your attention."

Kiera moved forward and stood by the side of the male but stayed alert, "How else were we going to get you to talk to us?" she said.

"You already had my attention" replied Sally, "I could smell you all over the village. If you wanted to talk to me, you should have tried knocking on my door instead of spying on me through my window. That usually works wonders in the civilized world."

Sally moved back slowly towards where Becky was sat but never took her eyes off her two opponents. The male just watched but Kiera tensed once again.

"Just one step princess," warned Sally. "You aren't in your wolf form now like you were in the woods. It's more of an even contest this time and you don't want to meet me on a level playing field."

Sally was hoping her hard-faced comments would do the trick because she really didn't know if she could handle two werewolves at once.

"We just want to talk," said the male.

Sally didn't answer. She just continued to make her way behind Becky then reached down, and with one quick flick of an exposed werewolf claw she sliced through Becky's bonds. Becky stood up quickly and moved behind Sally. Staying between Becky and the rogues she backed away towards the back of the building.

Kiera launched another lightning-fast attack but Sally seen it coming once again. She twisted and delivered a strong side kick into the face of the advancing attacker. The force of the kick together with Kiera's own speed lifted Kiera off the floor before she hit the ground flat on her back. There was no quick roll to get straight back to her feet upon landing this time. Kiera simply crawled away. The male helped her up.

"This conversation is over," Sally's voice contained another underlying, deep throated growl.

"No. Listen to us please, Sally," said the male, "My name is Blake and this is Kiera." He nodded towards the female. "We need your help."

"What in God's name would make you think that kidnapping my friend would make me want to help you with anything?"

"We didn't kidnap her to make you help us," he said, "only to get you talking to us." He paused. "I can see now it was a mistake."

"Too right it was," replied Sally.

"Look, I'm sorry. We were just desperate," said Blake. "We were just passing through when we first bumped into you."

"And she tried to eat my friend remember," added Sally, pointing a claw at Kiera who was starting to regain some of her composure.

"My wolf felt threatened that's all," said Kiera.

"So did my friend," Sally shot back, "But you didn't seem to care."

"Will you two calm down so I can explain?" Blake walked between Sally and Kiera again, trying to diffuse the tension a little. "Our pack has been taken prisoner by a government research laboratory. Kiera managed to escape and find her way home. We were on our way back there to try and get them out when we bumped into you at that party you were all sleeping off. We would have moved on straight away if I hadn't got your scent and realized who you were."

Sally's breath faltered a little when she heard that. She studied Blake's face intently, but she was certain she had never seen this man before in her life.

"How do you know me?" Sally asked.

"It's not easy to explain," he replied, obviously struggling to find the right words, "but once I realized who you were, I had to find a way to ask you to help. I know you're a powerful werewolf and with you on our side we at least stand a chance."

"I'm not going to help anybody who tried to eat or kidnap my friend. I certainly don't know you, I'm sure I would remember running into a nasty piece of work like you. Although, all you pack wolves are alike. You all disgust me."

Sally gave Becky a little shove and continued to move towards the rear of the building. When she and Becky reached the fire exit, she gripped the chain then with one powerful yank she pulled it free breaking the fire door handle and lock in the same motion. She took hold of Becky's arm and pushed her through the door, keeping her eye on Blake as she did so.

"No wait!" shouted Blake. "I know you probably don't remember me."

"There's nothing to remember" growled Sally.

"Yes, there is." He hesitated, "We have met. About three years ago, up north." He hesitated again, "I, I was the one who bit you."

Sally felt as though she'd been punched in the stomach. The shock of what she had just heard knocked all the wind out of her.

She let out a deep and powerful growl that seemed to shake the whole building. Her teeth started to elongate, and the growl turned into a vicious sounding snarl. Her whole body became tense.

"It was you?" Sally almost roared, "You ruined my life. You made me into this monster and then left me at the mercy of a pack of insane animals. And now, you expect me to help you. If your pack are anything like you then they are in the right place, away from innocent people."

Sally felt the urge to shift right there. She wanted to get her teeth around Blake's throat, to tear him apart and leave him on the ground bleeding and dying just as he had done with her.

'*We're not like him,*" said her wolf's voice from inside, "*come away. Let's escape while we can. We need to get to safety.*"

Sally puffed and panted, breathing in short shallow breaths, fighting the urge to kill the one who made her into a monster, and instead listen to the voice of her wolf. Every day for the last three years she had wanted to pay back this wolf for what he had done. This was her chance.

'*What about the human?*" asked her wolf.

Her wolf was right. She couldn't risk Becky being caught up in her anger. There would be another time for this. She had his scent now. She knew who he was.

"My pack are nothing like me," said Blake.

"That can only be a blessing."

"I mean they are innocent victims who find peace in each

other's company."

"Your victims," Sally added.

"Not my victims. Just people who I've helped who don't have a pack."

Sally bared her teeth again and growled. The displeasure she was feeling evident to all. She stared him straight into his eyes. A challenge from one wolf to another.

Blake stood his ground but looked more than a little concerned at the additional appearance of a set of elongated canines. He was an alpha and he didn't ever back down because of such a show of aggression. Kiera stood by his side growling but looked a little less confident than he did, which Sally found odd for a female alpha standing with her mate.

"Nothing in this world would ever make me help you or your pack," she said, the distain and disgust clear in the way she spat out the words. She flashed her elongated canines at the two werewolves and once more started ushering Becky to the doorway, "and if I ever see you again, I will kill you."

Sally pushed Becky out of the door and they made their way quickly back towards the village.

Sally noticed Becky rubbing her wrist as she helped her over the fence that would lead them to the back of Becky's house. There was no need to tie her hands that tight, Sally thought to herself. She could smell the blood from the cute, but at least Becky was away from the rogues and safe.

Once back in Becky's kitchen, the door locked and bolted,

Becky flung her arms around Sally's neck and sobbed into her shoulder.

"It's okay," said Sally, patting Becky on the back with her hand; a hand that was now claw free and looking like it should.

"You came and rescued me. Thank you, thank you, thank you."

"Of course I did. You don't think I was going to leave you with those two pieces of dirt, do you?"

"I don't know how I could ever thank you," said Becky.

"Well, you can start by putting the kettle on," laughed Sally.

Becky smiled, let go of Sally, then wandered over to the kettle, rubbing her arm once she had turned her back.

"Will they go now?" asked Becky.

"I have no idea. I'll give them tomorrow to get going then I'll go back to the mill and check.

"You promised to kill them," said Becky, "I think that would do the trick, and you looked so fierce. I thought you were going to tear them to pieces right in front of me."

"I've never killed anybody," said Sally, "and I'm not letting those two spoil my record, even though they probably deserve it."

Sally noticed Becky rubbing her arm again before she poured the boiling water into the teapot.

"Were those ropes a little too tight?" Sally asked, nodding to where Becky was rubbing.

Becky's face scrunched up and she started to cry once more. Her body visibly shaking.

"Hey, it's okay. You're safe now."

"I know," sobbed Becky, "It's not that."

"Then what is it?"

Becky rubbed her arm again.

"It's not the ropes."

She pulled up the sleeve of her coat to reveal a deep gash in her arm.

"One of your claws cut me when you were pushing me out of the door." Becky broke down in tears. "Am I going to be a werewolf like you now?"

Chapter 6

Becky wept, her body shaking uncontrollably. The smell of fear and the look of terror on her face was almost too much for Sally to handle.

"Hey, calm down, Bex," she whispered, wrapping her arms around her, "You're going to be fine. You're not going to turn into a werewolf."

"But you cut me," sobbed Becky, "and it's bleeding really badly. Oh, Sally, I don't think I can take the pain of changing like you do. You said it hurts a lot and I know I won't be able to do it, I just know I won't."

"You won't have to. Don't worry, Bex, you're not turning into a werewolf."

"But you got me with your claws."

Becky held out her arm for Sally to see.

"I know I did and I'm sorry, I didn't mean to. But you won't turn into a werewolf from scratches and cuts from my claws. Lycanthropy is only transmitted if you are bitten and the saliva gets in your blood stream."

"Really?" said Becky, calming down a little, her breathing still erratic.

"Really," repeated Sally, "Now let's get that cut cleaned up."

They went over to the kitchen sink and Becky held her arm under the tap while Sally ran some cold water on the nasty looking gash. It was deep and was still bleeding quite heavily.

"That looks deep," said Sally, "It may need a few stitches. I'll run over to The Black Bull and see if Tim will drive you to the hospital."

"I can drive myself," said Becky.

"You can hardly hold your hands still, Bex. I think it's best if somebody drives you there. It's at times like this when I wish I'd learned to drive."

Sally sat Becky down at the kitchen table and wrapped her arm in a clean tea towel.

"Here," she said, taking Becky's hand, "Keep pressure on there and I will go and get somebody to take you into town."

It was well into the early hours of the morning when Tim dropped them back at Becky's house. Six stitches had been needed, and the doctor hadn't looked convinced when she said she had cut herself on a broken glass. He'd started asking awkward questions and suggested that the cut looked a lot like a knife wound. Becky became a little feint at this point, but Sally suspected she was putting it on in order to distract the doctor from his questioning.

They stood on the pavement as Tim's car pulled away and Becky looked up at her house, then back at Sally.

"This sounds silly I know but..." Becky hesitated.

"Go on," prompted Sally.

"Can I stay at your place tonight?" Becky took another

glance at her house, "I don't want to be on my own."

"Sure you can," Sally smiled and put an arm around her friend.

They walked around the edge of the green, the air still thick with the remnants of the summer heat from earlier that day. She felt the familiar twitch in Becky's shoulders, the kind of shiver that came when a body was no longer its own. Since being bitten, Sally had stopped feeling the chill in the same way, her skin impervious, but she knew the signs when she saw them. She nudged Becky closer, the two of them walking the short stretch to the village shop. Once there, Sally led her up the side steps to the flat above.

They lay on Sally's bed, and soon Becky's deep breathing signaled she was asleep. Cutting Becky with her claws was the first time Sally had hurt someone close to her, showing how easily it could happen. The accident replayed in her mind, and when sleep finally came, it was restless and broken.

Sally heard a growl from the person lying next to her. Becky started to writhe on the bed as the change started. Bones cracked as they formed new shapes, forcing Becky's body into a form it wasn't meant to be. Becky let out a scream of pain as she shifted for the first time. The scream turned into a growl.

"No!" shouted Sally and tried to get Becky free of her clothes. The shock of seeing her friend becoming a wolf

caused Sally's hands to fumble, making it difficult to get Becky out of her garments so she didn't get tangle in them and die. "I'm sorry, Becky. I'm so sorry."

Tears rolled down Sally's cheeks as she tugged and pulled at Becky's tightening clothing. Becky instinctively fought back, adding to the difficulty of getting her free. The growls turned into a howl of pain and then a snarl of anger. Her clothing continued to tighten around her limbs and neck, pulling her into unnatural positions and slowly choking her.

"Stop struggling, Becky. Let me help."

Sally became frantic. Time was running out. Becky wouldn't last much longer. Then Becky howled again with the excruciating pain she must have been in and was suddenly silenced by a sickening crack as her neck broke and the lifeless golden orange eyes stared back at Sally.

"No!" Sally jolted upright, sweat running down her face and neck. She felt Becky's hand on her shoulder.

"It's okay, Sal. It was only a dream. You're safe now."

Sally relaxed and let her breathing slow before slipping from under the duvet and padding to the bathroom. She splashed some cold water over her face and stared into the mirror. Golden orange eyes stared back at her.

"Are you okay?" asked Becky from the doorway.

"Yes," Sally replied. "Like you said, it was only a dream."

"How long have you been having nightmares?"

"Since I was bitten," said Sally with a shrug.

She splashed more water onto her face then felt around for a towel. Becky stepped into the bathroom and handed her one from the rail near the door.

"What're they about?"

"Just stupid wolfy stuff, Bex. I'm fine now. Come on, let's get back to bed."

Sally lay next to Becky thinking of her latest nightmare and how easily it could have come true earlier. She couldn't get the image of Becky's twisted lifeless body, half human, half wolf, out of her mind.

Becky was soon back to sleep, but Sally thought it was best she stayed awake. Eventually, she got up and sat at the window, staring out in the direction of the derelict mill. Blake had ruined her life. He could have easily been the cause of ruining another life tonight. She looked back at Becky lying in her bed. If Becky had been hurt tonight during the rescue and turned, she would never have forgiven herself.

It was nearly lunch time by the time Becky surfaced. Sally had been up a few hours, and this was the first time she'd known Becky not to be up at the crack of dawn.

"Will you be okay today?" asked Sally, handing Becky a mug of coffee, "I have a shift in The Black Bull this afternoon."

"I'll be fine," Becky replied, "Thanks for letting me stay over."

"You can stay here until I finish work if you want."

Becky shook her head.

"No, it's okay," she said, "I have to go and get my car back from up the lane."

"Up the lane?"

"Yeah, where I stopped for…" Becky hesitated, "Where those two…" she stopped again, "I'm never stopping to help anybody by the side of the road ever again."

"They won't touch you again, Bex," said Sally, "They may even have gone already. I'll come with you if you want." Sally could see Becky didn't believe her. Sally didn't believe that Blake and Kiera had gone either.

"I'll be fine, and you need to get to work."

"Okay, but forget your car. We'll both go and get it later. I'll feel better if I'm with you along that way until I'm certain they have gone."

Becky just nodded and smiled.

Grabbing her black apron and till keycard, Sally headed off to work, leaving Becky in her flat with instructions to just drop the latch and go out through the shop.

The afternoon in The Black Bull went slowly. It was midweek, and the lunchtime trade was never more than a few regulars and the odd holiday maker from the cottages near South End Woods.

Sally couldn't get the two werewolves out of her head, especially Blake. She had finally met the werewolf who had ruined her life, and she wasn't happy that she'd let him get away. If Becky hadn't been with her she had a feeling she may have lost control. Other than small prey animals when she was out on a full moon night and been forced to take her wolf form, she had never killed anything before. Sure, she had done plenty of damage to other werewolves and local thugs she had ran into on her travels, but she had never killed any of them. The way she had felt last night though when she was faced with the werewolf who had savaged her and made her into a monster was new. She had a feeling she would have killed him then and there and that frightened her. She wasn't a killer and she didn't want to become one. But if she ever lost control, she didn't know what would happen.

When her stint in The Black Bull ended in the early evening, she left the pub and walked slowly round The Green towards her flat, her head still full of conflicting emotions and worry. It was then she caught the scent. Blake's scent and he was coming up from behind her. She spun round quickly and there he was, approaching slowly, his hands up in front of him and palms facing her.

"Easy now, Sally," said Blake, "I have something I need to tell you."

Her wolf growled inside and Sally could feel her teeth grinding together and her hands becoming fists. The intense anger and the desire to kill him began to increase again, just as it had last night. She felt her hackles rise and her skin prickle as her wolf pushed against the surface.

"Sneaking up on me isn't the way to do it."

"I didn't sneak up on you. I approached from up wind so you knew I was coming."

She was in the middle of Popwood with people going about their normal business, not the ideal place to sprout claws and attack a stranger. She fought her anger and forced her wolf back down inside. Blake may deserve to die for what he had done but she wasn't a killer, and she wasn't going to let him force her over the line that would mean she had become the monster she hated.

"What could you possibly have to tell me that you think I would be remotely interested in? Or where you going to ask when the next barbeque was so you could get another chance to eat my friends?"

"I told you last night that we were just after some food. Becky just came out of the tent at the wrong time and when she spotted Kiera as a wolf she started throwing stones."

"What did you expect her to do, tickle her behind the ear? She was scared."

"Kiera felt threatened that's all. She's had a hard time and been mistreated. When Becky started pelting her with stones…" He Paused. "Anyway, that's beside the point. I'm here because of Becky."

"Why? What's your interest in Becky now? Haven't you done enough to her? I thought you would've got the message last night that I want you to leave her alone."

Blake looked around, the sun had brought a lot of people out of their homes, and it was clear to Sally that Blake felt uncomfortable.

"We got that message loud and clear. Is there somewhere a little quieter we can go?"

The wolf inside her started to pace again. She felt the hackles rise and her heart begin to race.

This is the one. He's dangerous. Don't trust him.

The voice of her inner wolf bounced around her head and her skin began to tingle. Her wolf was rising, ready to defend them, wanting to get them both away. She took some convincing, but Sally managed to convince her to keep low for a little longer, while she found out what he wanted with Becky.

"Follow me." Sally said after a pause, "Any tricks though and I don't care who sees me rip you to pieces."

"You sure are one angry wolf," he said and let her take the lead.

Sally realised he was right. Ever since Blake and Kiera had turned up she had been on edge. Her determination to protect Becky and the village she had fallen in love with had made her territorial, normal for a wolf, but she didn't like it. Her feelings for the werewolf who had changed her life so dramatically was manifesting as anger and aggression. I'm never angry and aggressive, she thought to herself. He's making me like this. She was finding it hard to handle, everything she was capable of doing was being forced back into her mind.

They walked up the side of the church and into the graveyard behind. The trees that grew around the edge near the walls were enough to shelter them from the neighbouring houses, the family visits to pay respects to lost loved ones would be over for the day so there should be a little privacy. Sally found a bench towards the middle of the cemetery and they both sat.

"So," said Sally, "What's your interest in Becky?"

Blake took a deep breath. "We felt pretty bad about what we did. We didn't really think it through, but we were a little desperate."

"If this is supposed to be an apology you're speaking to the wrong person. Becky is the one you need to apologise to."

"I know, and just over an hour ago that's what Kiera went to do." He paused.

"There's a 'but' coming isn't there," said Sally.

"Yes, there is," said Blake, "Kiera did everything she could but there was too many of them."

Sally felt a thud in her chest, her wolf's ears pricked up and her hackles began to rise again.

"Too many of who? What's happened to Becky?" Sally demanded and stood up, looming menacingly over Blake. He remained seated and held up his hands.

"Calm down Sally and I'll tell you," he said, "We saw Becky picking up her car from the lane near the old mill and Kiera went to talk to her, to apologise. She took her for a walk to explain a few things without you there threatening to rip her insides out. They were walking by the cottages over there." Blake pointed towards the south end of the village.

"The holiday cottages near South End Woods?"

"Yes, I guess so. The research lab I mentioned last night has been trying to track Kiera since she escaped. Well, I guess they found her, and they attacked from the woods with nets, there were a lot of them. She managed to fight off most of them, but they must have thought that Becky was a werewolf too, because she was with Kiera I guess. When Kiera got the chance to look, Becky had gone."

"They took Becky?" Sally could feel her wolf rising and scratching under her skin. "She let them take Becky to save her own scrawny little neck, didn't she?"

"No, she didn't," Blake replied. "She fought as best she could, I think they simply made do with the easier target. Kiera tried to follow but they had a couple of vans waiting behind those holiday cottages. She lost them about a mile down the road.

"Which way did they go?" asked Sally and headed toward the graveyard gate, "South?"

"Yes, but it's too late Sally," he shouted, "They'll be over sixty miles away by now."

Blake got up and ran after her.

"I can't just leave her with them!" Sally didn't want to think of what Becky could be going through. First last night and now this.

"I don't expect you to, but running off after a van that could be anywhere isn't going to work," Blake grabbed Sally by the arm. She spun round and growled at him. "Okay, okay," he said, leaving go of her, "Look, Kiera knows where they'll be heading. Let's go and meet up with her and plan what we can do."

It was an effort, but Sally slowed her breathing and her wolf seemed to settle once she had calmed down a little, content to let Sally handle things for the moment but staying just below the surface, ready and waiting to be let out.

"Okay, but if anything happens to Becky I'll do more than just rip your mate's insides out."

They headed back to the old mill, Sally walked quickly, the thought of Becky being held captive by God knows who burning into her mind. Her breathing got faster, and her chest tightened. She flexed her hands and fingers, trying to distract her mind from the torment happening beneath her skin. Don't shift, she thought to herself, not here, not in the village, please. Her wolf could feel Sally's anxiety and was becoming agitated.

"You know, if you'd left last night when I told you to, this wouldn't have happened."

"I know," replied Blake, "and I'm sorry. We'd planned

on leaving straight after Kiera had apologized to Becky."

They entered the warehouse by the fire door which Sally had smashed the night before. Kiera was sat on a crate near the back of the building and as Sally and Blake walked in she jumped up to meet them.

As soon as she was within range Sally threw a punch and caught Kiera square on the chin. Her hand was in human form so there were no claws involved but it was enough to put Kiera flat on her back again.

"Hey!" shouted Blake.

"Back off!" Sally replied, "I'm not going to hurt her, but she deserved that. That's for not looking after Becky," said Sally as she stood over her.

To Sally's surprise, Kiera stayed on the floor, only sitting up and rubbing her jaw. She was ready for another fight, but Kiera didn't seem up for it.

"I tried my best to fight them off, but they took me by surprise, they had Becky in seconds," said Kiera, remaining on the floor. "By the time I got the better of the ones attacking me Becky was gone. I chased after them but lost the scent just on the edge of Buckley where the road joins the motorway."

"She couldn't have done any more than she did, Sally," said Blake, "Now if you want to get your friend back then I suggest we start working together."

"Then you'll be able to help us free the pack," added Kiera.

It crossed Sally's mind that Kiera, and maybe even Blake, could have set this up to force her hand again. Would they really try this kind of tactic again? If the research lab had been tracking Kiera since she escaped, then letting them know where she was would be a very risky decision. Kiera wouldn't have been able to guarantee she would get away or that the lab would be satisfied with just taking Becky, or even that they would mistake Becky for a werewolf at all. She dismissed the thought. Even these two wouldn't use that tactic, they can't be that desperate. No, on this occasion Sally came to the conclusion that Kiera was telling the truth and she decided that as long as she got Becky free and got her home unharmed, she would help them do anything. Hell, she would even help them steal the crown jewels if she thought it would save Becky.

"You promise you'll help me get Becky out?" she asked.

"Yes," Blake replied, "I promise."

"What about you?" asked Sally, looking straight at Kiera.

Kiera got up from the floor before answering.

"I'll take you to the lab and tell you everything I can about it. But I'm not going back in there,"

"Once we are there, me and you can handle things, Sally," said Blake, "Kiera will be our backup."

"That makes me feel a whole lot better," said Sally, not trying to hide the cynicism in her voice.

"She has her reasons, Sally, and I'm sure you will

understand once we get there."

"We need your help, Sally," said Kiera. She seemed to be almost begging. Sally couldn't understand the sudden change. "I can't help Blake in there and I need somebody who can. I don't want him going in alone. Blake says that you should be all the help he needs."

Sally looked from one to the other. Blake stood in front of her waiting for her decision, appearing to be full of confidence. Was it confidence that he knew she would help or confidence that he knew she would make a difference? Sally couldn't decide. Kiera, however, looked anxious. If Sally didn't know any better the look in Kiera's eyes could have been one of pleading.

"Okay," said Sally eventually, "I'll help with the pack." She turned to Blake, "But!" she added, "Becky is my priority and if that means getting her out and leaving the pack then that's what I do." Then, a little calmer she added, "But I promise I'll try my best to get the pack out too."

"Fair enough," said Blake.

"Once you see what's happening there," added Kiera, "you won't want to leave any werewolf, pack or not, in that place. Not if you're anything like the werewolf Blake tells me you are."

Sally turned her head to look at Blake.

"How would you know what kind of werewolf I am?"

"Because I've watched you all round this little village,"

he said. "You care about everybody, even if you don't know them all that well. I think if you can help somebody in need, you will."

Sally didn't quite know how to take that last remark. On the one hand she felt suddenly proud he'd seen her in a good light and had obviously read her quite well. On the other, she wasn't overly comfortable with the fact he'd been able to watch her without her knowing.

"I'll just go and throw some gear in a bag and meet you back here," she said, "Or are you picking me up on the way?"

"Picking you up?" Blake asked, looking a little confused.

"Yeah, I take it you have a car or a van or something. I can't drive so we will have to go in yours."

"We don't have a car," he replied, "If you come back here we can head off through the woods and into the hills."

"Hold the phone! You didn't say anything about walking all the way," said Sally, "Can't we just hire a car or jump on a train?"

"No!" Kiera snapped and looked at Blake, "We walk or I'm not doing this."

A little rumble of annoyance started in Sally's stomach at Kiera's outburst. What could be wrong with taking a car?

"You're the one who got Becky kidnapped," replied Sally, in just as strong a tone, "You will be going."

"I'm not going in a car, and that's final."

Sally knew they would be able to travel faster as wolves but because she couldn't control her wolf once she was in her wolf form that wasn't an option. They needed another form of transport because walking would take too long.

"Fine, we'll take a train then," Sally stood square on but to her surprise Kiera didn't shy away this time.

"No trains either."

"Why?" said Sally, "What's wrong with that? Are you trying to stall?" Sally took a step closer to Kiera.

Blake stepped between them both, breaking up what was starting to become another very heated argument. A situation like this between two werewolves could quite easily result in fur and claws.

"Let's just calm down shall we," he said, "We'll be walking because I promised Kiera that was what we would be doing."

"That's just stupid," replied Sally, "It'll take too long, and Becky could be getting hurt right now. We're just wasting time."

"Kiera doesn't do well in enclosed spaces," he said, "So we have to walk."

"That's her problem not mine," said Sally, "She can meet us there. I need to get Becky out and spending time strolling down the country isn't going to help me do that quickly is it."

"You won't get there any quicker without Kiera because

she's the only one who knows where this research lab is. We also need her knowledge of the inside, so we can get in and out quickly without attracting the attention of the guards."

Sally threw her hands in the air; her wolf was pacing again out of pure frustration. She turned and walked away shaking her head.

"I still don't understand why we can't go in a car. We can open a window if she's that scared."

"It's not that simple," said Blake.

"Why?" shouted Sally, spinning around to face them again, "Give me one good reason. Just one."

"Because I was locked up in nothing more than a cupboard for nearly two years," shouted Kiera, tears starting to well up in her eyes, "They tortured me daily just so they could watch me shift and take notes and blood samples." The tears started to trickle down her cheeks. "That's why! I have nightmares about it every night and being in small spaces brings it all back. Do you have any idea what it's like to have nightmares every time you go to sleep, to not want to sleep because you know what is waiting for you if you do?" Kiera's voice almost became a growl. "Do you have any clue?"

Sally knew about nightmares alright. Her breath caught at the memory of what it was like to not have any control over dreams that came and haunted her as soon as she closed her eyes when it became impossible to stay awake any longer. She stood and watched Kiera break down in tears and collapse into a sobbing heap on the floor. Blake went and knelt beside her, just stroking her hair and whispering a few words of comfort.

Sally stared at the werewolves for a while but saw only two people, two friends, one comforting the other. She walked over and knelt at the other side of Kiera, placing her hand gently onto the girl's shoulder.

"Yes," she said quietly, "I know exactly what it's like to have nightmares." She rubbed Kiera on the back, "It's okay, we'll walk."

Sally got up and headed for the door.

"I'll be back in fifteen minutes," she shouted back as she left.

Chapter 7

Blake was outside the warehouse on his own when Sally got back.

"You have nightmares too?" he asked.

"Don't go there," replied Sally, placing her rucksack on an upturned oil drum next to him, "That's something else I have you to thank for."

Kiera came out of the fire door all packed and ready. She still looked like she'd been crying but had pulled herself together while Sally had been away.

"Come on then," Blake patted Sally on the shoulder, "We need to get a move on if we are going to get far enough into the hills to make camp before nightfall."

"Can't we keep going?" asked Sally, "We're werewolves, we don't need much sleep."

Blake shook his head. "I would rather only travel during the day," he said, "That way we have less chance of running into vampires."

Sally stared at him and wondered if she had heard him correctly.

"Vampires? You can't be serious."

"Of course I'm serious," he replied, "If we stick to the more remote areas we should be okay, vampires prefer towns and cities."

"You're telling me vampires really exist?"

"Sally, you're a werewolf. Do you think we're the only kind of supernatural creatures to roam the earth?"

When Sally thought about it, which she hadn't before, it made sense. If the myths about werewolves were true, then why not the myths about vampires?

"But what about the bodies?" asked Sally.

"What bodies?" Blake had a confused look on his face.

"The bodies of the people that vampires kill. If they live in towns and cities there must be bodies all over the place with marks on their neck?"

"Vampires don't need to kill people to feed," Kiera added. "They have people they use as donors. Some are volunteers, some they collect from the area."

That made Sally think a little more. Maybe some of the missing persons on police files have been, 'collected', by vampires.

"Do they live in packs?" Sally asked.

"They call their packs families," said Kiera.

The investigative journalist in Sally was starting to get more interested in the supernatural world of which she was part, and yet knew very little of. She started to wish she'd brought her notebook.

"So, if werewolf and vampire myths are both true," she said, "what other supernatural creatures don't I know about?"

"Oh, there's plenty. I've not come across that many myself but if I were you, I'd keep an open mind. Anyway, vampires and werewolves will give us enough trouble without worrying about any of the others. There's etiquette we can use to handle the werewolves. Vampires on the other hand, well, they will be more of a challenge and one we should avoid until we get to the lab."

"What etiquette?" Sally asked.

Blake stared at her for a few moments.

"That pack I left you with really told you nothing did they."

"That pack you left me with were no better than wild animals. Their only interest was who was going to be top dog or how they were going to knock the top dog off their pedestal."

"Didn't you have any questions?"

"Loads, but not many of them were interested in explaining things to me. They were too busy fighting over who was going to 'own' me."

Blake looked at her and shook his head.

"You should have been too strong for any of them to 'own' you," he said.

"I was, I guess," Sally replied, "The only trouble was that once they realised that, I became a threat. They asked me to leave or they would hurt my family."

"Why didn't you just kill the alpha and then lead the pack?" asked Kiera, "They couldn't hurt your family then."

"I'm not a killer," Sally snapped.

"You're a werewolf," said Kiera.

"That's no reason to kill anybody."

"You threatened to kill us last night."

"You two are an exception," said Sally. "He turned me into a monster and you tried to eat my friend then you kidnapped her."

"This is getting us nowhere." Blake's voice was deep and authoritative for once. "If we don't work as a team neither Becky nor the pack get rescued. Now we can work out the details on the way but right now I think we need to get going."

The two girls stopped bickering and Sally turned to Blake and nodded. Kiera did the same.

"Good. That's agreed then," said Blake. "Keeping to the remote areas will probably keep us clear of the vampires for a while but we will definitely run into werewolf territory and when we do we go around it if we can. If we must go through a pack's territory, then we hunt out the alpha and let him know we are there and that we are simply passing through. An alpha tends to get in a very bad mood if other werewolves waltz through his land without informing him and asking for permission. An alpha pair in a bad mood is not something you want to come across if you can help it."

Kiera disappeared back into the warehouse to get Blake's rucksack and to make sure they hadn't left anything behind.

Sally thought of all the disagreements with werewolves she'd had during her search for a place like Popwood.

"That explains a few things," she said quietly to herself. "Is the research lab in a town?" she asked.

"No," Blake replied, "Kiera said it's in a small valley, away from prying eyes."

"Good, then I needn't worry about vampires too much."

"Actually…" Blake started to say something but stopped when Kiera appeared.

"I'm ready when you are," she said, and threw Blake's rucksack to him.

They made their way around the back of the old mill warehouse and headed off across North Farm towards the surrounding hills.

As they left, Sally phoned Tim in The Black Bull. If neither she nor Becky turned up for work he would worry and end up calling the Police or the Mountain Rescue Team or something. The best story she could come up with was that she'd been called back home urgently because her mother had just had a serious accident and Becky had offered to drive her straight there. She could tell Tim wasn't very happy with two of his staff taking off together at such short notice, but he told her not to worry, that he would get the shifts covered and to take whatever time she needed. It was only after she had hung up that she remembered that Becky's car was still parked in the village. It was behind her house though so with a bit of luck nobody would notice.

Sally walked behind the other two, staring at the back of

their heads, her wolf telling her not to trust them. She blamed Blake for what she was, so not trusting him was going to be easy. It was Kiera who was going to be the problem. Seeing Kiera breakdown as she did had made Sally's resentment for her start to fade just a little. She was still annoyed with her for being part of the plot to kidnap Becky, but Sally could tell Kiera's head was a mess. With everything Kiera had been through for the last two years, Sally supposed she could cut Kiera a little slack for a while. The journey was going to be a long one if they were constantly at each other's throats. They all had more or less the same goal, which was to get into this research lab and rescue a friend, a goal which would only be achievable if they worked as a team. Sally decided to bottle her feelings for the two werewolves for a few days, then once Becky and the pack were free she wouldn't have to see either of them again. She could then, hopefully, get back to some sort of normality.

They walked in silence through the last of the fields and into the trees. Sally's senses were filled with the sounds and smells she now loved, fresh pine, damp earth and animals; she didn't need to be in her wolf form to appreciate the scent of the wild. This was one change since becoming a werewolf that she didn't mind, something she enjoyed sharing with her inner wolf. She often came up here when she needed to clear her head or think about an article she was writing, the sights, sounds and smells helped her relax and wind down. Now that

Sally's temper was calming a little, she decided to make an effort to get to know something about her two traveling companions.

"So, how did the pack get captured?" she asked.

Blake's head lowered, but he said nothing. Sally looked over at Kiera hoping she would answer for him, but she only shook her head, a look of warning clear on her face, telling Sally not to take the conversation any further. So much for her efforts to get a discussion going.

Sally tried changing the subject. "So how far is this place then? The research lab I mean."

"Somewhere in Dartmoor as far as I can tell from what Kiera has told me," Blake replied.

"Dartmoor!" Sally stopped. "That's going to take us about a week."

"Six day's I reckon," Blake replied, "As long as we don't run into any trouble."

Running into trouble on her travels was something Sally had always been very good at.

"But full moon is in seven days." Sally started to get a little agitated. "If we do rescue them all by then, Becky is going to be in the middle of a pack of werewolves on a full moon night with only me to protect her, and I don't even know if I can do that when I'm a wolf."

"It will be worse for her if we don't," said Kiera. Sally turned, there was a look of real concern on Kiera's face. "I've just remembered," she continued. "At full moon all the werewolves are put in one large holding area so that the scientists can study the carnage and fights that happen when they put live meat in with them. If they still think Becky is a werewolf by then, well, she will be put in with the pack."

"No!" Sally was starting to pace back and forward, mimicking what her wolf was doing inside. "Surely they won't still think Becky's a werewolf by then. Once she doesn't change they will know they have a human."

"I resisted the change for three weeks when I was there," said Kiera. "There's a chance that they may just think she's just a very strong-willed werewolf."

"They'll tear her apart," said Sally.

"No, they won't," said Blake. "My pack won't do a thing like that. They know I don't allow them to attack humans."

Sally huffed, "Come off it, Blake. They're werewolves, you're a werewolf, I'm a werewolf. I think we all know what's going to happen."

"My pack are different."

"I sure hope so," Sally replied, "For Becky's sake." She put both arms through her backpack, making it more secure. "Let's get going. I don't want her anywhere near your pack and we're wasting time."

They set off again, but this time Sally was setting the pace, fast and determined. Her attempts at making conversation weren't making the situation between the three werewolves any easier. She figured if they weren't talking they may as well pick up speed.

The further they travelled the more miserable the weather became. Sally would have given anything to be able to be sat in front of a warm fire now with Becky, each with a glass of Prosecco in their hands and some Nachos on the table.

The light was beginning to fade, a rumble in her stomach reminded Sally she hadn't eaten since before starting her shift. Her wolf was awake too and the smell of the animals in the undergrowth was making them both hungry.

Kiera sniffed the air. "I think it's time to go hunting," she said, "I'm starving."

Sally kept on walking. "After you two dragged me on this trip you don't think you're getting me to eat skinny little rabbits and rodents do you. There's a town in the next valley." She turned to Blake, "You can treat me to a nice pub meal. If we pick one that rents rooms, we can have a decent night's sleep too instead of having to find some shelter out here."

"I told you, we're staying away from towns and cities because of the threat of vampires," replied Blake.

"Come off it, Blake," said Sally, "I know this town and I haven't caught the scent of anything I didn't recognise. I'm sure if I'd come across the scent of the living dead, or whatever they are, I would have noticed. The only thing you will come across down there is a small pack of werewolves."

"I'm in charge and we aren't going into a town," he said,

in what Sally guessed was his best alpha male voice meant to show his supremacy. The only trouble was it wasn't going to work on her.

"You keep forgetting, Blake," she said, "I'm not one of your pack lackeys. We eat in the town and you're footing the bill."

Kiera gave Sally a long cold stare at the use of the words, 'pack lackeys'. Sally could feel the tension rise a little once more, but she had meant what she said and the fact that Kiera didn't like the tag wasn't her concern.

They made their way through the trees, which were all planted in regimental rows in a manmade forest and came out onto a small country road leading into the town. When they reached the first of the houses, Blake stiffened and sniffed the air.

"This is where the local werewolf pack's territory starts," said Blake. It probably extends up into the hills on the far side of the town. We need to find the alpha."

Sally gave a sigh. "More stupid pack politics," she said, "I'm so glad I'm not part of all that rubbish."

"That rubbish, as you call it," he replied, "is the way we do things and it has stopped packs tearing each other apart for centuries. You'll do well to learn some of it."

"How are you going to know where to find the alpha?" asked Sally. "There must be half a dozen different werewolf scents here."

"Take a long sniff Sally," said Blake. "Can you make out which scent is more prevalent than the others? A scent that seems to have been left on purpose?"

She lifted her nose and sniffed around. There was a scent that seemed to stand out, it was male, and the more she sniffed the more she realised it was all around them and not simply passing the place they were standing.

"Yes, I can. But it doesn't seem to lead anywhere."

"He has marked his territory," said Blake. "Most alphas do that."

Sally screwed up her face. "So, you're telling me he's pee'd all over here? That's disgusting."

"Come with me Sally and I'll show you how to track for an alpha."

Sally just laughed. "No way. You go and do what you need to do," she said, "Me and Kiera will go and find a pub that serves food and we'll meet you there. I think it's called The Royal Oak, if my memory serves me correctly." She wanted to get Kiera on her own to find out a little bit more about Blake.

"Have you been here before?" asked Kiera.

"I just passed through, before I settled in Popwood."

"You really should come too," said Blake, "I've told you that there's certain etiquette."

"Which I'm sure you know much more about that I do so I trust you to handle it."

Sally patted Blake on the arm and gave him one of her looks that always appeared to get up the nose of anybody she was trying to annoy. It seemed to work on Blake just as well.

"Anyway," she added, "I want to have a talk to Kiera. I think me and her have gotten off on the wrong foot."

She smiled at Kiera and got a confused and unsure look from her in return. She clearly trusted Sally as little as Sally trusted her.

Blake wandered off muttering something about acting like a child, his nose in the air tracking the scent of the alpha. Sally and Kiera set off along the high street towards what Sally thought she remembered as being a town square surrounded by bars and bistros.

The smell of the restaurants, Italian, Greek, and a steakhouse drifted over the square filling the two girls' noses and making their mouths water in anticipation. Then another smell hit them from close by, the scent of a werewolf.

They both caught the scent at the same time and looked around in search of its source.

"He's on this side," said Kiera and Sally turned to see a medium sized male approaching.

"Well, well, well," he said, "If it isn't our little troublemaker, Sally Bowers." He walked around them, his eyes flicking from one girl to the other and looking them up and down. "And I see you've brought a friend with you." His eyes settled on Kiera. "Very nice too," he added and reached his hand out to touch her face.

Kiera pushed his hand away and stared him straight in the eye.

"Feisty little thing isn't she," and he raised his hand to Kiera's face once more. Kiera pushed it away again, this time with a little more force. "Fine," he said, then slapped her hard across her face, knocking her to the floor. "Have it your way."

"Hey!" shouted Sally, "That's enough of that," and she stepped in between Kiera and him.

"I see you haven't changed," he said. "Still sticking your nose into other people's business. You want to be careful somebody doesn't rip it off and spoil that pretty little face of yours."

"Well that won't be you," Sally replied.

He just laughed and turned slightly as if he was moving away. Then, with one swift movement he swung a fist, aiming it at Sally's face. Her arm was up before the punch even got close, blocking the attack easily and countered with a punch to his stomach. The force doubled him over before an uppercut straightened him back up. As his head came up level with hers she brought her forearm round with blistering speed, smashing it into the side of his head and he hit the ground.

"As I said," she repeated, "that won't be you."

Kiera was up and at her side now and the two girls stood over him together. He staggered to his feet and pointed a finger in Sally's face.

"You know you shouldn't be here," he said, almost spitting the words at her.

Sally grabbed his hand and twisted then squeezed. There was a crunch of bone, and the would-be hard man dropped to his knees, his face contorted in pain.

"I'm not staying don't worry. We're only passing through. We'll be gone in the morning."

Sally let go and once again he got to his feet, cradling his hand and backing away slowly. When he was about ten yards away he turned and walked off quickly.

The look on Kiera's face was one of shock and amazement.

What?" said Sally.

"You keep your werewolf strength even in your human form don't you," she exclaimed.

"Yes," replied Sally, "Don't you?"

"No, I don't," said Kiera, "and as far as I know, other than Blake, nobody else does either."

"Really?"

"Yes, really. How do you do it?"

"I don't know," Sally answered, "I've always been stronger and faster since I was bitten."

"I've noticed your eyes change colour too," said Kiera, "Why do you do that?"

"I don't know," said Sally, "I was going to ask you how you stop yours changing."

"I don't have to. It doesn't happen to me. You're a curious werewolf, Sally."

There was a long silence between them. Kiera stared at Sally, obviously deep in thought.

"Come on," said Sally when she couldn't bear the silence any longer, "I'm hungry. Let's go and get something to eat."

When they reached the Royal Oak, Kiera sent a text to Blake telling him where they were and asking if he wanted her to order him some food. The two girls found themselves a table in the far corner, their wolf instincts wanting a position where they could see any potential threat coming.

They tucked into their food as soon as it hit the table. Neither thought about waiting for Blake to arrive. They put his plate to one side. Their moods brightened as they ate and Sally relaxed in Kiera's company, who seemed to do the same.

"Back in the warehouse," said Kiera, "your hands and teeth changed. I thought you were going to shift but you didn't. You just sort of partially changed. How did you do that?"

"I just let the lycanthropy flow into the places I need it. My wolf moves closer to the surface but just watches and gives me help where I need it." Sally laughed. "That sounds so weird."

"You have very good control over your wolf," said Kiera, "If I start to change then it's a full change and I can't do anything about it."

"I don't have any control over her," said Sally, "The

powers I get to use she lets me use. If she's determined to come out, then she does."

"Well, I'm impressed anyway," said Kiera, "The only thing I have in my human form is a good sense of smell, hearing and eyesight, I think that's true of every werewolf though. I'm nothing special."

Sally hesitated and watched Kiera pick at what was left of her food, which wasn't much. Werewolves are not known for their lack of appetite. There was something sad about Kiera. Sally couldn't tell if it was the fact she was a werewolf, which should have been enough to sadden any person, or if it was the things she had been through at the hands of the research lab.

"Who told you that?" asked Sally.

"What?"

"That you're nothing special."

"Nobody has to tell me. I just know it."

Sally studied the girl across the table. Kiera obviously had lots on her mind. None of which Sally wanted to know, but she was starting to see Kiera in a different light.

"How many others escaped from the lab?" asked Sally.

"None," replied Kiera," only me.

"I think that makes you pretty special then. Don't you?"

"I just took my chance and ran for it." Kiera said, "There's nothing special in that."

"You didn't just run away though. You avoided getting

recaptured and made your way back to Blake to get help. Now, you're on your way back to get the rest of your pack out. If you want my opinion that shows just how special you are."

Kiera looked up and smiled. Sally hadn't seen Kiera smile once since they met.

"What happened the night the pack was captured?" asked Sally and Kiera's smile disappeared.

Kiera didn't answer, she looked down and stared at her empty glass, tapping the sides and twisting it round and round.

"I was just too slow," said Kiera eventually and stood up. "Do you want another drink?" she asked.

End of conversation again, Sally thought to herself.

"Yes please," she said, handing Kiera her empty glass.

She watched Kiera make her way to the bar. She couldn't understand why the night of the pack's capture should be such a no-go subject. Both Blake and Kiera refused to talk about it or changed the subject as soon as it was raised. She assumed it must have been a well planned attack. Why Blake's pack though? The research team must have passed dozens of pack territories before they reached Blake's pack way up north. It looked to Sally as if they had traveled the length of the country to capture one particular pack. Blake must have been targeted. That raised another question in Sally's mind. Why hadn't they taken Blake too?

Blake arrived at the same time as Kiera returned with the drinks.

"Have you two been at each other's throats again?" he said as he sat at the table.

"What do you mean?" asked Sally.

He nodded towards Kiera and at the mark on her face where she had been struck earlier by the local werewolf.

"That wasn't me," said Sally.

"We ran into a bit of trouble with an old friend of Sally's," said Kiera.

"Acquaintance," Sally corrected.

"You should have been looking after her while I was gone," he said, looking straight at Sally.

"Hey, I did, don't worry," Sally replied, "He went away with his tail between his legs. Besides, Kiera is well capable of looking after herself."

"It was handy you were there though," Kiera added.

"He probably wouldn't have attacked if I wasn't there," said Sally, "You would have been okay."

"Why would he attack because you were there?" asked Blake.

"Oh nothing, I just had a little run in with them last time I was here."

"A little 'run in'," said Blake, emphasizing the last two words.

"Yeah, it was nothing."

"I've just spent half an hour with the alpha convincing him we wouldn't be causing any trouble," said Blake, "What happened last time you were here? What do you class as nothing?"

Sally paused, wondering if she should tell Blake the whole story but decided the edited highlights would be good enough.

"It was just a misunderstanding."

Blake remained silent, staring at her, waiting for Sally to elaborate.

"I just helped out a couple who own a café at the other end of the high street," Sally continued, "I'd only just arrived and decided on a coffee while I got my bearings. These two guys came in and wanted the owner to handover some of their takings as protection money. I didn't like it."

"And these two guys were werewolves?" asked Blake.

"No," replied Sally, "Just two local villains."

"Then why would the pack have any trouble with you stepping in?"

"I gave them a bit of a pasting and they came back with a few others. I didn't know at the time, but they were a kind of local mafia. They had a protection racket going all over the town. The guy we came across earlier was amongst them. He was the pack's mafia representative, for want of a better description. They had some sort of deal going I think."

Blake put his elbows on the table and dropped his head into his hands. "Please go on," he said, "but I don't think I'm not going to like it."

"You're probably going to hate it," replied Sally. "Look, he thought he could handle me himself, he was wrong. The others got involved to help and when the other business owners saw them attacking a 'poor defenseless' young girl they all came out and helped me. The protection racket was sort of over by then I guess. All the locals decided to stand together and the gang were chased off."

"I still don't understand," said Kiera, "Why would the pack be annoyed with you that some gang of criminals had been thrown out by the locals?"

"Because," said Blake, "the pack alpha was probably getting a rather large cut for allowing the protection gang to operate. I've seen it before with some packs, they have an understanding with the local villains and they don't get in each other's way. Our little heroine here cut off what I'm guessing would have been a rather substantial income." He turned to Sally. "Am I right?"

"You might be," Sally replied, a little sheepishly, "Look, I wasn't just going to stand there and let this couple be robbed of most of their weekly takings, was I?"

"So, what happened with you?" asked Kiera.

"The alpha guy and some of his cronies came looking for me. As it was a crowded place, and the locals had already stood up for me once they didn't want to 'teach me a proper lesson' as they put it. They said I should leave and never come back or they would carry out my sentence."

"Which was?" asked Blake.

"I don't know," said Sally, "They never said."

"And you didn't think to tell me about this order for you never to return before we came here and before I went off looking for the alpha?"

"I thought it was just words to scare me off. I didn't want any trouble, I just wanted a place to live in relative peace and quiet. So, I decided to leave. I didn't think they would remember me. That was over a year ago."

"Please promise me you won't be keeping anymore secrets from me on this trip." said Blake. "It would make our travels much easier and faster if I didn't have to find out things as we go."

"Okay," she agreed, "no more secrets."

Blake got up from his seat. "Come on, we're leaving. Now."

"Why?" said Sally, "Just over one little scuffle with an arrogant little bully?"

"No." said Blake, "Because of the fact the arrogant little bully is probably with the alpha right now telling him you're back. The alpha will put two and two together and come up with us three."

"Your maths is rubbish."

"This isn't a joke, Sally!" Blake raised his voice, the alpha in him suddenly appearing. "I don't want us to be here when the pack turn up. We're leaving, now."

Kiera got up and put on her jacket while Sally huffed and puffed and under her breath said, "I'm sick of being told to move on everywhere I go." But she got up and made her way out of the pub behind them.

They headed along a side street and behind the pub where they found a little alley way leading onto some rough ground. When they rounded the corner at the other end of the alley all three of them stopped. "Shit!" they said in unison when they caught the scent of werewolf. Five people stood in front of them blocking their way. Three were large males, the smaller male was the bully from earlier and the last one was a female. Sally recognised them all. The alpha pair and their lieutenants were the ones who had asked her to leave when they last met, not too far from this very spot as it turned out. At least they were in their human form, Sally thought to herself.

"You didn't tell me she was one of you little pack, Blake," said the male in the centre of the five.

"It's okay, Mitch," said Blake, "we're just leaving."

"Mr. Mitchell to you, now that I know you're traveling with this little bitch."

Mitch looked at Sally. "Dean here tells me you attacked him."

"I think the bump on his head has affected the way Dean remembers things," replied Sally.

"Are you calling me a liar?" shouted Dean.

Blake stepped forward, his hands in front of him, his

palms facing the pack.

"Nobody's calling anybody anything," said Blake, "Please accept my apologies for anything we've done to upset you. We don't want any trouble; we were only looking for a place to rest for the night. Sally has just explained some of the details of your last encounter with her. We'll find somewhere else."

Mitch pointed at Blake and Kiera and flicked his hand to the side in the direction of the surrounding trees. "You two can leave," he said, "but she stays." He looked directly at Sally. "She's trouble, Blake. You don't want to be traveling with her. She'll cause you more trouble than she's worth. You just leave her here with us and I'll make sure she never causes you anymore hassle."

Sally knew she couldn't handle all of them at once on her own. Her stomach started to churn, and she could feel her wolf getting agitated. It sensed danger and wanted to get them both out of there. From where Sally stood, running wasn't an option. The pack had maneuvered so Sally had her back to a wall. For the first time since she became a werewolf Sally felt a fear inside starting to rise.

Blake took a deep breath and sighed, giving Sally a quick sideways glance, "I'm sorry, but she comes with us," then he added, "and the name is Mr. Mulligan to you."

Sally felt a little relief that she wasn't going to face them alone, but the fear remained when she sensed the hostility of the pack suddenly build. The scent of werewolves grew stronger as inner wolves started to rise to the surface. Everybody was getting a little twitchy. Blake's words and the tone in which they were said, a clear indication that the talking was over. The five pack members spread out around the three visitors. The female alpha moved round close to where Kiera was standing. Mitch and his largest lieutenant lined up in front of Blake, the remaining lieutenant moved round to cover Sally, Dean joining him.

All eight werewolves stood looking at each other, the air almost crackling with the tension. Sally shut out all the noise around her, the cars driving by the alley on the road a little way off, the laughing and shouting of the people in the nearby streets, she focused on the sounds of the five werewolves facing her. She heard their breathing change to slow calculated breaths; her breathing had done the same. She could hear faint growls coming from deep within each of them. She watched the hands of the five pack members closing into fists as they prepared for battle. The alpha male let out one last breath and the area went silent. Then, with just one single snort from the alpha, the pack attacked as one.

Chapter 8

Mitch's lieutenant launched himself straight at Sally but she was ready for him. Her werewolf reflexes kicked in and she side stepped the large, clumsy male easily. Sally had hoped he would hit the wall behind her as it was clearly his intention to crush her against it in the first place. He didn't. He stopped just in time and spun himself around using his hands to push his great bulk away from the wall as he turned. Sally was ready for him again and punched him hard in the face, the lycanthropy allowing her to get enough force behind the punch to stop him dead. She followed up immediately with a second punch and he was knocked back against the wall. Her third punch cracked his head against the brickwork, his eyes glazed, his body went limp and he slipped down to the ground.

Sally spun around expecting to find Dean attacking her while her back was turned, and sure enough that was his plan. He grabbed her wrist and threw a punch, hitting Sally on the side of the head. It was a weak punch and she ignored it. Grabbing the hand that had hold of her wrist so Dean couldn't let go she twisted it on the joint and he squealed in pain as his recently heeled wrist broke again. He went down onto his knees and Sally kicked him in the chest, sending him flying. He landed on his back a few feet away. He lay there whimpering and clutched his wrist to his chest.

She looked over at Kiera, who was on her back and the

female alpha had her pinned to the ground with a hand around Kiera's throat. Kiera was doing her best to block the punches that were being repeatedly thrown at her face, some were starting to hit their mark.

Blake was on the floor with Mitch and the other lieutenant punching and kicking him with everything they had. Sally had to make a quick decision on who to help first. She decided she would apologize to Kiera later and ran towards Blake. She slammed into the side of the lieutenant, the force of the impact knocking him away from Blake and onto the ground. They rolled over a few times and Sally got to her feet in one swift move at the end of a roll. She was a lot more maneuverable than the much larger and slower male, who was only just pushing himself up with his hands. Sally aimed a kick at his exposed and unprotected face. The thud of the impact echoed off the walls on each side of the alley. The lieutenant was straightened up by the force of the blow and Sally's next kick caught him square on the chin. He fell backwards onto the ground with a grunt.

She looked over at Kiera as she blocked one of the female alpha's punches and managed to get a good grip on her wrist and twist. The look on the alpha's face turned to one of agony as Kiera put more and more pressure on it and the alpha leaned to the side and then onto the floor. Kiera was up in a flash and on top of the alpha, this time it was Kiera's fists that were raining down and all of them were finding their mark.

Sally looked over at Blake, hoping to see him getting the better of Mitch just as Kiera was doing with his mate. He wasn't. The first lieutenant Sally had left on the floor, had recovered and both he and Mitch were now on top of Blake, punching and kicking him again. Once again Sally set off at full speed, heading directly for Blake and his two assailants. She hit the lieutenant at full speed with her shoulder just under his arm, knocking him off Blake. Sally rolled and was up in a flash once again but this time her opponent did the same and caught her on the side of the face with a backhanded punch. Pain shot up the side of her face and small lights flashed in her eyes as she landed on her back. Sally shook her head and her vision quickly returned to normal to see the lieutenant standing over her.

"Orange eyes," said the large male as he bent forward. "I've not seen that before."

With one fast, powerful and well aimed kick to the side of his knee from Sally, the lieutenant's leg buckled and he fell heavily onto his back right beside Sally. She threw out and elbow using as much force as she could muster a heard the satisfying crunch as it made contact with his nose. His head was forced back onto the hard tarmac with a sickening crack and his body went limp again.

"Don't talk while you're fighting," said Sally to the unconscious male as she got back to her feet, "it gets me annoyed."

Blake was now in control of his fight with Mitch and was backing the alpha across the open grassed area with a combination of jabs and punches like a well-trained boxer. Kiera was in trouble again though. The other lieutenant had also recovered, dragged Kiera off the female alpha and was holding her while the alpha pummeled Kiera's stomach with punches.

Sally ran over and jumped onto the lieutenant, put her arm around his throat and squeezed with all her strength. He dropped Kiera and reached for Sally's arm, trying to get it away from his windpipe but Sally held on tight.

As Kiera hit the floor the female alpha was once again on top of her trying to use any advantage that she could.

Sally continued to squeeze the lieutenants throat and try as he might he couldn't break her grip. In a desperate attempt to get Sally off he moved quickly backwards, picking up speed as he went in an obvious attempt to crush her between his substantial bulk and the brick wall behind them. Just before they reached the wall Sally let go and dropped to the ground, crouching down low behind the retreating lieutenant. Before he could stop himself he tripped over her and fell back against the wall. Sally was straight back on her feet and as he pushed himself off the wall she threw a punch and heard another satisfying crunch of a nose as her fist landed full in his face. He fell back onto the wall again and as he bounced back off it Sally spun round, bringing her leg up as she did so and slammed the heel of her foot into the side of his head. The force of the kick sent him back against the wall and his head struck the brickwork once more and he slid into a heap on the pavement.

Glancing quickly at Kiera, Sally saw she was once again on top of the female alpha hitting her wherever she could find an available target.

Sally now turned her attention to Blake and saw again he had two opponents and was defending himself with his back to the wall.

"Jeez," said Sally, "Don't these guys ever stay down?"

This time targeting Mitch she ran across the road and slammed into the alpha male's side. To Sally's surprise it was like hitting a tree trunk and all she managed to do was make him stagger slightly. She launched herself at him again, but he caught hold of her in a bear hug and squeezed. She felt the air being slowly squashed out of her lungs and could hear her ribs and spine creak and groan under the pressure he was exerting. She found it hard to get a breath and kicked and wriggled trying to get free. Mitch just continued to squeeze and laughed in her face.

"I should have killed you when we last met," he said. "A mistake I'm not about to repeat. This is where it ends for you, Sally."

She looked around, hoping to see Blake coming to her aid but he was still busy with one of the lieutenants. Kiera was being dragged off the female alpha by the other lieutenant who had recovered again so she wasn't going to be any help. Sally was on her own and the pain was increasing as the life was being squeezed out of her.

Almost in a panic Sally slammed her forearm into Mitch's face but it had no effect. She tried again but the second impact was weaker than the first. Her strength was failing along with her ability to breathe. This battle was beginning to look hopeless.

Sally cried out in pain and Mitch leaned his head back laughing. She saw one chance as his head went back and rammed a finger right up his nostril then ripped it to the side with all the strength she had left.

Mitch's laugh turned to a roar of pain and anger and he let go of her. Sally dropped to her knees, gasping for breath, desperately trying to inflate her lungs. She heard another shout of anger from Mitch then felt a large fist hit her across the face and she was sent rolling backwards over the ground. Small flecks of light once again flashed in her eyes and disrupted her vision. She felt herself being picked up again and this time she was thrown through the air like a ragdoll. She hit the wall and landed on the floor. Pain raced through her body and her vision blurred.

"Don't pass out," said a voice inside. *"Let me out and I'll get you away from all this."*

It took a few seconds for her sight to clear again and

when it did she could see her two companions being beaten by two pack members each.

"No," said Sally, "We need to help them."

Her wolf was almost bouncing off her insides to be let out so she could run and get them both away from danger. The growls came from inside her, she couldn't shift now, not in a town, not in the middle of a fight. Her wolf continued to growl, wanting to be out or to offer help.

"*If we help them it must be done quickly,*" said her inner wolf. "*The other wolf ran off at the start but could soon be back. If you won't let me out, then let me help a little. I don't think we have much time.*"

Sally decided that the offer of help would be enough and accepted. She reached down inside herself and let a small amount of lycanthropy flow to her hands and fingers. Powerful paws appeared, and her fingernails started to grow into razor sharp claws. She felt even more werewolf strength flow into her muscles than usual. Her breathing slowed and a deep, menacing growl came from her throat. She raised her head slowly, surveying everything that was happening and deciding who to take out first.

She launched herself at the closest lieutenant, who was hitting Blake with some sort of extended baton, and she opened the side of his torso with her claws, ripping through his shirt into his skin and scraping bone all in one move. He dropped the baton and held his side, screaming with pain.

Stay Away

Sally raked his leg, opening his thigh in the same manner with her other claw covered hand, and he fell to the ground.

She went straight for the other lieutenant but the cry from his friend had alerted him, and he saw her coming. He managed to grab her arm and use her own momentum to spin her around and land on top of her as she hit the floor. Sally just lifted him off her and threw him away like he weighed almost nothing. She was up and on him before he could defend himself. The claws of one hand ripping into his abdomen while the other followed immediately and slashed across the side of his face.

The other lieutenant was still on the ground a short distance away and the one at her feet was going nowhere either. Kiera was once again on top of the female alpha, raining more blows down onto her face and Blake had pinned Mitch against the wall and was hitting him with a vicious flurry of punches. With one final, swinging, punch he hit Mitch on the chin and the alpha hit the ground.

Kiera got off the beaten female alpha and stepped back breathing heavy. The three companions moved together to the middle of the field of battle, bloody and breathless but victorious.

Mitch got slowly to his feet and looked around at the best fighters in his pack on the floor, in pain and bleeding.

"I didn't want it to come to this," said Blake, "We could have just talked about it.

"You're still not staying," replied Mitch. He pointed at Sally. "She was barred from returning."

"Yes' I know," said Blake, "and when I found out I decided we should go but you and your boys," Blake nodded to the two lieutenants who were still on the floor clutching at their wounds, "decided to put on a show of strength. Five on to three? That wasn't fair odds, was it?"

"No," said Sally, the growl still in her voice and blood dripping from her claws, "You should have brought more."

Mitch looked around as if trying to find somebody.

"If you're looking for your little weasel, Dean, he did his usual trick and high tailed it out of here when the fun started."

"You have no respect for pack laws," added Mitch.

"No, I don't," replied Sally, "and-"

"And she's young," Blake interrupted before Sally could get into full flow once more, "but I am trying to teach her few things that her original pack failed to mention."

"Good luck with that," said Mitch, getting slowly and somewhat painfully to his feet.

Sally was still wondering where Dean was and if he had gone to find some more of the pack. She thought it was best they make a hasty retreat just in case he was on his way back with reinforcements.

"Come on," she said, digging Blake on the arm and nodding her head in the direction of the road back up into the hills. "Let's get going. I wouldn't stay here if you paid me." She tried to get as much disdain in her voice as she could without it turning into a growl.

"Watch her," shouted Mitch as they made their way in the direction of the road out of town, "she's dangerous."

Chapter 9

They left the town behind them and made their way back up into the tree covered hillside. The smell of bricks, concrete and car exhaust fumes, was slowly replaced by the scent of pine trees, damp earth and wildlife once more.

For the next hour they climbed higher into the hills, going deeper into the ever-thickening trees. They said nothing to each other as they walked, and the silence was grating on Sally's emotions. She couldn't tell if the other two were annoyed at her for getting them into a fight with Mitch and his pack or if they were simply weary from the battle.

Sally noticed Kiera kept holding her side every time she needed that extra bit of effort to get over a rock or up a steep section of ground. Kiera's fight with the female alpha had been especially vicious from what Sally had witnessed.

"You fought well back there," said Sally, trying to break the silence. "That female alpha was a nasty piece of work."

"Thanks," said Kiera, "You didn't do too bad yourself, once you stopped playing around with them."

"I wasn't playing around with them."

"Then why did those two guys keep getting back up?"

"I don't like hurting people," said Sally, "and I thought they would give up after a while when they realized that they weren't winning."

"You threatened to rip my insides out not so long ago.

Don't you class that as hurting somebody?"

"That was different. I thought you were trying to hurt a friend of mine."

"Yeah, well I wasn't, and for your information pack alphas and their lieutenants don't just give up in a fight. Why didn't you get your claws out earlier?"

"I don't like to unless it's absolutely necessary."

"Well, when you're fighting with me and we're outnumbered I would prefer it if you did. So, think of it as necessary from now on."

Kiera clutched at her side again and screwed up her face, obviously in pain.

"Are you okay?" asked Sally.

"I'm fine," replied Kiera, the anger starting to grow in her voice.

"Fine," said Sally. "Forgive me for asking."

Sally moved off ahead of Blake and made sure that she walked with the male alpha between her and Kiera until they reached a suitable place to make camp. When they did, she disappeared into the forest by herself while Blake and Kiera got a fire going. She felt the need to keep out of the way of the other two for a little while, to have some time on her own to mull things over. Walking to the lab was taking too long and thinking of Becky held captive in that place was driving her crazy. Kiera's attitude towards her wasn't helping matters and neither was being in the company of two supernatural creatures. They were a constant reminder of what she was and the world to which she now reluctantly belonged.

Her attempt at talking to Kiera clearly hadn't worked and she needed a new approach. On her way back to camp Sally caught three rabbits and as she entered the makeshift camp she threw one at Blake and a second at Kiera.

Kiera looked down at the animal on the ground near her feet.

"A peace offering?" asked Kiera, "From you? I didn't expect that."

"That's because you don't know anything about me."

"Obviously." Kiera picked up the dead rabbit then added, in a low voice, "Thanks."

Sally wasn't that hungry so she offered her rabbit to Blake. After all, he had missed his meal earlier because of the trouble with Mitch and the others. Blake, of course, being a gentleman, wouldn't take it.

They ate sitting around the campfire discussing the route they would take the next day then turned in for the night. Sally lay on her back and looked up through the trees. The thought of where Becky was still bounced around inside her head, preventing her from sleeping. Blake seemed to be asleep, but Sally could hear Kiera moving about on the ground close by and huffing in frustration.

"You know, if you'd have killed a few of them instead of being so gentle with them we may not have had to leave the town at all," said Kiera, appearing to be trying desperately to get comfortable on a pile of leaves she had managed to arrange into a crude little bed but failing.

"I've told you before," Sally's tone was rather forceful, "I'm not a killer."

Kiera gave up trying to get comfortable and moved to sit near the fire, closer to where Sally lay.

"You may think you're not a killer," said Kiera, "but sooner or later that's going to have to change."

"And why would that be?"

"They aren't just going to let us walk in there and get the pack out you know."

"I'm not killing anybody!"

Blake turned over as the two girls' voices began to rise again.

"Are you two at each other again?" he said.

"You haven't told her about the guards, have you?" said Kiera, looking over at Blake.

"I was waiting for the right moment," he said.

Sally sat up.

"You told me there was a team of security guards." She looked between Kiera and Blake. Kiera with a look of 'are you telling her or am I?' on her face. Blake's expression was calm and emotionless, as usual.

"What aren't you telling me?" asked Sally.

"I will if you don't," said Kiera. "She needs to know

what's waiting for her."

"What's waiting for me?" asked Sally. Blake hesitated so Sally added, "When I agreed not to keep anymore secrets from you I was assuming you hadn't kept any from me. What's so special about these guards?"

Blake took a deep breath. "They're all vampires," he said.

"Okay," said Sally, "So, they're vampires. Are you saying I should have brought a crucifix and some holy water?"

Blake cleared his throat. "What do you know about vampires, Sally?"

"Only what I've seen on the television," she replied. "But seeing as what I've seen on television about werewolves is mainly a load of rubbish, I guess I don't know much."

Sally noticed Kiera go very quiet, deep in thought. She'd obviously had a lot of experience with vampires, these vampires in particular she suspected.

"They're the ultimate predator," said Blake, "Strong, silent, very fast, difficult to kill."

"You mean because they're already dead?"

"No. Their healing powers are almost instantaneous. The wooden stake through the heart does work but that's not easy unless they're asleep and their lairs are difficult to get into. That won't be an option for us. The only other way to kill one would be to remove its head from its body. We can do that easier in wolf form, but we can't get into the lab and free the pack as wolves."

Stay Away

A vision of Becky flashed into Sally's mind, alone in a place run by a team of mad professors, a pack of scared, and probably hungry werewolves, and a vampire squadron. Could this get any worse? Sally shook her head in frustration.

"What else do I need to know about them?" said Sally.

"The main weapon they have is obviously their teeth," said Blake, "so avoid those at all costs. They can empty a body of all its blood within minutes. As I said, Vampires are very fast and powerful so don't let one surprise you. If you don't see him coming, then you're probably too late. It's game over."

Blake reached into his rucksack and pulled out a small Japanese sword.

"This is a Wakizashi," said Blake. "Carry it with you when we go into the lab."

He held the sword out to Sally. Carrying a weapon was not something Sally liked the idea of.

"I won't be needing it," she replied and pushed it away.

"I know you don't like to kill anything, Sally," said Kiera, seeming to snap out of her thoughts, "but you can't play about with vampires. They won't show you any mercy and they don't stay down if you manage to put one on its back. You saw the trouble you had with the lieutenants in that pack we just met. If you have to fight a vampire, you have to kill it."

"If it's any consolation, Sally," said Blake, "They're already dead. You'll probably be doing them a favour."

He offered Sally the sword again.

"Take it," he said, "just in case. If you need it, use it."

"I'll try," said Sally quietly, taking the sword.

"No," said Kiera, "There is no try. If one attacks you then you kill it, no hesitation, no mercy. You take its head off with that." She pointed at the sword in Sally's hand. "You hesitate; you die. It's as simple as that."

"And remember," added Blake, "Don't let one catch you by surprise. It really is all over if that happens."

"You're both making me feel so much better you know."

Sally wasn't sure if her sarcasm was to hide her fear from Blake and Kiera, or to hide it from herself. Being a werewolf had always frightened her, but the way these two described vampires had made them sound almost invincible.

Blake gave a little smile and patted Sally on the shoulder.

"Don't worry," he said, "you'll be fine. Besides, I have a plan and if it comes off then hopefully we can be in and out before the vampires realize what we're doing."

"What plan?" asked Sally, "Are you going to tell me or is that a secret too?"

"It will be easier to show you once we get there and you can see the layout of the place. Plus, we have a contact in there who'll be a great help if we can get his attention."

"Who's the contact?"

"One of the pack," said Kiera, "He got himself in the good books with the guards and staff. A sort of good behavior thing. He gets a little more freedom around the place than the others."

"Good behavior?" asked Sally, "You mean he does as he's told, or he grasses up the rest of the pack?"

"He just doesn't cause any trouble," said Kiera.

"Come on," said Sally, "I may not know much about this place but I'm betting you don't get freedom to roam around just by being a good boy. Who's he sold out?"

"He wouldn't do a thing like that," said Kiera.

"Wake up," said Sally. "He'll smell us coming a mile off. He knows your scents. As soon as he gets so much as a sniff he'll know what's going down and he'll be straight to the vampires."

"He won't go against his alpha," said Kiera, "You don't realize the pull your pack has on your wolf inside."

"And you don't seem to understand the human trait he still has of saving his own skin."

"I don't believe it. Not one of our pack. We don't work like that."

"Well, I hope you're right."

"Come on you two," said Blake, "Can it for a few hours will you. Let's get some rest."

He turned over and settled back down as easily as if he was in his own bed back home. Kiera huffed as she lay back down on her pile of leaves. She appeared to settle too but Sally could still sense her agitation and knew she was just lying there. Tucking the wakizashi into her rucksack she lay back and continued to stare at the sky. Clouds had covered the stars and blocked her view. She thought that Kiera's mind was clouded when it came to her little goodie goodie pack wolf, who seemed to have a freedom in the lab that none of the others did. Sally eventually dropped off but visions of Becky in a corner of a room surrounded by wolves disturbed her sleep and made her restless.

Becky backed into the corner while Sally stood between her and the many wolves that were approaching. There were too many of them. She couldn't protect Becky from them all. She was outnumbered and in danger herself. Her inner wolf wanted to be set free and was tearing at the surface, but Sally couldn't let her out. If she shifted now, she didn't want to think about what would happen to Becky. The wolves closed in slowly, snarling and growling, showing their teeth, spreading out so there was no escape. Sally's inner wolf knew they would be killed unless she was let out.

Sally could feel her wolf's panic building inside and tried to stop the change she could feel getting closer. She gritted her teeth and concentrated on something other than the wolf fur rising under her skin. She looked down and watched in horror as her hands started to change into wolf paws, she could feel her teeth elongating and the familiar pain as her body started to crack and change shape.

"No! Not now," she cried.

The change was happening and there was nothing she

could do to stop it. She managed to claw her way out of her clothes just in time. Her wolf was out.

The wolf looked round at the advancing pack then stared at the human in the corner. There was something familiar about the female, but she was hungry and ignored the memory. She started to snarl and growl with the rest of the pack, her hunting instincts taking over. The human held out her hand and was saying something she couldn't understand. The wolf growled once more and then lunged at its prey.

Sally woke with a start, sweat running down her face and her breathing was fast and urgent.

She looked around, checking where she was then wondering if she'd woken her two companions. Kiera was still asleep, Blake wasn't there. She picked up the jacket she had been using as a makeshift pillow and wrapped it round her shoulders. A small note that had been pushed under her jacket flew up in the air and landed at her feet. She opened it as Kiera turned over and stretched.

Sally

I've gone ahead to do a little scouting. Follow the trail south and I will meet you at Scarne Point.

Blake

P.S. Talk to Kiera. I need you two focused if we are going to get Becky and the pack out.

"What's that?" said Kiera as Sally tossed the note into the remains of the fire.

"It's a note from Blake. He wants us to meet him further south at Scarne Point. He's gone on ahead to scout around."

"He left you a note instead of me?"

Sally could see the fact that Blake had left the note for her was winding Kiera up again and she was a little ashamed of the pleasure she felt inside but, keeping Blake's P.S. in mind, she didn't play on the point.

"It didn't have a name on it. I just assumed it was to both of us."

She hated missing out on an opportunity to twist a knife into Kiera's feelings, but she wanted Becky free more than she cared about what Kiera was thinking. Blake was right. For Becky's sake she needed to be focused and could put on a brave face and pretend to get along, until Becky was safe that is.

They gathered their few belongings, put out the fire and set off south along the trail. They had all agreed it was the best way the night before. Sally led the way and set a less than leisurely pace. She wanted to get to the lab as soon as she could so Becky didn't have to stay there longer than was absolutely necessary.

The morning sun was well above the horizon and the sky was a clear blue; one of the best days of summer the year had offered so far. By the time they'd climbed the hill and passed through the trees, finding at last the winding trail that led toward the southern reaches of the Pennines, they were hot, and their bodies drenched in sweat.

Sally slowed her pace and took a mouthful of water from a steel bottle while Kiera caught up with her. She held out the bottle to Kiera. After a hesitation Kiera took it and had a few sips before handing it back.

"Thanks," she said.

Remembering Blake's P.S. once more Sally felt she should make another effort to get along with Kiera. They had something in common through their lycanthropy but in every other way they were different. The way Sally felt about being a werewolf, about werewolf packs and about the supernatural world she was just starting to discover, was the total opposite to how Kiera felt. But, Kiera knew things that Sally didn't. She knew about werewolves, vampires and the supernatural. She knew about Blake and the pack's history. Kiera may be the best chance Sally had of finding some answers to the questions that had plagued her mind over the last few years. If she was going to get those answers, then she had to get on better terms with her travel companion. She could see this was maybe why Blake had left early, forcing the two girls to walk together, to get to know more about each other.

"Can I ask you something?" said Sally as they started walking again.

"What about?" replied Kiera.

"Your pack, and the night you were all captured."

"I don't like to talk about it."

Kiera picked up her pace and headed off along the trail. Sally matched her stride for stride.

"I know you don't. Neither does Blake. You both clam up every time I mention it."

"We have our reasons. Take the hint."

"I'm sure you do, but I get the feeling there's something important in all of this that you're still not telling me. The questions I have in my head keep mounting up because of it."

"How would knowing more about that night help you? You've already said that you don't care for pack politics."

"You're right I don't. But I can't understand how a full pack can be captured so easily. You saw the problem we had with just a few pack members last night."

Kiera slowed down and Sally could sense that she was struggling with the memory. It was making her agitated and Sally could smell Kiera's fear. A fear of what? She didn't know, but it had to have something to do with the night of the capture. She kept quiet until Kiera eventually broke the silence.

"The pack was in a panic when the attack came and not

fighting as a unit. With no alpha there to lead us the pack disintegrated. Blake was away somewhere on business."

"But you were there."

"Yes," said Kiera, "but there was so much panic without an alpha, and I didn't realize what was going on until it was too late."

"Sorry," said Sally, "I'm getting confused. If you were there the pack had an alpha. Or do you mean a pack needs both alphas?"

Kiera stopped walking and looked Sally directly in the eye.

"You think I am an alpha?"

"Yes. You're with Blake so I assumed you were the female alpha. I thought that pack alphas were always a pair."

"No!" replied Kiera, "I'm not with Blake. He is my alpha. Apart from that and him being a good friend that's as far as things go. Helena was the female alpha. They were a couple."

"Oh, sorry," said Sally, "I assumed you two were an item." After a little pause she pressed on. "So, was Helena away with Blake too?"

Tears started to well in Kiera's eyes. She wiped them away with the back of her hand and started walking quickly along the trail again.

Sally had never for a second thought that Kiera and Blake weren't the alpha pair. If that was true, then where was the female alpha now? Sally thought she should probably let it drop if it was upsetting Kiera so much but there was something inside her that felt the need to press the point. This was probably the best chance she was going to get to find out the truth of what happened that night, and the new information about a female alpha raised even more questions in her head.

"Hey, come on," said Sally, catching up with Kiera and placing a hand on her shoulder. "I didn't mean to upset you. Sorry. I'm just being nosey. The investigative journalist in me keeps popping up now and again."

Kiera stopped and looked up at the sky, ran her hands through her hair and sighed. Sally let her take a few deep breaths to regain some of her composure before she spoke again.

"I've obviously touched a nerve. I'm sorry. I'm just interested that's all."

Kiera slipped off her rucksack and threw it against the base of a tree then sat on one of the large, exposed roots. Sally sat opposite on another of the roots that spread out like fingers digging into the earth to hold the tree in position.

"Come on, Kiera," Sally prompted, "What really happened that night? It may help me understand why this pack thing is so important to you."

Kiera wiped the last of the tears from her cheeks then sat forward, resting her elbows on her knees and picking the dirt that had accumulated over the last two days out of her fingernails. Sally could tell Kiera was still hesitant about telling her anything, but she had her right on the verge of spilling the truth and she wasn't about to let go now.

"Why isn't Helena here now helping you and Blake rescue the pack?"

Kiera looked Sally in the eyes then lowered her own to look at the ground between them.

"Because she's dead," said Kiera. "She was the first of the pack to be killed." Kiera's eyes filled once again. "They took her out first. She was targeted and shot, many times, with silver bullets."

Sally felt her own heart almost stop, the shock of what she had just heard making her speechless. How do you respond to something like that? Sally knew the pain of touching silver even by accident so to have it shot into you in the form of a bullet, or in this case many bullets, must have been excruciating.

"Blake blames himself for not being there, he is carrying the guilt of Helena's death with him," Kiera continued and snapped Sally out of her thoughts. "But if he had been there they would have only targeted him at the same time."

"You mean like, take out the commanders and the army will have no direction sort of thing?"

"Yes. With Blake away and Helena dead we all just ran about aimlessly. We were in a clearing in a forest in Northumberland close to where we lived, a bit like the clearing you had your barbeque the night I... the night I met you. We used it as a meeting place for pack runs and on full moon nights. It was a place we felt safe."

We didn't see them or smell them coming but suddenly Vampires and men with nets and tranquiliser guns appeared from the trees all at once. How they got there without us knowing I don't know but they took us by surprise. Some of the pack started to shift while they were still clothed and died too, tangled up and strangled in their clothes with their bones all twisted and broken. It was a horrible sight. Others panicked and ran, only to be rounded up by the vampire guards. Some of the pack decided to attack but only ran straight into the nets and tranquilisers. It was mayhem."

Kiera's tears started to drip onto the ground between her feet and Sally found her own tears following Kiera's example, trickling down her face before dropping onto the ground where she sat. The pack had obviously been targeted and their capture planned out in great detail. The team of vampires and soldiers must have already known who the two alphas were before the attack had been given the go ahead. Could this have been an inside job? That was a crazy idea surely. Sally decided not to mention that particular suggestion.

"I tried so hard, Sally," Kiera sobbed. "I got some of the pack free from the nets, but then a tranquilizer dart hit me from behind. I can still hear the screams of my friends as everything around me went black."

Kiera broke down into uncontrollable sobs. Sally moved

closer and knelt on the ground in front of her. She put her arms around the sobbing girl and hugged her close. The grief and sorrow flooded out of Kiera like a Tsunami and all Sally could do was hold onto her until it all calmed down.

That's why Blake never spoke about the night the pack was captured. He lost his mate that night too, and he blamed himself for not being there. Sally could only imagine the pain Kiera must have felt, watching her friends either killed or taken. Whether it's a pack or a family, the experience must have been unbearable.

Sally stood up and walked over to her rucksack, pulling out a couple of tissues. She handed one to Kiera and used the other to wipe away her own tears. While Sally was all too familiar with the trauma of her own story, she knew Kiera's was just as haunting.

"Come on, Kiera," said Sally, lifting her rucksack onto her back and holding out a hand to help Kiera to her feet. "We have a pack to set free."

She pulled Kiera onto her feet before helping her on with her rucksack. The two girls set off along the track at a fast, determined pace, this time side by side.

Chapter 10

They made their way along a well-worn trail above the trees under which they'd been sleeping. Sally suspected the weekend rambling brigade from the cities and towns found this trail a popular Sunday stroll with its views across the valley. It was well away from any civilization and the ground was compacted and solid so it must have been in constant use. The early morning dew glistened on the grass either side of the track and reminded Sally of the family walks she enjoyed before she became a werewolf. The two girls sniffed the air as they went, checking for any unseen dangers but Sally also reveled in the scent of the countryside. The smell of the trees or wet grass carried over the fields on a light breeze always relaxed her. Her inner wolf was content to curl up and let Sally do the work and take them to their next destination.

They walked in silence. Not the stubborn silence they had been used to throughout the journey but a silence that meant the hostility between her and Kiera had dissipated somewhat. It was Kiera who broke it this time.

"So, what happened with this pack of yours when you were first bitten that has you so dead set against being in a pack now?"

Sally shrugged. "Nothing really," she said. "It was just the whole 'I'm superior to you', thing that got to me the most. They tried to force me to move in with them on a farm they had just outside of town, but I wouldn't."

"That doesn't sound bad enough for the resentment to pack life I see in you." said Kiera.

"Well put that together with the guys all fighting about who was going to be my 'mate' as they put it and me stopping all their advances by breaking a few of their ribs or wrists and you can start to see why they, and me, were having a kind of clash of interests."

"Getting on your bad side isn't the most sensible mistake to make, is it?" Kiera laughed. "I still don't see why any of that should make you anti-pack though. You are strong enough to put a stop to anything they tried I'm sure."

"Yes, I was," replied Sally, "the female alpha tried to make me apologize to one of the guys I talked out of any ideas he had of a relationship. I refused. The alpha pair had a discussion and decided, for my own good obviously, which of the pack males I was going to belong to. I told them what they could do with their idea. She decided to make an example of me, but I hurt her pretty badly in a fight."

"How badly?" asked Kiera.

"Without realizing it I partially changed during the fight and my claws sliced her open as easy as the proverbial knife through butter." Sally gazed down at her hands. They were small and delicate. Not the hands that anybody would believe were capable of such devastation. "I knew then I could never trust myself not to get out of control and hurt somebody I cared about." She put her hands in the pockets of her jacket, out of sight. "It was then the male alpha decided I was too strong to be in their pack and probably a threat to their leadership. He told me to leave the area. When I refused, they threaten to kill the people I cared about. It all got pretty ugly but, to protect my family, I agreed and started the search for a place I could settle that didn't have any silly little werewolf pack rules."

"But I don't understand," said Kiera, "You could probably have just taken over the pack anytime you wanted. They wouldn't have been able to touch your family then."

"Yes, I know," said Sally, "But to do that I would probably have to kill the alphas and as I've said I don't do killing. Plus, I got the impression there would be challenge after challenge. I didn't want to spend the rest of my life fighting and possibly killing other people on a weekly basis. Anyway, I was happy with the agreement."

Sally could feel Kiera's eyes on her. She was obviously waiting to hear more details of the agreement. Sally ignored her, hoping Kiera would get bored and drop it but she was out of luck.

"Which was?" asked Kiera.

"Which was," said Sally after a deep breath, "that I leave the area and never return and they would promise to protect my family. If they failed in that duty I would come back and tear each and every one of them to shreds. A little dramatic I know."

"A little," laughed Kiera, "but I have a feeling you would."

"They're my family, of course I would."

There was another short silence while the images of each of her family spun around in Sally's head. The devastated look on the face of her sister as Sally told her she had to leave, etched into her memory.

"You must miss them though," said Kiera, "Your family I mean."

Sally nodded. "Yes, I do."

"Not all packs are like that you know."

"So you keep telling me."

With that Sally picked up the pace. That conversation was over, she had no wish to discuss packs with Kiera anymore, not while she was in the middle of a determined effort to get along a little better with her.

They kept walking until lunchtime. The trees had disappeared as they got higher and the terrain became more rugged and harder to negotiate. They found a rocky outcrop which gave them a view of the valley below and the other surrounding hills in all directions and sat down to rest. The small amount of food they'd brought with them was starting to run low. As much as Sally didn't like shifting between full moons she realized they may need to go hunting later that night. She wasn't sure how her own wolf would react to running with the two wolves she had considered a threat just a few days earlier.

Sally sat quietly eating her lunch, deep in thought. She couldn't get Becky out of her mind. What was she going through? Was she frightened? Did she expect Sally to come and rescue her again or had she given up hope after it had taken so long?

"Are you okay?" asked Kiera.

"Yes," replied Sally. "Why?"

"You're a little quiet that's all."

"I was just thinking about Becky and what she might be thinking."

"She'll know you're on your way."

"Do you think so?" Sally sighed, "I just don't want her to think I've abandoned her."

"Are you kidding me?" said Kiera with a laugh, "When she was with us she left us in no doubt that we'd made a mistake and when you got there we were in big trouble. She knew you'd be on your way to help her as soon as you got our note."

"I can just imagine her giving you both one of her lectures," Sally joined in the laughter.

"She has a lot of faith in you, Sally, and so does Blake."

"Really?"

"Yeah. Becky was so sure you were going to, 'teach us a lesson' as she put it, that she didn't seem frightened of us at all. Blake seemed sure about you before we even got to know you properly. The night of the barbeque we were just passing through until Blake caught your scent. I was all for heading off straight away after our little scuffle, but he said that if we could talk you into coming with us then we couldn't fail."

"I'm pleased those two have faith in me. I'm not sure I share their confidence. You make these vampire guards sound impossible for just the three of us to handle."

"That's because you're thinking like a human," said Kiera. "Lycanthropy can be a very powerful weapon if you use it right. It doesn't have to be a disease you know. It can be a gift as well. It's enhanced every power you possess and evidently given you new ones."

"All it's done is given me problems and ruined my life," Sally replied.

"Give it a chance Sally. Run with us for a while. You'll see it can be useful too."

"You have until I get Becky back to convince me," said Sally. "Good luck."

With that Sally packed away the remains of her lunch and headed off up the trail leaving Kiera to pack away her own things and catch up.

During the afternoon they made slow progress. Valley after valley slowed them down and in some cases a river running through the bottom of the valley was too deep to cross, which meant they had to take a detour to find a bridge.

Kiera suggested adding a little competitive edge to their journey and challenged Sally to see who could get up a hill first or jump the furthest across a stream as they went. Sally wasn't particularly interested in playing games at first. She simply wanted to get to Becky as fast as possible. After some encouragement from Kiera in the shape of a few slightly derogatory comments, Sally eventually agreed. The results of the challenges were surprisingly even. Sally won any of the speed and strength challenges, but Kiera had the longest and highest jumps. Both girls took to cheating to try and get one over on the other and by the time they reached the final valley that led to Scarne Point they were messing about and joking, making the other one laugh so she couldn't concentrate on the challenge they had been set.

"Well, you two seem to be getting along a lot better," said Blake, walking around a bend in the track ahead of them.

"Just trying to pass the time while we catch up with you," said Sally. "I thought we were meeting you up the next ridge."

"I could hear you coming miles away so I thought I would come and tell you to be more careful. If I can hear you then you could be drawing the attention of somebody less friendly. Besides, there's something not right on that hill ahead but I can't figure out what it is. I didn't' want you walking into something."

Sally didn't like the feeling of being told how to behave. She thought Blake was trying to exert his alpha male authority again. She decided to let this one pass because she could see his point.

"Why? What's wrong?" asked Kiera.

"I'm not sure. Something just doesn't feel right."

Sally pricked up her ears and sniffed the air but couldn't sense anything out of the ordinary. The three of them remained silent and alert as Blake led them back up the hill he had just come down and they headed for Scarne Point.

As they got closer Sally's wolf started to pace and her hackles began to rise. Blake was right. There was something strange about this place, Sally couldn't put her finger on what it was. The area felt empty, like it should have an echo but it didn't. The air was thin, almost as if they had climbed a huge mountain. They all stopped when they were close to the top and squatted low to the ground.

"This isn't right," said Kiera. "My wolf knows there's something wrong; we should get away."

"It's not just me then," Blake replied. "I don't know what it is, but this place just feels wrong. I've never known anything like this before."

All three of them sniffed the air together.

"Haven't you noticed?" said Sally. "There's no birds in the trees. This place is silent. I can't even hear any animals scurrying about." She sniffed the air once more. "I can smell them, so they've been here recently. It's as if everything has simply left and gone someplace else."

"I think we should go," said Kiera.

Blake agreed so they turned to leave but Sally stopped and turned back.

"There's pain here," she said. "Somebody is hurting really bad."

Blake and Kiera both looked at each other then back at Sally.

"What do you mean?" said Blake. "How do you know somebody is in pain?"

"I can just feel it. Can't you? Somebody is in pain and they're scared. I can smell a fear getting stronger."

She looked around and pointed to the top of the hill. "It's coming from over there. Wait." Sally paused, trying to home in of the vibrations she was getting. There was definitely something. She couldn't get a scent, which worried her wolf because she was down wind, but she could sense the pain of someone or something out there.

"It's getting closer," she said. "There is something approaching us from that direction."

Sally pointed dead ahead, and three noses sniffed the air and they all got closer to the ground.

"I can't smell anything, Sally," said Blake. "Are you sure?"

"I don't like this," said Kiera.

Sally saw the creature attacking out of the bushes a fraction of a second before the other two and pushed Kiera out of its path. Blake swerved to his right just in time but Sally's move to save Kiera was all the time the creature needed. A paw, roughly the size of that of a bear, grabbed her arm and threw her to the floor with speed and power Sally had never known. Before she could react, she was pinned to ground, the whole weight of the creature on top of her.

Chapter 11

Sally couldn't move. She put all her werewolf strength into the effort to get away, but it was no use. The creature's massive arms were wrapped around her like a vice and they were pulling her tighter against its body. Everything went dark, her breathing virtually stopped and even Sally's hearing lost its sharpness. She could faintly hear voices shouting but they seemed to be far away. There was a pounding noise all around her as if she was inside a tree trunk and somebody with an axe was trying to chop it down. As the pounding continued, one of the voices seemed to turn to a growl but it was still too far away for Sally to make out properly. She could feel nothing but the pressure on her body as she was being slowly crushed. Then, suddenly, the pain and pressure stopped.

A low rumbling noise started. It whipped around her like a swirling wind before focusing on her head. Vibrations rebounded off the inside of her skull and Sally thought her head was about to explode. She became aware of a strange sensation like another consciousness inside her brain, examining it, searching it. Random memories flashed through her mind as somebody would look through a bookshelf, taking volumes out and searching the pages, looking for something specific but not knowing what.

Memory after memory was pulled out and searched. Memories Sally had tried to tuck away, not to be seen again, were brought out into the open and viewed. The attack from Blake, Sally's fear that her mother now thought she was a monster, worries about ending up with nowhere to live and nobody she could call a friend. After the fears and bad memories came memories of times she had helped people and animals in whatever small way she had. Everything from rescuing a bird from being eaten by the cat when she was a little girl to the time she had fought to protect some complete stranger from another werewolf.

"You like to help others." The voice was low and powerful yet almost a whisper. It wasn't a sound as such. It was more like a thought. "You're not like any others I've met."

Something was putting thoughts into her mind, communicating without talking. Sally tried to talk back but no sound came from her mouth. She couldn't even tell if her lips were moving. She tried to speak again but still there was nothing.

This is impossible, she thought to herself.

"What is?" asked the voice in her head.

Sally knew she hadn't said anything, only thought it. Was that the way to speak to whoever this voice belonged to? She spoke again but this time inside her mind only.

"Who are you?" she asked.

"I don't have a name," said the voice.

The words echoed around her head, no more than small vibrations, not a real sound but Sally could hear them all the same.

"What are you then?" she continued.

"I'm a Neuromancer," said the voice.

"What's a Neuromancer?"

"It's just what I am. What are you?" said the Neuromancer.

"I'm a human," Sally replied.

There was a pause as if the creature was considering Sally's reply. She felt more searching of her mind then sensations all over her body as if she was being physically scanned from the inside.

"You aren't human," said the voice.

Those three words hit Sally like a steam train. She knew she wasn't human but didn't like to admit it to herself. Hearing the words as vibrations in her head was like being labelled for all to see. A monster, just as she believed her mother now saw her.

Sally felt a sensation of sorrow, then pain, great pain, but not hers. There was a loud cry and everything around her began to shake. The Neuromancer squeezed her tighter as it tensed and cried out. The feeling of pain and sadness was so great that Sally couldn't stand it any longer and tried to cry out but again, no sound came out.

The Neuromancer's pain started to ease, and she felt him relax.

"How do you heal so quickly?" the Neuromancer asked.

"It's because of the Lycanthropy. I don't know how it works."

She felt the Neuromancer begin searching through her body again, searching every bone, blood vessel and organ.

"What's this?" he asked.

Sally didn't understand what he meant.

"What's what?"

"This warm light?"

"I don't see any light," she replied.

She felt invisible hands holding her head and the image of a cave was projected into her thoughts and she was suddenly standing in the middle of a huge cavern. She felt as if she was in a dream. She looked around but apart from her the cave was empty. The ground on which she stood was loose dirt and there was no light, although she could see perfectly. Looking around she noticed the walls were full of little passageways heading off in all directions. All the external sounds she had been hearing, the shouts and growls, the pounding, everything had gone leaving a calm and comfortable silence. The faint sound of footsteps started in one of the passages to her right and she listened more carefully, trying to figure out from which passageway the sound was coming. She sniffed the air but could smell nothing, there was no scent at all, not even her own. The footsteps grew closer and Sally backed away from the opening. Concentrating on her hands she attempted to make them change and grow werewolf claws. but nothing happened, they remained the same small and delicate hands they should be. She became aware she couldn't sense her wolf either. She felt suddenly alone. The wolf inside she had become so used to wasn't there. She missed her, she missed her terribly for a reason she couldn't fathom.

A dark, slim shape appeared at the entrance of a passageway. The shape wasn't fully formed, it was more like a black mist floating just above the ground and in the shape of a tall thin bear. The voice was unmistakable, but the Neuromancer looked nothing like the bear sized creature she had seen spring out from the bushes.

"Don't be afraid, Sally. We can't hurt each other here. This is inside your subconscious."

Sally backed away still further as he stepped into the cave. She began to realize her wolf was the one who gave her the survival instinct and her courage. Without her wolf, she was just a frightened teenager. Kiera may have had a point about Lycanthropy being a gift.

A large gap opened in the black mist where the Neuromancer's mouth should have been and she heard a loud cry, a cry of intense pain and the Neuromancer fell to the floor. She felt nothing. The pain and fear she could sense before were gone. In her subconscious, if that's where she was, she felt and sensed nothing. The Neuromancer was writhing around in pain and the features of the face in the mist were contorted and twisted.

Sally watched helplessly until she could take it no longer. She ran over and knelt down beside the misty form.

"What is it?" she asked. "Can I help?"

The misty image of the Neuromancer slumped and relaxed and Sally could see the pain was easing once again. Eventually he rose up and floated freely again.

"I have seen in your memories that you can heal very quickly. I have been searching for somebody with a healing power like yours for some time. How do you use the warm light inside to heal yourself?"

"I don't know," said Sally, "The Lycanthropy just heals my injuries without me needing to do anything."

"Then what is the purpose of the light and why do you hide it down here?"

"I've never seen a light. I'm not sure what you are talking about. Where am I?"

The Neuromancer held out his arms indicating to Sally that she should look around.

"All this is your subconscious. You create many passages as you go through life. This is where you keep your memories. I have opened a doorway, so you can come in and search easier. You also keep this light here. I've never seen it before in anybody's memory cave."

"Do you look in people's memories often?" asked Sally.

"That's what I do. I'm a Neuromancer and I feed off

people's bad memories and leave them with just the good ones."

"I'm not sure I like that," said Sally, "Bad memories help people to learn from their mistakes and the mistakes of others."

"It was one of my many mistakes that has led me to you so to speak. I encountered a demon a few weeks ago and made the mistake of trying to get into his subconscious to search for his bad memories. He was full of them. Everything he had ever done was bad. He fought back in a way I didn't expect, and he's killing me."

"Killing you?"

"Yes. He has a skill to possess all manner of creatures and reach inside them. A little like I can."

Sally was confused. She didn't believe in all this demon and devil mumbo jumbo or anything along those lines.

"I don't believe in demons," said Sally.

The Neuromancer laughed.

"That's what I am. A demon. Not all demons are evil. Merely misunderstood."

"How can another demon possess you and kill you?"

"It depends on the type of demon. This one is feeding on me. He's eating my soul."

The misty shape shuddered again as if another wave of pain had started to swell inside.

"Eating your soul? Is that even possible?"

"I sense many doubts in you, little one."

Stay Away

The Neuromancer sank to the floor again and cried out in pain. The dark mist looked a little lighter than it had when she first saw it and it was flickering. Sally thought it was as if the image was losing the connection with its host. The Neuromancer seemed to be getting weaker.

When the pain appeared to ease again the Neuromancer rose up.

"Please tell me how to use this warm light. I know it's how you heal yourself, but I can't get it to do anything."

"I've told you," replied Sally "I don't know anything about a warm light."

"The Neuromancer indicated the passage behind him, the one from which he had appeared.

"It's along there. Come, I'll show you."

As they stepped into the passage the illumination from within the cave followed them. Where Sally had once seen only a dark passage there was a long corridor with many more passages leading off it on both sides. The Neuromancer led her through the passages turning left and right at what Sally thought were just random turns, but he seemed to know where he was going.

Up ahead, Sally noticed that one of the openings had a faint glow which framed the entrance. When they reached it the Neuromancer stopped and turned to face her. The misty form was becoming less dense, even as Sally watched.

"There," he pointed, "That is the warm light that holds

your power of healing."

Sally looked in amazement at a small ball of light the size of a tennis ball. It flickered like there was a tiny flame inside it. Even though it was so small she could feel the glow from it warming her skin and the heat seemed to seep through her whole body from head to toe.

"I can't get near it," said the Neuromancer," it simply moves to another corridor if I approach it."

Sally moved forward a little, stepping into the passage and walked slowly towards the glowing ball. As she got closer she could feel little vibrations and hear a gentle hum. She held out her hand to touch the light and it floated to her and settled in her palm.

"Bring it back to the main cavern," said the Neuromancer, his voice getting weaker.

Sally followed him out of the passage, but he flickered a few times then vanished. Sally had no idea how to get back to the main cavern. She closed her eyes to try and visualize the route they had come but it was no use. She couldn't see the way back, only the cave she first stood in. When she opened her eyes again she was already back there. How did I get here, she thought?

"You can always get back to this cavern," the voice of the Neuromancer said. "It's your safe place."

"My what?"

"Your safe place. With a little practice you can come in

here anytime you want to."

"Where are you?" asked Sally.

"I am too week to keep the connection. Time is running out."

"What shall I do? I don't know how to use this thing," shouted Sally.

"Put it in the cabinet and then come back outside."

The Neuromancer's voice faded and Sally could tell that she was once again on her own.

"But there is no cabinet," she shouted, "and I don't know how to come outside. There're no doors. Only passageways."

"Visualise what you need."

The voice was no more than a whisper now. She looked at the globe in her hand and closed her eyes. She thought of a small glass cabinet like the one where her mother kept her most precious bone china ornaments and crockery. She opened her eyes slowly.

A cabinet, the same as the one she had visualized right down to the glass door and brass handle slowly appeared close to where she was standing. Had the Neuromancer done that? How could he? He was no longer there. She gently placed the little ball of light into the cabinet and closed the glass front. The light immediately grew and filled the cabinet, the vibrations got stronger and Sally felt the warmth grow inside her too.

She looked around the cavern at the passageways. All of

them were dark and there were just too many for her to try one by one.

This would be so much easier if there was a door, she thought to herself. A single wooden paneled door slowly appeared in the wall to her left. It can't be that easy. She opened the door and saw another passageway. This one was different. The floor was paved, the walls were smooth and she could feel a light breeze on her face. The scent of a forest hit her senses and she could hear the distant growls and shouting again. Sally stepped into the passage and closed the door behind her. She felt a sudden surge as if she was being pulled forward by her navel and the walls of the passage flew past her at terrific speed. The light all around her became brighter and suddenly there was the sun above her.

Sally lay on the ground, gasping for breath with her senses reeling and the sound of growling loud in her ears.

"Sally! Sally!" shouted Blake and his face appeared above her. "Are you alright?"

"Yes," said Sally, coming round a little more and recognizing her surroundings. "Yes, I'm fine. Where's the Neuromancer?"

"The what?" asked Blake.

"The Neuromancer. The bear type thing that attacked us."

"Kiera is handling that thing," said Blake and nodded his head in the direction of the growling and snarling.

Sally looked over and saw Kiera, now a fully shifted

werewolf, biting and slashing at the flesh of a huge bear like animal while it lay unconscious on the ground.

"No!" shouted Sally, "No! Leave him alone!"

Jumping to her feet Sally rushed over and dragged Kiera away from the Neuromancer then knelt beside him. Kiera backed off but kept low and alert, the snarl deep in her throat a warning that she was ready to go again at any moment if needed.

Sally leaned close and could hear a weak voice, nothing more than a whisper.

"Use the warm light."

He must mean my healing power, Sally thought to herself.

"I can't it's back in the cavern in the cabinet," she said.

"You are the cabinet," was the whisper she heard.

"What light? What cabinet?" asked Blake, his keen hearing picking up parts of the conversation.

Sally didn't answer but sat back on her heals trying to think what the Neuromancer was meaning.

"You brought it out to your safe place for you to use. Just think of being in your safe place."

Sally remembered the Neuromancer had called the cavern she had been in her safe place. Was the Neuromancer saying she could go in there whenever she wanted? She closed her eyes and imagined going back deep down inside herself again and opening the cabinet. The little ball of light floated out into her hand and when she opened her eyes her hand was vibrating. A gentle warmth radiated over her palm from within and a few small scratches she had received whilst initially trying to get away from the Neuromancer disappeared instantly.

What to do now? Did she have to just touch the Neuromancer? She tried it, but nothing happened.

"What're you doing?" asked Blake.

"I need to heal him using my Lycanthropy.

"That's not possible, Sally," replied Blake.

"I think it is but I'm not sure how. He thinks I can." She nodded at the Neuromancer.

"Well, he's wrong. Anyway, even if it was possible. Do you really want that thing to attack again? We tried everything while he had you in that bear hug but nothing we did had any effect on him."

Sally considered what Blake was saying. If she could heal the Neuromancer, would he feed on her bad memories? She may not like some of her recollections, and some of them may well be the cause of her nightmares. Without them, would she remember why she didn't like what she was, why she didn't want to be part of a pack? If she healed him would he do what Blake had said and attack them again? She'd been the one talking to him though, not Blake. She hadn't sensed any ill will, but her senses were more or less blocked at that point. Her wolf seemed settled and she would be pacing if they were in danger. That was good enough for her. If her wolf wasn't worried, then she didn't see a reason why she should be.

Just touching him hadn't worked. She guessed there would need to be physical contact but maybe she needed to connect subconsciously as well. She laid her hand back on the Neuromancer and closed her eyes once more.

Going deep within her own mind again she travelled down to the depths of her power. The cave appeared and she was holding the glowing ball in her hand. She thought of a passage out of her body and into the Neuromancer's. Immediately one of the passageways to her right started to glow. She walked over to the opening and entered. The passage wound its way into the distance and Sally followed it, picking up speed as she made more progress until she was eventually running. When she came to the end it opened out into a room. She saw a large glowing pearl almost completely covered in what looked like black tar. The tar was moving, pulsating and Sally could sense a presence. The tar was alive.

As she approached, the tar stopped pulsating and Sally got the feeling it was looking at her. She didn't need her wolf to warn her of this danger. It was as if she could sense all the evil the tar was harboring and was preparing to unleash upon her. Sally took a few steps backwards and the tar started to pulsate, its attention once again on what she now assumed was the Neuromancer's soul. If she was going to do anything it would have to be from a distance because she didn't fancy getting too close to this demon.

Sally held up the small glowing ball and willed it to rise out of her hand. It rose up then moved slowly across the room towards the Neuromancer's soul. It hadn't floated more than a few feet when the pulsating from the demon stopped once again and the demon's attention refocused upon Sally. She quickly brought the glowing ball back to her hand, but the demon continued to watch her. There was a short agonizing pause and Sally held her breath before the demon returned its attention to the Neuromancer's soul once again.

Obviously, the slow approach wasn't going to work so Sally considered her options. She was fast but even if she made it to the demon before its attention changed to her, what was she going to do? She didn't have claws here. The only weapon she had was her healing power and she wasn't totally convinced that hitting the demon with it was going to make a great deal of difference. It was the Neuromancer who needed it, not the demon. She needed a way to get her healing power into the Neuromancer's soul before the demon realized what was going on. If the ball of light was something pointy instead she could stab the large glowing pearl with it.

She looked at the ball of light in her hand and it started to change shape. The ball became a handle and out of it grew a long thin blade. Taking hold of the dagger shaped light, she looked at the tar moving slowly over the Neuromancer's soul and took a few deep breaths.

Stay Away

Squatting down she began to concentrate on her goal then with a sudden surge of power and speed she sprang towards her target. She buried the dagger deep into an area of the Neuromancer's soul that wasn't covered by the tar and was surprised at the intensity of the glow from the wound. Her surprise caused Sally to hesitate and before she could retreat the demon lash out at her, striking her in the abdomen and hurling her through the air across the full width of the room. She landed heavily on the floor but while she was here inside her own head she felt no pain.

She looked back at the soul, which now had a dagger sticking into it which had started to pulsate. She felt herself smile, proud of her success until she saw the black tar pouring onto the floor and rising up to take the shape of large man. He turned towards her and began to approach slowly. She was laying in the opening of the passage leading from the Neuromancer back into herself. Sally could feel a panic building inside when she realized the passage wasn't one way, the demon now had a way to move into her body as well. She couldn't risk the demon getting into her body but how could this thing be stopped? She had to think quickly but nothing useful came to mind. She couldn't move back inside herself and close the passage because that would leave her healing power inside the Neuromancer. She wasn't sure how her werewolf healing power worked but she was quite sure she needed it within her own body. The demon was getting closer and Sally was running out of time. She shuffled backwards to try and keep the ever-closing gap for just a little longer. Getting past the demon to retrieve her healing power should be possible with the speed advantage she seemed to have but it would leave the passage unguarded. If she managed to get back to the passage with her healing power and close it, then the Neuromancer would be left to die. She wasn't there to let that happen.

"Not on my watch," she said, more to give herself some confidence than threaten the demon.

She had no wolf gifts to help her and she had no idea how to defeat such a powerful demon, but she stood facing him ready to fight anyway.

The demon closed to within a few feet then stopped. He stood facing her as if studying what she was. Sally prepared herself for the attack and wondered if any of the usual places she would strike would have any effect upon a demon made purely of a tar type substance.

"Let's get this over with," said Sally but the demon didn't move.

When the attack didn't come Sally looked more carefully and noticed the demon seemed to be pulling against a force that was pulling him back away from her. Suddenly the demon lost his balance and fell backwards onto the floor. Sally could now see the demon was still attached to the Neuromancer's soul. The tar had run onto the floor like a liquid but was still coating the soul, continuing its feeding. The soul, along with her own healing power still in the shape of a dagger, were both glowing much brighter than before and the light within them both had a rhythmic beat.

The demon tried to detach itself from the soul but couldn't. It produced more hands and arms and clawed at the ground, trying in what looked like desperation to find something to hold onto to stop itself being dragged back to the light. It was shrinking before her very eyes. She watched her healing power appear to turn up and glow almost too brightly to look at. The walls of the room began to hum and Sally was sure she heard a faint cry of terror as the demon was dragged away. Wolf paw shaped beams of light reached out and smothered what was left of the demon, dragging it into what seemed to be a solid wall of light.

As the light faded Sally saw the Neuromancer's soul, pulsating bright and translucent. There was no sign of the demon at all. Sally held out her hand and her healing power moved out of the Neuromancer's soul, turned back into its usual ball shape and floated slowly and gently back to her before settling in her outstretched palm.

Leaving the soul behind, Sally turned and walked back along the passage to her safe place then broke the connection. She watched the glow from the passage fade then placed the small glowing ball back into its glass cabinet before moving back out of herself and opening her eyes. She was still kneeling next to the body of the Neuromancer and was aware of Blake's voice asking if she was alright. She stood up a little shakily and Blake took her arm.

"I'm fine," said Sally and shrugged his hand away from her.

The Neuromancer sat up and both Blake and Kiera crouched down, ready to spring into action.

"No," said Sally, "leave him."

"Thank you, Sally," said the Neuromancer. Sally knew it wasn't a voice that Blake or Kiera would be able to hear as it came from inside. "I owe you a life debt."

"You owe me nothing," said Sally.

"What?" said Blake.

Sally just shook her head and the three of them stepped away to allow the Neuromancer to rise to his feet.

"Nevertheless, I intend to repay you some day," the Neuromancer added.

The three companions watched as he turned and walked away into the trees making no sound at all as he moved.

"Thank you!" shouted Sally as the Neuromancer disappeared into the thickening trees.

"What was that all about?" asked Blake.

"I'll tell you when we reach Scarne Point," replied Sally. "She needs to rest and shift back." Sally nodded her head towards Kiera, who was stood panting as a large brown wolf.

They made their way up the last few hundred yards of

dirt track and settled down where they had a view of the whole valley before them. Sally told Blake everything that had happened and what the Neuromancer really was while Kiera lay behind them and slept off her hurried shift into a wolf.

"She was worried about you," said Blake, nodding behind them at the sleeping wolf.

"Kiera?"

"Yes. She had a panic shift and just got out of her clothes in time. She bit and slashed trying to get you free but nothing we did seemed to have any effect on him."

"I think I could hear you both, but you sounded so far away. Then you were gone."

"We never stopped trying to get you free."

Sally didn't know what to say so she just smiled. Why would these two werewolves who had nothing to do with her try so hard to get her free? Would she have done the same for them? Sally had a strange feeling inside that she probably would have. It was small but there was a connection of some sort now that she came to think about it.

Things were starting to feel different between Blake, Kiera and herself. Things also felt different inside now. She could still sense the cavern and passages inside she had recently been wandering around. The Neuromancer had left the door to her subconscious, to her safe place unlocked. She could feel the space inside now, waiting for her to return. The werewolf healing power was still safe inside its glass cabinet on the shelf where she had left it. She could see it there, pulsing and glowing. Sally was now even more aware of the power she held within and, if it was possible, felt a much stronger bond with her inner wolf.

When Kiera had shifted back to a human and woke up all three of them ate together before setting off again to start the decent into the next valley. Kiera was full of questions and bombarded Sally, wanting her to explain everything in minute detail. Sally had the feeling that her own wolf was sat listening to her story and studying Kiera at the same time.

Since her encounter with the Neuromancer Sally could feel the wolf inside not only as a presence, but she could sense the animal's mood and feelings more deeply than ever. Her wolf seemed to be surprisingly comfortable with the situation. What shocked Sally more than anything was that she felt more comfortable with the situation too. She didn't feel so alone anymore. It was as if her and her inner wolf were now standing side by side, facing what was to come and determined together to see this quest through.

Chapter 12

Blake wanted to get through the next valley before nightfall and Sally was in favour of anything that meant they were moving closer to the research lab and Becky's rescue.

The hills on either side of the valley were nothing more than gentle slopes and the trees on the west side thickened the further down into the valley they went. A river ran through the bottom of the valley and meandered lazily south. The water was slow moving and looked deep in places. They followed its western side and the further along they went the rockier the banks of the river became.

After a couple of hours they reached a small bridge and the all too familiar scent of werewolf territory markers hit their senses. The terrain on the opposite side of the river looked easier to navigate so, in the hope of making faster progress and getting away from the werewolf pack territory as quickly as possible, they crossed the bridge and continued on their way.

The river seemed to serve as a natural boundary to the pack territory and, on Blake's suggestion because of Sally's previous performance when encountering a pack, they followed the river making their way around the west side of the pack's marked area and continued to head south. They remained downwind of the pack markers to hide their presence.

The river kept snaking further away from the trees and dragged them more out into the open and closer to the road which also wound its way through the valley. Keeping their scent from the local pack was more important than staying within the cover of the trees so they followed where the river took them and kept a watchful eye on all sides.

Back in Popwood, rural police were always on the lookout for strangers, so it came as no surprise to Sally when they spotted a patrol car coming down the hill on the opposite side of the river. They quickly moved away from the river and back to the cover of the woods and waited for the car to pass.

Blake watched the police officer drive safely by and tapped Sally on the shoulder as he made a move to leave the woods.

"Come on, Sally. Let's go," he said.

He and Kiera stepped out of the cover of the trees but Sally didn't move, she was tense and sniffed the air. She could feel the hackles start to rise under her skin.

"What is it?" he asked, coming back and squatting down next to her.

"Can you smell that?"

Blake sniffed the air and shook his head.

"Just the pack. Nothing special. Why, what can you smell?

"I can smell fear." Sally sniffed again and turned to face into the woods. "Somebody's in trouble."

"Fear?" He gave her a puzzled look. "You can smell fear? You surprise me more and more, Missy." He looked around, checking for any signs of danger and then tapped her on the shoulder again. "We should go. If you're right and there's trouble brewing, you can bet your sweet butt that there's a pack involved; and we have already wandered too far into their territory. Come on, let's go." Blake moved off again.

Sally knew she should follow, she knew she wanted to rescue Becky as soon as possible. Her inner wolf, however, was pulling her back, she wanted Sally to find out where the fear was coming from and who needed help. Sally had always been able to hear her wolf speaking inside her head but somehow it was clearer now than ever before. She was torn between the desire to help somebody in need and her own need to get to Becky.

"Why should I go in there and help somebody I don't even know?" she asked her wolf.

"Something is very wrong," replied her inner wolf. *"Something is happening that shouldn't be. I don't know what, but I can feel it. So can you."*

Her wolf was right, she could feel something. A niggle inside that was stopping her walking away. She felt a strong hunger inside all of a sudden, a need to go further into the trees. A need to stop the pain and suffering.

Sally moved off but not in the direction Blake was going. She made her way slowly and silently deeper into the woods and towards the scent that was filling her nostrils and pulling at her senses.

"Where are you going?" said Blake, following her. Clearly getting annoyed.

"We can't just leave. Somebody needs help."

He grabbed her arm and she gave a quiet growl as a warning. She stared him straight in the eyes. A challenge? Maybe. But more a confirmation that she was there under her terms, not his.

"Look, there's one thing I've learned over the years that's helped to keep me safe and alive." He didn't drop his gaze. He was an Alpha and obviously used to getting what he wanted. "You don't get involved with anything in another pack's territory. I thought you would have learned that too by now. Even if it's just been in the last few days. Come on, we're going."

"I'm not leaving until I know what's going on." She pulled her arm out of his grip and started to move once again towards the scent.

"You're going to get yourself killed," Blake warned.

"Then come with me and watch my back."

Sally slipped through the bushes. With a sigh, Blake followed while Kiera covered them from the rear, grumbling her disapproval.

The scent of a werewolf grew stronger as they got closer to the source of the fear. After a few more minutes they were close enough for Sally to be able to distinguish between two wolves, one male and one female. She caught the scent of what she thought was a mix of singed hair and burning flesh, then heard growling and whimpering, a yelp of pain and the smell of fear increased.

Keeping low to the ground the three companions moved quietly to the edge of a clearing but remained just out of sight. What they saw stunned them all into silence. There was a small, female, werewolf in her wolf form tied to two wooden stakes. Both front legs were tied together to one stake and both her hind legs were tied to the other. The stakes were set far apart causing the wolf to be stretched out between them, forcing her onto her side and unable to move.

The male werewolf was still in his human form and stood over her, holding what looked like a branding iron into the flames of a small fire close by. Pulling the iron out of the flames he spat on it and smiled as it hissed angrily. As they watched he pressed the hot metal onto the defenseless wolf's hip, holding it there while the young wolf yelped in pain, a look of pleasure on his face there for all to see.

Sally was horrified. She could feel the wolf inside her climbing to the surface, trying to get free. The rage at what she was witnessing grew quickly and uncontrollably. She could feel her change starting to happen, the skin on her arms and legs started to prickle and sting, bones creaked and cracked as they got ready to change shape and thickness, her wolf inside was trying to claw her way through Sally's skin. Sally closed her eyes and her whole body tensed and trembled as she fought to stay human, determined to stop the change. She was still in her clothing and to change now could be fatal if she was to get tangled up in the material. She had seen a werewolf die like that before, strangled by his own clothing as his body changed shape and he struggled against the constraints of garments that weren't designed for the creature he was about to become. Blake placed his hands on her shoulders and whispered gently into her ear.

"Steady now girl, calm down. Hold it in. It's fine, I'm here. That's it."

The touch and sound of another human helped to focus Sally's mind on the form in which she wanted to stay. With the help of Blake's touch and words she managed to calm herself just enough for the change to recede. The anger, however, remained.

There was another yelp as the hot iron was once again pressed onto the young werewolf's rump and Sally snapped back to reality.

"The alpha gave you to me," said the male who stood over the suffering animal. He removed the iron and watched the young wolf whimper on the ground in front of him, "and that means you don't go running back to your previous master every chance you get." He touched the hot iron to the wolf's ribs, smiling as the animal at his feet yelped and squirmed in pain. "If you want the pain to stop, you pledge your allegiance to me now. Only I have the power to end your suffering."

"That's not strictly true!" shouted Sally, stepping calmly into the clearing.

Turning quickly, a look of surprise on his face, he pointed the branding iron at Sally.

"Who's going to stop me?" he replied. "You?"

"As I'm not tied to a couple of wooden stakes, I guess that's a yes."

Sally walked slowly but confidently directly at him, her werewolf swagger and instincts kicking in automatically. Showing him who was boss and that she wasn't going to back down easily. He took a step back when she was close enough for him to catch her werewolf scent but then his expression changed and he lunged forward, aiming the hot iron at Sally's face. With one easy sidestep and spin, Sally avoided the iron and slashed his face with her fingers, fingers that now had razor sharp werewolf claws. He dropped the iron and put his hand to his face, feeling the warm flow of his blood.

"You bitch!" he said, then noticed the partial change of her hands. "How did you do that?"

"Oh, I'm full of little tricks. Want to see another?"

She ran at him at full speed. He reached down quickly and picked up the still hot iron, swinging it at her head as she reached him. Sally dropped down low, avoiding the weapon easily and with a single roll on the ground she took his legs from underneath him. In the same move she bit into his leg with her now elongated canines, then finishing the move by continuing the roll and using her momentum to end up on her feet. She spat his blood at him while he rolled around on the ground clutching his leg.

"You taste like vermin." She said as she stood over him.

Her hand, which was now a fully formed werewolf paw complete with claws and the full strength of the supernatural predator she was, closed around his throat. Her claws bit into his flesh and blood started to slowly trickle down into his shirt collar. She lifted him up off the ground until his face was level with hers.

"If I ever see you treating another wolf like that, I'll tear the flesh from your bones piece by filthy piece."

A wet patch appeared in the front of his jeans and spread down both legs. Sally looked down and laughed.

"Such a brave member of your pack you are. Your Alpha must me so proud."

She threw him to one side and turned her attention to the whimpering wolf still tied to the stakes. He crawled away from the clearing and disappeared into the trees. Sally knelt down next to the injured wolf.

"Be careful!" Shouted Blake, entering the clearing now the pack wolf had fled. "That's a fully changed werewolf and she's in pain and frightened."

"It's okay, pet," said Sally as gently as she could,

"you're safe now."

She gently stroked the injured animal and before Sally had time to react the wolf's head snapped round and she sank her teeth deep into Sally's arm. Sally winced at the pain and gritted her teeth, but she didn't pull away.

"Hey hey!" said Sally, "it's fine, pet. The danger's over. He's gone. I'm not going to hurt you."

Sally continued to talk softly and stroke the wolf's head gently. Slowly the wolf released her grip, letting go of Sally's arm and laying back onto the ground. Sally spoke quietly, reassuring the wolf as she untied the paws from each of the stakes, her own blood now running down her forearm and dripping from her fingers. The wolf lay there, letting Sally inspect the injuries, jumping occasionally when Sally's hand got too close to the worst of the burns.

"She's badly burnt," said Sally when Blake and Kiera reached them, approaching from downwind so as not to frighten the wolf with the scents of two more strangers.

"We have to move," he said. "I wouldn't put it passed that low life to come back with more of the pack. I don't want to be here when he does."

"What happened to you two?" asked Sally. "Why didn't you come and help?"

"I was going to," said Kiera, "but Blake stopped me. Besides, it didn't look to me as though you needed much help."

"If we had all come out of the trees together, he would

have run off for help before we got near him and the rest of the pack would already be here. I would have come out if you needed me."

Sally turned to the injured wolf, put her hand under her head and tried to help her up.

"Come on. Let's get you out of here too."

Slowly the wolf rose and, limping badly, followed Sally and the others out of the clearing.

They made their way to the edge of the woods and down the hill towards a farm that stood on the outskirts of a village. The injured wolf stumbled often but Sally helped her up and used gentle words of encouragement to keep her moving.

They found a barn stacked with straw bales and settled the wolf in the middle so she could rest and change back slowly. Blake disappeared to find their guest something to wear once she had changed back into a human and Sally stood guard. Kiera did a quick sweep of the farm buildings, but the only signs of life were in the farmhouse set away from the barn. They were downwind from the woods, so they would be able to smell any supernatural company coming long before they got near.

The girl woke about an hour later and dressed in the clothes Sally had laid out for her. It's difficult to judge the size a werewolf would be once they had changed back to a human but Blake had got the sizing of the clothes just about right. She didn't ask where he had got them from but suspected that somebody in the village was going to find their washing missing from their clothes line.

The girl was smaller than Sally by a few inches, about twenty years old and a bit too thin. Sally thought she looked a little undernourished. The girl's long brown hair reminded Sally of how Becky had been wearing hers when they first met, which made her wonder how her friend was coping as a prisoner of the research lab still many miles away. She was starting to feel guilty for taking so long to get there. She should be making her way to Becky instead of rescuing a total stranger.

The burns on the girl were already starting to heal but her movements were stiff, and the wounds still looked sore. She winced each time the material brushed over her injuries as she dressed. Sally cleared her through to let the girl know she was there. Hearing a noise behind her, the girl spun round and crouched low, despite the obvious pain.

"It's okay, pet," said Sally, "it's only me. How are you feeling?"

"I, err, I'm okay thanks."

The girl looked around nervously, checking her surroundings.

"Don't worry. You're safe. Nobody's going to get close without us knowing about it. Not with him on watch."

Sally's eyes looked up to the top of the barn where

Blake sat watching the area around the farm. The girl followed Sally's gaze.

"I'm Sally."

She extended her hand and waited for the girl to take it. Slowly she did, and the handshake was gentle and uncertain.

"Lucy," said the girl looking down at the blood stain on Sally's sleeve, "sorry about that."

"Don't worry about it. You were in pain and scared. I would have done the same probably."

"Biting you was wrong though," said Lucy. "You were only trying to help."

"You're still aware of things? Even as a wolf?" asked Sally.

Lucy nodded.

"How do you do it?"

"I don't know. I just do."

There was a long pause while Sally just stared at Lucy, wondering if it was a skill that she could learn. Lucy appeared to get uncomfortable at Sally's stares and broke the silence.

"Who's that?" she asked, looking up again towards the figure sitting on top of the hay bales.

"That's Blake," said Sally. He won't hurt you.

Hearing somebody else approach, Lucy stiffened and sniffed the air then backed away when she caught sight of Kiera walking into the barn.

"It's okay," said Sally, sensing Lucy's nervousness at

being surrounded by three strange werewolves. "That's Kiera, she's one of us."

Lucy remained tense, her eyes flicking from Sally to Kiera.

"Nobody is going to hurt you," Sally added.

Lucy settled a little, but Sally could still smell the unmistakable scent of fear emanating from every pore of the girl's body. Lucy lowered her head in a very submissive wolf like gesture.

"What are you going to do with me?" said Lucy, sounding even more timid and scared.

"What do you mean?" Sally replied.

"Well, you won me from Charles. That makes you my new master."

"Nobody is your master, Lucy,"

Sally was a little shocked at Lucy's remark. What sort of people were in this pack if they fought each other to win the ownership of another human being?

"That's how some of the older, more traditional packs get their mates and minions," Kiera chipped in. "My guess is that Lucy here was this guy's prize for some help he gave the Alpha. Or, he challenged her previous master and won her in a fight."

"That's awful," said Sally.

She turned back to Lucy, who still hadn't looked up, and put her hand gently under Lucy's chin, raising Lucy's head so she was looking directly into her eyes.

"You are your own person. Nobody owns you. Just you remember that. You're a werewolf and werewolves are strong."

"Not as strong as you," Lucy tried a smile but still looked nervous. "You beat Charles in a fight. I couldn't have done that."

"He was just a bully," said Sally. "All bullies are cowards. If you stood up to him I bet he would have backed down."

"It's not that simple," said Kiera, "In a pack there's a hierarchy that you must respect. That respect keeps order within the ranks."

"Respect!" snapped Sally, "Don't make me laugh. Are you saying that branding a defenseless young werewolf is a way of keeping order and that should be respected?"

"I didn't say what he was doing to her was right," said Kiera, "It's just pack politics and we, as outsiders, don't have the right to interfere in another pack's politics."

"I have no time for these pack politics as you call them," Sally turned to Lucy again. "Don't you worry about pack politics either. You are free to do what you want and come and go as you please."

"Go where?" asked Lucy.

"Anywhere," Sally replied.

Lucy just looked at her, a confused expression on her face, her eyes searching for answers.

"All she knows is her pack, Sally," said Kiera, "She has nowhere else to go. I think your little rescue earlier has saved her some suffering but denied her a home. Like she says, where can she go? Not back to her pack that's for sure."

Sally looked down at Lucy and saw a very confused girl, then at Kiera and up at Blake. All three of them were waiting for Sally to answer the question. Where could Lucy go now?

Sally just patted Lucy gently on the arm, "You can come with us."

"So she goes from one pack to another?" said Kiera.

"We aren't a pack," said Sally, "I was starting to hope we were friends."

"That's what a pack should be," Blake jumped down from the hay bales, "A collection of family and friends. But somebody needs to be the head of every family."

"I've been in a pack, remember, the one you left me with," said Sally, "I know what a pack is like and it's got nothing to do with family and friends."

"That's because you were with the wrong pack," Blake added, "You belong in my pack."

Sally just laughed, dismissive, full of disdain and dislike.

"I don't belong in any pack."

"I bit you Sally, you're my responsibility."

"I didn't ask you to bite me and make me into this monster and I relieve you of your responsibility."

Blake sighed, "Look, all I'm saying is that you're welcome in the pack at any time, whenever you need it. You're one of us."

Sally turned away and patted Lucy on the shoulder as she walked past.

"She stays with us if she wants to. But we aren't a pack."

With that Sally climbed the hay bales and looked out over the farm, taking her turn on watch.

Chapter 13

It was dark when Kiera climbed up on top of the hay bales to join Sally. Blake was resting below and Lucy had fallen asleep again, her injuries needing a little more healing time due to the ferociousness of her torture at the hands of her would be master.

"You go and get some sleep, Sally," said Kiera, "I'll take over the watch."

"I'm not sleepy."

"Then I'll just sit with you if that's okay."

Sally simply nodded and continued to look out over the fields for any sign that the local pack were on the hunt, but there was nothing to see. Strictly speaking they were outside of the pack's territory, but Sally didn't think that would prevent the pack from keeping a close eye on them at the very least.

"I get the impression you don't like being a werewolf," said Kiera.

Sally laughed.

"Can you blame me? It's ruined my life."

"Do you really mean ruined? That seems a little strong."

"I had a life, and the future was mine to take, Kiera. I had a family that I loved and who loved me. Now, my life has totally changed. I don't do the things I used to enjoy, I don't see the friends who I was close to, I lost the chance of a career

I wanted more than anything and my parents are frightened to be anywhere near me so I don't see my family at all. Yes, I would class as a life ruined."

"I wouldn't call it ruined," said Kiera, "Things have changed that's all."

"Oh, it's certainly changed, I'll give you that."

A dog started to bark in the distance and both girls sat up, looking out over the fields, their werewolf sight cutting through the darkness and their hearing homing in on the direction of the dog's bark. They both sniffed the air at the same time. Sally couldn't smell the scent of a werewolf, only sheep along with other animals that came out at night.

"It's probably just a fox wandering through the farm over yonder," said Sally.

Both girls relaxed, Sally felt confident that there was no imminent danger of a werewolf attack.

"So," said Kiera sitting back down on the bales next to Sally, "what exactly do you miss apart from your family? What did the pre-werewolf Sally Bowers like to do in those days?"

"Lots of stuff. I had a few friends I spent a lot of time with. I liked to go running and keeping fit. I loved playing the piano. The one hobby I miss more than any other is karate training. I loved training and competing. I haven't been able to find a club around Popwood to go to."

"Karate!" said Kiera, "Well that explains some of the

fight moves you have, and why I always ended up on my back."

"What about you?" asked Sally.

"What about me?"

"What did Kiera… sorry I don't know your surname."

"Chapman."

"What did Kiera Chapman do in her pre-werewolf days?"

"Nothing."

"Nothing? You must have done something, had a pastime, friends, family."

Kiera just shook her head and took another bite of a sausage roll that Blake had stuffed quickly into her bag before they left Popwood.

"You don't have a family?"

"No," said Kiera with an emotionless shrug. "I never knew my parents. I grew up in an orphanage or I was passed on between different foster parents. I was never in one place long enough to make any friends."

"That's rather sad," said Sally, "No wonder you hang so much hope on the pack."

"Yeah, I guess so. They really are the only family I have. Given the chance I'm sure you'll do anything for your family. Well, I'll do anything for mine. Mine just happen to be a pack of werewolves."

This explained a lot to Sally about why Kiera defended the pack life that Sally so detested. It was becoming obvious Kiera needed the pack because she literally had nobody else in her life. Blake and Helena being her substitute parents in a way. Sally was trying to stay away from her family because of a pack. She still didn't understand all this pack politics rubbish. To her it was nothing more than a collection of rules made up by alphas to keep their minions in line.

"You should join our pack Sally," said Kiera, "They can be like a family to you too."

"You're starting to sound like Blake," said Sally. "Besides, I already have a family and if I didn't, the last person I would want in a replacement family would be him."

"He's not as bad as you make out, Sally. I was bitten by a rogue," said Kiera, "and Blake took me in, even though I wasn't his responsibility. The pack protected me and helped me get used to my, 'condition'. I think that's something you've missed out on."

"Well, I had a slightly different experience," said Sally. "I wasn't just bitten. I was half eaten and left for dead," Sally nodded back down to where Blake was resting, "and that hero of yours is the one who did it. Forgive me if I don't feel the same sort of connection as you do."

"I feel sorry for you, Sally," said Kiera, "Not because you were bitten, although I can see how that can make you a little bitter. No, I feel sorry for you because you haven't had the experience of a true pack."

"There's no need to feel sorry for me. I'm fine."

"I know you are, and you will continue to be fine. I'm

not sure you understand how or why you will be fine though."

Sally looked at Kiera trying to read her body language, trying to grasp onto something that would explain Kiera's sudden change towards her. This had got to be some kind of trick, and it made Sally feel uneasy.

"What do you mean?"

"You have one of the strongest strains of Lycanthropy there is," said Kiera, sounding a little envious, "Even Blake has trouble controlling it and he is one of the toughest werewolves I have ever met. That was why he was unable to control his wolf when he came across you that night. You know yourself that when you are in wolf form it's difficult to override basic wolf instinct."

"He managed to override it enough to stop eating me and leave me to turn into this monster."

"He didn't leave you to become a monster. It's not something he does on purpose you know."

"That makes me feel a whole lot better," said Sally, a little more sarcastically than she intended.

"Blake has only made three werewolves. The first one was when he was first turned and had to go through his first full moon on his own. The Lycanthropy was driving him mad and he bit Damian. He's still locked up at the research lab."

"Who was Damien?"

"He was like you I guess," replied Kiera. "He was just somebody who was in the wrong place at the wrong time. I think he would like you. He's got the same accent as you."

"I see your hero has a habit of making werewolves out of innocent bystanders."

"He doesn't!" said Kiera. The anger starting to show in her voice. "Blake regrets that every day and swore to himself never to infect another living soul."

Sally raised her arms and pointed at herself.

"He didn't quite manage that did he."

"Well, it's not always easy. You know yourself there's things you can't control even in your human form."

Sally just huffed and turned away then remembered her eyes. They changed to a golden orange whenever she was angry or scared or felt any strong emotional feelings.

"You said there was three," said Sally, turning back to Kiera.

"There was Helena, his wife. She was kidnapped and when Blake tried to rescue her they threw her off a cliff. She was nearly dead when he found her, so he bit her to keep her alive."

"He bit his wife?" asked Sally.

"It was the only way he could save her life."

Kiera went quiet and gazed back out over the fields. Sally knew this had hit a nerve so she let Kiera take a moment then continued.

"And the third?"

"The other one is you. I know you probably don't

believe it but, like Damien, you were just in the wrong place at the wrong time. Blake was trying to get away from the local werewolf pack and using all his strength to control his wolf so that he didn't turn and kill any of the pack. His wolf attacked you before he could stop it. The lycanthropy you and him share is the most difficult to control and he struggles with it daily. But you, you take it all in your stride and can control it and use it in ways that I've never seen."

"Oh yeah," said Sally, "Like what?"

"You can partially change, your claws grow, and your teeth elongate but you don't shift."

"So, what, it's just a simple werewolf thing."

"No, it's not, Sally," Kiera turned to face her fully, "You are the only werewolf I have seen do that. Even Blake can't do that."

"Really?" Sally had never thought she could have powers that other werewolves didn't have.

"Yes really," said Kiera, "and I've watched you take out three massive male werewolves who were there to kill you, but you controlled your lycanthropy and refused to kill them. The strain you have should have taken over and you would have woken up not knowing you had ripped them to pieces. You didn't let that happen."

"I don't like killing," Sally replied.

"No, but your wolf will if it feels threatened. Or at least it would normally. It's as if you are its Alpha and it will only do as you say."

"She has a mind of her own, and sometimes I can't stop her coming out." Sally looked down at her body. "We seem to have an understanding most of the time and I let her out when it's safe to do so and she can have a run."

"You're amazing," said Kiera, "and the best thing, is that you don't realize just how amazing you are."

The two girls talked for the rest of the night, each telling small parts of their history to the other while keeping an eye open in the direction of the local pack territory. Blake joined them as the sun started to rise and warm the tops of the trees.

"Any sign of our branding iron friend?" he asked.

"No, nothing," said Sally, "they've not been anywhere near."

"Well, I doubt that will last. Come on, let's get going. I don't want to hang around here for much longer," said Blake.

Lucy sat up with a start when they came down from the hay bales. She didn't say anything, only lowered her eyes to the floor.

"Are you coming with us?" asked Blake, standing at her feet.

Lucy kept her head down and simply shrugged her shoulders.

"Of course she is," said Sally, "I thought we'd agreed that last night."

"Well, she doesn't look that sure," said Blake, staring

down at Lucy.

Lucy threw a quick glance at Sally and then found another interesting spot on the ground. Sally walked over and crouched down beside her, noticing how Lucy was keeping from having any eye contact.

"You can stay if you want to you know," said Sally gently, "or you can come along with us."

"Can I?" asked Lucy, "Come along with you I mean?"

"Of course you can," said Sally.

Blake huffed as he turned and picked up his coat.

"I hope you've explained to her where we're going," said Blake. "She may want to change her mind."

"She doesn't have to go in there," snapped Sally.

Lucy looked up at Blake's back then at Sally.

"Why?" asked Lucy. "Where are we going?"

Sally felt a little anger and frustration growing inside. There was no need for him to say that while Lucy could hear. It was a cheap trick to pull just to try and convince Lucy that she should go back to her pack, a pack that obviously only looked upon her as a piece of meat. Well, she wasn't going to play along with his pack politics.

"Don't worry," said Sally, turning her back to Lucy. "We're just going to rescue a few of his friends." She stared straight into his eyes as he looked back at them from the door. "I'm sure they can't all be as grumpy as him."

"A rescue?" Lucy's eyes widened.

"Yes," replied Sally, "But that's my job. There's no reason for you to get involved. I'm only involved because he brought a friend of mine into a disagreement we had, then he failed to protect her. Now she's locked up with his lot."

Kiera stepped between Sally and Blake with a look on her face as if she was going to cry.

"That was my fault," said Kiera, "and you know I'm sorry for what happened to Becky."

"You did what you could, Kiera," said Sally. "It's not your fault. He, on the other hand, disappeared at the crucial moment didn't he? He's good at that."

A low growl sounded from the direction of Blake. Kiera spun round and stepped back. Lucy shot her eyes back at the floor, looking as submissive as ever. Sally stood and stared straight back at him. He might be an alpha of his pack, but he wasn't her alpha and if he wanted to try and push the point here and now then he was welcome to try.

With another growl, Blake punched the wall of the barn, loosening a wooden board as he did so, then turned and walked out.

"That was unkind," said Kiera and followed him out.

"What was all that about?" asked Lucy.

Sally's inside tightened a little at Kiera's comment and she closed her eyes and shook her head. She hadn't meant it to sound the way it had come out but her frustrations at Blake always trying to be, or suggest that he could be, her pack alpha had gotten the better of her.

"Just Blake having trouble with his alpha mentality," said Sally. "Don't you worry about him. Come on. Let's get out of here."

They made their way off the farm and out of the valley in silence. The longer the silence went on the more guilty Sally felt. Kiera was right. What she had said back at the barn had been unkind. She hadn't meant to draw on the similarity with his not being there the night his pack had been captured but the similarity was there, and Sally felt bad about it. What made things worse was the fact she couldn't apologize to him properly because that would tell him that Kiera had been talking to her about it. She had to make some sort of apology without letting on she knew about the details of the night his pack was taken.

Chapter 14

As they made their way south, Sally watched Lucy closely. She seemed to be acting as if everything was new, unusual, scary even. It was as if Lucy had never been out of the little town where Sally had found her. Lucy jumped at every bird that flew out of a bush or squawked from up in a tree. Any sudden sound had her hiding behind Sally. As night approached, Lucy started to fidget and look up at the sky, searching for something she was either afraid of or secretly excited about.

When they settled down for the night Sally made sure she was close to Lucy so that she could keep an eye on her. Having an unknown, unstable and frightened werewolf travelling with them was not what she'd planned when she'd invited Lucy to tag along. She staggered into a restless sleep.

Sally ran as fast as she could. Her legs were like lead and the effort it took was like running through waist deep water. The wolf was gaining easily. She could hear its growls and feel its breath on the back of her neck. Teeth snapped at her heels and she knew it was only a matter of time before she was caught. She screamed as powerful jaws closed on her leg and she was tossed from side to side like a ragdoll. The wolf let go and she hit the ground, rolling onto her back. Wild eyes stared down at her, wolf's eyes. She waited for the final attack, but the wolf slowly began to rise up onto its hind legs as it's form slowly changed. A young girl played with her hands as she looked down at Sally. The look on the girl's face was sad and familiar.

"Lucy?" asked Sally.

Lucy smiled down at her before the eyes changed again, they were once again the eyes of a wolf. With a growl and a lunge, the wolf pounced once more.

Sally woke with a start panting as if she had actually been running. Sweat was seeping from every pore of her body. She looked around as she sat up trying to judge if any of the others had noticed the effects of her latest nightmare. Lucy was asleep closeby and Keira was curled up quietly on the other side of the dying campfire. Blake was nowhere to be seen. He had the habit, Sally had noticed, of going off during the night to scout the area. An Alpha keeping watch over his pack? An instinct that hadn't disappeared when his pack had. Or was it now a determination on his side not to let the same thing happen again? Sally lay back and drifted off into another restless sleep.

The following day was more of the same with Lucy sticking close to Sally as much as she could. She seemed more comfortable with, if a little unsure of, Kiera and whenever they stopped for a rest or some food she would sit with Sally or Kiera but always kept her head lowered if Kiera spoke to her. Blake, she kept away from totally and seemed to always make sure that she kept Sally between her and Blake as they travelled.

"I think Lucy has attached herself to you," said Kiera, on one of the rare occasions when Lucy left Sally's side.

"She's just getting used to us all," Sally replied.

"It's more than that. I think she sees you as some sort of role model."

"Me?" Sally almost laughed. "She doesn't want to be looking up to me. She can do a lot better that."

"You saved her life, as she sees it. You are strong and brave. Everything I'm sure she wishes she was."

"Putting up with the life she was living and getting through what she suffered is very brave and far more courageous than anything I've done if you ask me."

"I'm just telling you what I see," said Kiera, "Be careful, Sally or you could be turning into Lucy's alpha, even though you don't want to be."

Sally looked over to where Lucy was sat, her back against a tree trunk and her eyes closed while she rested in the shade. Sally started to wonder if she had done the right thing. Had she forced Lucy into leaving a pack that she was going to find it hard to be without? All Sally had seen was the way she had been treated on one particular occasion. Maybe the pack alpha would have punished Lucy's abuser once he found out. Just because one person acted that way didn't make the whole pack bad. There was no way of knowing what that pack was really like just with a snapshot of a single incident. Was she wrong? No. She hadn't come across any pack yet that acted anyway other than the animals they really were. Surely Lucy was better off out of all that stuff.

"If she needs an alpha, she can choose either Blake or you," said Sally.

"I'm not an alpha," Kiera replied.

"Neither am I."

"Through Lucy's eyes," Kiera looked at their new travelling companion, "you could be."

For the rest of the afternoon Sally watched Lucy closely. She was never far away and would wait for Sally before she did anything. Is this the same werewolf from her dream or was the dream the werewolf that Sally was turning Lucy into? A werewolf who would find her confidence and, because of the pack she had come from, see a challenge to an alpha the right and natural thing to do when she was ready? Sally shook her head, not wanting to believe she was making Lucy into a werewolf she wasn't destined to be. She was almost certain helping Lucy gain some confidence and a little independence could only be a good thing.

They reached a good spot for a camp so Blake decided that they should stop there for the night and they each found a tree they could rest against. Lucy, as usual, picked a tree closer to Sally than to Blake or Kiera.

It was getting dark and the rumbling sound coming from her stomach reminded Sally she was starting to feel hungry. She assumed the others must be feeling the same way. The food they had packed before they had set off from Popwood was long gone and they were a full night's walk from the nearest town. She decided this would be the ideal time to get Lucy on her own and find out what was going on in the young werewolf's head.

"I'm hungry," said Sally, getting to her feet and dusting off her jeans. "Who's up for a little hunt?" She looked over at Lucy. "Lucy?" she said, "what about you? Do you want to come along with me for the groceries?"

"Me?" Lucy asked. "Go with you on a hunt?"

"Sure. Why not?"

"Okay," said Lucy. The excitement showing in her voice.

Lucy started to unbutton her clothes but Sally stopped her.

"It's okay," said Sally, "we won't need to shift for this."

"I've never hunted as a human before."

Lucy looked a little confused.

"Then I'll show you how to catch a few rabbits without the added complication of a wolf."

The two girls slipped off through some trees, Sally taking the lead and Lucy falling in behind. They hadn't gone more than a few hundred yards when both girls caught the scent of rabbit, quite a few rabbits if Sally wasn't mistaken. She looked over at Lucy, who had a broad smile on her face. Anticipation and eagerness written all over it.

"What do we do now?" asked Lucy.

"You head left, and I'll head right. Wait for my signal and then we go. If we come at them from both sides we should be able to grab a lot of them. There's plenty there from the scent.

"You can tell how many there is?" asked Lucy. "Just from the scent?"

"Not the exact number. Only that there is a fairly large group.

"That's unreal." Lucy added a quiet, excited little giggle.

They were both downwind so creeping up on their prey wasn't difficult. Sally waited until Lucy was also in position then gave a nod and the two girls leaped out from their hiding places. Sally managed to grab four rabbits before the others had run off in all directions. Lucy stood in the middle of the opening in the trees where the rabbits had been without a single one. She looked at Sally with a look of admiration on her face.

"You were brilliant," said Lucy. "How did you do that?"

"You just have to be focused. Shutout all the other sounds and smells and plan what you are going to do. In your mind see yourself catching your prey and believe you can do it."

"I don't think I would be able to be that fast."

"Have you ever tried before?"

Lucy shook her head.

"I wasn't really allowed to practice that kind of thing."

"Why not?"

"Our Alphas said it wasn't my place."

Sally suspected the alphas didn't want to allow any potential threat a chance to develop any meaningful skills. Although, how they could see Lucy as a threat Sally couldn't think.

Lucy gazed again at the collection of rabbits in Sally's hands.

"I would love to be able to do that."

"Then I'll teach you."

Sally stored the rabbits in the trunk of a tree and set off again, Lucy close behind her. When they got the scent of rabbits once more, Sally dropped to the ground and Lucy did the same.

"You lead this time, Lucy."

With a little reluctance Lucy crept forward and the two girls closed in on the scent of their prey. They stopped behind some bushes and stared through the leaves to where two rabbits were munching on some leaves. Sally put her arm around Lucy's shoulder and brought her lower to the ground.

"Now, dig your feet into the ground so you can get a

good push off," Sally whispered.

Lucy did as instructed.

"Pick which rabbit you are after and close out everything else. Keep focused on that rabbit." Sally's voice got quieter and quieter. "See yourself lunging forward and grabbing the rabbit. Decide which hand you are going to use. See yourself being successful. Believe what you see in your mind and when you are ready just go and don't think of anything else."

Sally heard Lucy's heart slow and her breathing virtually stop. Almost before Sally herself knew what was happening Lucy was on top of the rabbit. It didn't stand a chance. The second rabbit was grabbed in midair as it tried to escape.

Lucy got to her feet holding the two animals in her hands, a look of surprise and joy all over her face.

"I did it."

"Yes, you did," said Sally as she came out from behind the bushes and hugged a triumphant Lucy. "See, you can do anything I can. You're just as strong and fast as me."

Lucy looked like a different werewolf and practically strutted back into the camp, tossing one of the rabbits over to Kiera. She sat by Sally and offered her the other rabbit. A typical offering to an alpha.

"No," said Sally. "That's yours. You caught it."

That night, Lucy fidgeted even more and while Sally took her turn on watch she noticed that she didn't get much sleep. None of them had trusted Lucy to take a turn guarding the camp. Lucy seemed uncomfortable and Sally began to wonder what had the had her so spooked.

"It's the full moon," said Blake when Sally asked if he had noticed Lucy's strange behavior. "The closer we get to the full moon the worse she's getting."

"That's normal though," said Sally, "I get a little twitchy myself on the nights running up to the full moon. But we're still two days away from it."

Blake pulled Sally to one side; a move that told Sally there was bad news coming.

"Well, when the full moon does arrive, it's going to give us a problem."

"Lucy will be fine," Sally replied, "I'll take care of her during the full moon."

"Lucy isn't the one you should be worried about."

"Why? Are you going to go all alpha on me once you shift because I should warn you that my wolf won't put up with it any more than I will." From the look on his face Sally could tell Blake had something else on his mind.

"Rescuing Lucy has taken time and she is slowing us down. We're still quite a way from the Lab, according to Kiera. If we don't get there before the full moon…"

"Your pack is going to rip her to pieces."

"Normally I would say they won't. I know them and they aren't like that. But they have been mistreated... by humans. We need to get there soon, Sally."

Sally didn't want to think about the danger Becky was in right now and she was ashamed she had wasted time rescuing a total stranger. She could almost hear Becky telling her she had done the right thing because that was the person Becky was, caring and kind. Now was the time to finish this quest and save her best friend.

"Then let's go. I need to get there and stop them," said Sally and jumped to her feet.

Chapter 15

Sally grabbed her rucksack and headed out of the clearing. pushing her way through the dense bushes as she went. Blake followed.

"Wait, Sally. We still need to get some rest and some food inside us before we get going. We don't want to get to the lab without plenty of energy."

Sally ignored him and kept going.

Blake caught up and grabbed her by the arm, Sally snapped her head around and growled.

"We need to eat," was all he said.

"Then you stay and eat," said Sally. "I'm going to get Becky."

"Not without some food inside you you're not. You've not eaten much for a couple of days. Those little rabbits aren't going to give you much energy. We're no match for those guards unless we're at full strength. If you're killed by a vampire before you get to her, you'll be no use to Becky."

Sally looked Blake straight in the eye.

"If Becky gets killed by your pack of monsters you better hope I do get killed, because if I'm still alive, I'll be coming for you."

Sally shrugged herself out of his grip and set off once more. By this time Lucy had caught up and had fallen into step behind her.

Stay Away

"Sally you don't even know where the lab is" he shouted after her.

"I'll ask when I get closer," replied Sally over her shoulder.

The pace Sally set was steady and determined. It was almost an hour by the time Blake and Kiera had packed up their gear at the camp and caught up.

"Sally, we'll give it another hour but then we must rest and get some food inside us," said Blake as he walked beside her.

Sally pulled out the small Japanese sword Blake had given her. She cut her way through a line of bushes that surrounded the field in front of her and pressed on. There was no time to go around it in Sally's mind, only a strong urge to get to Becky.

"We're hungry. We're losing our strength. Let me hunt and I'll get us some food."

Her inner wolf had always been right in the past. She was like the voice of conscience or reason, not always what Sally wanted to hear but something that kept her walking the right path. Sally hesitated and considered her wolf's words then pressed on across the field, cutting through the line of bushes opposite. She didn't have time to listen to reason.

"We're fine," Sally replied.

Her body was beginning to agree with her inner wolf. Her stomach groaned and complained at the lack of nourishment and her energy level started to fall. Still, she couldn't bring herself to stop. She had to get to Becky as soon as she could.

Inside, Sally could feel a connection with Becky that had been growing all day, getting stronger and more urgent. Becky was alive, Sally was sure of it. She was also sure that Becky was in serious trouble. A danger that had not yet surfaced, a danger that was waiting for the full moon to rise. She picked up the pace still more.

An hour later she sensed Blake walking alongside her. She knew what he was going to say. Her stomach twisted and growled some more because of the lack of food. She didn't want any. The only thing she wanted was still miles away and the full moon was approaching. Time was running out.

"Sally, we need to stop," said Blake.

Looking over her shoulder she saw Lucy falling behind. Kiera was quiet but keeping up with the pace. Sally could smell the fear building inside her travel companion. Kiera didn't come across as the kind of werewolf who would scare easily, but something was bothering her.

She waited for everybody to catch up. Kiera continued past a few paces and stopped, her eyes staring straight ahead. Sally followed her gaze but could see nothing out of the ordinary.

"She's frightened of something ahead," said Sally's wolf.

"Are you alright?" asked Sally and placed a hand on

Kiera's shoulder.

Kiera turned quickly and growled.

"Hey, what is it?"

Kiera hesitated, then seemed to snap out of her thoughts and shook her head.

"Sorry, Sally," she replied. "I'm not myself.

Lucy caught up and sat heavily down on the ground panting. She looked tired and weary.

"She can't go on much further," said Blake, noticing Sally looking at Lucy.

Even Blake looked tired. His eyes were dark, but he stood up straight as an alpha would, refusing to show weakness. Kiera looked around and sat on a fallen tree trunk. Sally was walking her team into the ground. She needed to get to Becky as quickly as possible, but she also knew she would need help from the others when she got there. She had no idea what she was going to be up against, but she was sure the more they had in the team the greater the chance of success.

"We'll rest here for half an hour." Lucy looked up at Sally with a thankful look on her face. "I'll go and get us something to eat."

"I'll go with you," said Kiera to Sally's surprise.

"Are you sure?"

"Yes, I need to clear my head."

The two girls dumped their rucksacks and headed off into the trees together, Sally leading the way. Her nose searching for the scent of any prey that may be close by. They hadn't gone far when she caught the scent of a small group of rabbits.

"You take the left and I'll go right," said Sally.

Sally approached the animals from downwind and stopped at the line of bushes. Kiera went too far and the rabbits spotted her and scattered.

"Sorry, Sally."

"It's okay," Sally replied. "There will be more."

Sally sniffed the air again.

"This way," she said.

Once again Sally took the right and Kiera circled round to the left. They got into position and when Sally gave the signal, they both pounced. Sally got two rabbits, but Kiera missed her targets and the rest of the prey scattered once more.

"What happened?" asked Sally.

"I don't know. I got distracted. I thought I heard something approaching from up ahead."

Sally looked around and listened and sniffed the air again.

"There's nothing there, Kiera."

"No, you're right. Sorry."

Kiera looked round from side to side then focused her attention up ahead again.

"What is it you're so scared of?"

"I'm not scared," Kiera replied.

"Well, something's got you spooked."

"I'll be fine."

Kiera was twitchy and if Sally could see her hackles, she was sure Kiera's would be up. This wasn't the same confident werewolf she'd set out with from Popwood. Kiera was becoming a nervous wreck in front of her eyes.

They tried a few more times to catch some prey but each time Kiera either made too much noise or lost her concentration. Sally had the only catch, four small rabbits. Enough for a snack but nowhere near enough food to build the strength of a team of hungry werewolves.

"What's the matter?" Sally asked, noticing Kiera rubbing her hands together then picking at her nails and playing with her bottom lip.

Kiera glanced all around as if expecting an attack. Sally sniffed the air as a precaution again but could still smell nothing unusual.

"Come on tell me," Sally prompted again.

"I can't go back in there."

"Where?"

"The lab? I just can't."

"You won't have to. Blake and I can deal with that part."

"You don't know what it's like in there, Sally. The things they do to werewolves. The guards…" Kiera stopped talking and rubbed a stray tear from her eye then ran her fingers through her hair, pushing it back off her face. She took a deep breath to steady her emotions. "Sorry, I'm not usually a coward."

"Nobody's saying you're a coward."

Even though Sally hadn't known Kiera for long, a coward was not a word she would use to describe her in any way. She had changed though. Kiera didn't seem to trust her senses and was on a constant lookout, searching ahead of them and keeping an eye on the trees on either side.

"It's okay, Kiera. I can't smell anything. There's nothing coming."

"You can't always tell they are coming," said Kiera almost in a whisper, her eyes wide and searching. A wild look on her face.

"Kiera, we're still a full day away. The vampires won't be around here. You're safe."

Kiera didn't look convinced. Sally knew they were getting closer to the lab, probably less than fifty miles away now. The closer they got the more stressed they were all getting. Kiera knew more about these vampires than Sally so should she be getting more wary herself? She knew about vampires from what she'd seen on the television and at the cinema. Could it be as simple as a steak through the heart or was it a little more complicated than how it was portrayed on the big screen? After all, what she knew about werewolves before she was bitten was from the television, and that had proven to be a lot different in reality. Would vampires turn out to be more of a surprise as well? There was no denying vampires were seen as a formidable enemy, but since Sally had become a werewolf her own abilities had increased tenfold. She was certain she could handle a vampire one on one. Seeing Kiera like this though was making her feel uneasy.

They made their way back to the others and Sally gave out the food before settling herself down next to Lucy, who looked a little less weary.

"After this we'll have a few hours sleep before we get going again," said Blake.

"Not a chance," replied Sally immediately. "We don't have much time before the full moon and I'm not wasting any of it here while Becky is with your animals."

"He's right. We need to rest. To build our strength up."

"They're not animals," said Kiera.

"Whatever," said Sally. "We leave as soon as we've finished our meal."

"These scraps are no meal." Blake waved what remained of his small rabbit in the air.

"Have mine," said Sally, throwing her half-eaten dinner over to him, "and next time you can catch your own prey." She nudged Lucy. "Come on. Let's get going."

Sally ignored the frustrated complaints from Blake and the voice from within herself and got to her feet. Lucy was up beside her in a second, obviously trying to appear refreshed but Sally knew she wasn't.

Looking around at her ragged band of comrades she saw a disheveled little group. Should she let them rest or press on?

She wasn't sure exactly how far she had left to go and the pull on her insides in the direction of Becky was getting stronger. She couldn't waste any more time. They had to go.

Swinging her rucksack over her shoulder she turned and set off again.

"They aren't the only ones who are still tired. We are too."

"I know," said Sally quietly to her wolf. We have to get going.

"We're getting weak."

"We'll be fine. We may not even come across any vampires. Once we have the pack free, we'll have all the strength we need to get passed a few undead guards."

Sally felt less confident of what she had said than she tried to look. Her wolf knew it but remained quiet.

She didn't want to sleep. She didn't want another nightmare about how Becky was being torn apart, by the pack or by her. She just wanted to get there and get her friend to safety before the full moon. She didn't allow the others to rest, she just kept trudging on, getting closer and closer to their target. Blake made a constant effort through the night to assert his alpha male influence and make her rest, but Sally was having none of it. She kept walking, sometimes not even answering him, just increasing the pace.

Lucy started to drop off the back and even Kiera was hanging back. Sally didn't think it was because of weariness or a concern for Lucy, but Kiera was the one bringing up the rear.

Blake dropped back to walk beside Kiera. Sally knew he was worried about his pack member. It wasn't eves dropping, her werewolf senses were not something she could turn off and the keen hearing came as part of the package, but she didn't try to stop herself from listening in upon their conversation.

"Come on Kiera," she heard Blake say, "You need to keep up. We're getting close."

"We're too tired for this Blake," Kiera replied.

"I know but Sally won't slow down. Short of physically pinning her down I've tried everything. She just won't listen."

"Then let her go. We don't need her."

"We do, Kiera."

"You can get the pack out."

"I can't. Not by myself. And we can't let Sally go there by herself either."

"Why can't we?"

"Because she'll get killed. If she dies, then our last hope of getting the pack out has gone. I need her."

"I'll help."

"You? Look at you Kiera. You're a mess. You'll be useless in there."

Sally could feel Kiera's hurt the moment the last remark came out.

"That'll do!" shouted Sally. "We go there together. Kiera

will be fine. She can stay outside and be our backup. Me and you can handle things in there. Now leave her alone."

Sally took Kiera by the arm and dragged her to the front to walk with her, setting off once more at a fast pace and in silence. She couldn't understand why she had stood up for Kiera. All she knew was that it felt right.

After another hour Blake tapped Sally on the shoulder.

"Lucy is struggling," he said. "We need to stop and rest."

"There's no time," Sally replied.

She looked over her shoulder towards Lucy who was starting to fall behind again. One look from Sally, however, and Lucy seemed to get more encouragement. She was obviously still trying her best to impress.

They pressed on through the night. They had a short rest when Lucy fell to her knees, out of breath and retching with the effort it was taking to keep to Sally's schedule. It wasn't long before Sally was urging them on once more.

The following day was no different. More walking and not enough rest or food. Kiera once again slipped to the rear, startled by the smallest of sounds, the scent of fear from her getting stronger the further they went. It got suddenly darker as the sun sank below the surrounding hills. Even Sally felt uneasy now. This place wasn't safe and her inner wolf could sense it.

"Sally!"

Kiera's shout made Sally stop and look round. Kiera was

standing motionless, staring at her with a pleading look in her eyes.

"We have to stop, now."

"Why?" Sally asked.

"Because the lab is just over that ridge and the sun has gone down."

Sally looked up the hill. They were fifty yards from the top where there was a covering of more bushes and trees.

The sudden darkness seemed to seep into her skin. Sally had never really felt the cold since she was bitten but there was a chill in the air, a cold unearthly chill. Sally felt uneasy and her inner wolf was alert. She felt her hackles start to rise. Her mouth became dry. She listened for any sounds around her searching for danger but there was nothing. No birds, no animals, just the spooky sound of the breeze moving through the leaves on the trees.

"You two stay here," said Blake to Kiera and Lucy. "Sally, with me. Let's have a look."

Lucy collapsed to the ground and leaned up against a tree trunk. She looked anxious and Sally could smell fear. Kiera remained standing, rooted to the spot, staring up the hill. Sally and Blake turned and made their way slowly towards the ridge.

Removing her rucksack Sally squeezed under some bushes and peered over the ridge. A large complex of grey buildings stretched out from the lower slopes of the hill and were surrounded by tall wire fencing. The buildings were of different sizes and in the middle was a large, three-story office block.

Staying low, Sally scanned the compound from a distance. The security was strangely non-existent. There was a gate which could obviously be locked, but there was no CCTV that she could see. either on the outside of the buildings or around the grounds. There was a lack of patrolling guards and the building looked deserted. Not one single light illuminated any of the windows. She couldn't understand why her two companions hadn't just walked in before they came looking for her, they could have easily got in and out of there. Why was there no security? It didn't make sense. Then, she saw something appear in one of the windows, the figure of a man, walking from office to office but staying back from the windows slightly. As Sally watched he suddenly disappeared into thin air.

"What the hell was that?" she whispered to herself.

"That, my dear, was a vampire."

Blake crawled up beside her.

"How did he just disappear?"

"He didn't," said Blake. "They're very fast. That's why I told you not to let one surprise you."

"Do you think he saw us?"

"No. I doubt he could see us from here. There will be one on the roof too I'm guessing."

Sally waited and watched, then just as she was about to

look away, she saw a movement. Another figure of a man had appeared on the roof and was looking over the edge of the building. They were downwind of the building and she got the scent of something she hadn't smelled before. A stale, cold smell, of something old, something dead, like an animal skin that had been vacated and left to rot.

"Can you smell that?" he said, and Sally nodded, "That is the stench of a vampire. Learn to recognize it."

Sally wasn't going to forget that smell as long as she lived. Her wolf seemed to recognize it too and started to panic a little inside. This smell was dangerous, the most dangerous thing she had ever come across and her wolf wanted to be out, to run. Sally moved away slowly. For the first time since becoming a werewolf she felt fear. Blake followed and they made their way back to the others.

The scent of the vampire had unsettled Sally's wolf more than she had ever known before. She could feel her pacing inside, going over and over the same paw prints each time, unable to calm down and it made Sally more nervous.

Looking around at her small band of brothers she saw only a tired and disheveled bunch of misfits. Lucy was exhausted, Kiera was a wreck, Blake and herself were far below their best. She'd made a mistake. They weren't ready to confront a team of vampire guards. Sally knew that now. She had driven them too hard and ignored too many of Blake's more experienced warnings. There was no time left though.

Tomorrow night was a full moon and Becky was still in there somewhere, expecting her best friend to come to the rescue. Sally didn't want to let Becky down, but it wasn't going to be as easy as she had first thought. It was going to take some serious good fortune, if not a miracle to pull this one off.

Chapter 16

Sneaking into the lab wasn't going to be as straightforward as Sally had thought. For one thing, she didn't know the building layout. For another, she didn't know the security arrangements it had. Now, she also realised she had no idea of the tracking skills of a vampire or what they were really capable of?

"We need to go and check the place out," said Sally. "Find a way in and scout around for a while."

"It's too late now, Sally," replied Blake. "The vampires are up and about. They'll spot us too easily. We don't know enough about the geography yet."

"Kiera knows her way around," said Sally, looking over to where Kiera was sat.

The pain inside started immediately. It wasn't a physical pain; this was more of an emotional pain. A pain that came from within and tightened Sally's stomach and chest. Kiera had made her feelings clear regarding how she felt about going back into lab. Sally knew she'd promised Kiera she wouldn't have to. But that was before she fully understood the dangers they would be facing. This was no time to be feeling guilty.

"It will just be you and I, Sally," said Blake.

Sally looked over at Keira. She could smell the fear of being this close to the lab pouring through Kiera's skin. The twisting pain inside grew a little stronger and Sally did her best to ignore it.

"We need her."

"She's not going in. You promised."

Sally thought about Becky and how she could be locked up with a pack of werewolves and being guarded by vampires. She couldn't bear to think of what Becky must be going through by now. She would be frightened. Becky was too sheltered a person to be able to cope with the fear she must be feeling. Blake may be right about his pack and they may not hurt Becky for all Sally knew. The vampires, however, were a totally different pull on the rope. Sally had seen the films on television. Vampires preyed on girls like Becky.

"I know I did," said Sally, "but we need all the help we can get. I have a very bad feeling about those vampires."

"And so you should have. They're very unpredictable. But it'll still be just the two of us, and it'll be tomorrow. Not tonight."

Sally wanted to argue but deep down she knew Blake was right. She couldn't ask anybody to put themselves in such danger. Even though she hadn't got on with Kiera for most of this journey, she couldn't bring herself to try and force her into going to the lab. An alpha may force her, but that wasn't the kind of werewolf Sally was. She was beginning to see Blake as not that kind of alpha either now.

"Okay," said Sally eventually. "Just me and you."

Stay Away

She looked back up at the ridge from where she had seen her first vampire and caught its scent.

"How are we going to do this then?" she asked.

"First, we rest," said Blake.

Sally made a move to protest, but Blake merely held up his hand and carried on.

"Then, once the sun is up, we go to the lab, we make contact with Bren, our friend on the inside Kiera told you about, he can tell us the best way in, then we stay calm and come up with a proper course of action. Then it's just a matter of getting in, freeing Becky and the pack, and getting out."

"Just like that?"

"Yes, Sally. Just like that. Now go and get some rest."

Blake seemed to know what he was doing and starting to take charge. Sally felt tired and nervous and she was happy to share the stress of the mission for once. Knowing Becky would be counting on her to stage a rescue and steal her away from under the noses of, what Blake called a perfect predator, was starting to play on her mind and the pressure she was keeping herself under was beginning to build inside.

She knew she wouldn't be able to talk Blake into doing anything tonight, so she chose a space beside the now sleeping Lucy, settled down and started to drift off, It was not quite sleep but just sort of on the brink. It didn't last long. The memory of the vampire was too fresh in her mind and her inner wolf wouldn't relax.

"Vampires are dangerous."

"What do I do?" answered Sally quietly to the voice inside.

"I don't know, we've never faced anything like these before."

"I don't know if I can kill one."

"They're dead already. I'm not sure how you could kill one."

"I have the little sword."

"Have you ever used a sword?"

"No."

Sally felt a shiver start up her back. Her hands were shaking and she found herself biting her bottom lip.

"How am I going to do this?" she asked her inner wolf.

There was no answer, just a feeling from inside of wanting to shift and run, get away to safety.

Blake was keeping watch and Kiera had found a spot next to him and curled up. Kiera was on edge too, Sally could see her fidgeting, the vampires and the lab clearly still on her mind. Blake's plan to rest was all well and good, but the only one to be getting any sleep tonight seemed to be Lucy. Sally didn't think Lucy fully understood what was just over that ridge, or the danger they were in and the dangers to be faced in the morning.

The night was quiet. Even for such a small gathering of trees like the one they were in it was too tranquil. Sally couldn't hear any nighttime animals scurrying about and there was no scent of any prey. It was as if all the wildlife had cleared out. Even the breeze through the trees seemed to be making its way surreptitiously.

After coming across a vampire, even at such a long distance, Sally was sure they were the reason for the emptiness here. Nothing would want to be in the vicinity of such a dangerous predator if they could help it.

Something else had been building inside her ever since that first encounter. A strange ache in her stomach which was almost a sickness. As it grew, images of the vampire prowling the building flashed into her mind. She could almost feel something pushing at her skin and slowly seeping out through the pours. From the day she'd been bitten, Sally had been able to smell fear in other people, but this was the first time she had been able to smell her own. Her hands were physically trembling and then tears overflowed her eyelids, trickling down her face in a constant procession. She was frightened. How could she help Becky if just the sight of a single vampire had made her like this? Sally put her head down and wept silently in the darkness.

Sally wiped her eyes quickly when she heard Kiera disappearing through the trees, leaving Blake on lookout. Sally assumed she must have needed some space or wanted to get a little further away from the lab for a while. She didn't blame her. The stale, dead scent of the vampire was still lingering in her nostrils and the enormity of the task ahead was like a weight pressing down heavily on her shoulders.

After what could only have been thirty minutes, Kiera returned and whispered something to Blake before they both made their way over to where Sally and Lucy were resting.

"There's no prey round here at all that we can hunt," said Blake.

"I've looked everywhere," added Kiera, "the place is dead."

"I've not been able to smell anything either," replied Sally. She didn't mention the smell of her own fear.

"Kiera tells me there's a small town further to the west," said Blake. "I suggest we all go there, get something to eat in a pub and see if we can pick up any info on the lab from the locals."

Sally's stomach rumbled as if it had heard the suggestion and was giving its approval. If Blake was right and there was nothing they could do until the morning, then getting some food and intel was probably a good idea.

"Okay," she agreed, "let's get going.

She gave the sleeping Lucy and gentle shake and explained what was happening and they set off. Lucy, as usual, fell into step closely behind Sally.

The town was about twenty minutes' walk away. They cut across a few fields and picked up a road that ran into the center of the town. The town square looked deserted but

Stay Away

looking around they found some pubs and takeaways open with plenty of people inside. They hunted out a pub that was still serving food and took up a table in the corner where they could monitor the door. The last thing they wanted was to be surprised but a couple of vampires out searching for fresh blood.

"Can you smell werewolf?" Sally asked Lucy once Blake and Kiera had gone to the bar to order some food and get drinks.

The smell of flame grilled burgers and curry was very strong in this place, but Sally was sure there was a faint scent hiding behind the other odors. Lucy sniffed the air and shook her head.

"Well, I can. I'm sure of it."

Sally scanned the crowd in front of her and started to home in on a scent. It was then she spotted Kiera running across the room toward a small group Sally had been homing in on. When she reached them, Kiera threw her arms around a tall guy's neck and hugged him tight. He hugged her back but with a little apprehension Sally thought. He definitely hadn't expected to see her. The look on his face changed from that of shock to total disbelief when Blake stepped out of the crowd near them. This was a meeting of friends that hadn't seen each other in a long while.

"Kiera! Blake! What… how…" the shocked werewolf managed to splutter.

Kiera let go and stepped to the side. The two males stood face to face then hugged like brothers.

Sally stood slowly and moved a little closer so she could better hear what was going on. She kept a little distance. She hadn't been introduced to this new wolf and didn't feel she should interrupt the emotional reunion taking place.

"Bren," said Blake. "How did you manage to get out? Is the pack free?"

Bren shook his head and threw a quick glance at Kiera. Sally got the impression he wasn't convinced he was totally comfortable, but she had suffered from misunderstanding werewolf mannerisms and reactions before, so she let it pass.

"I'm allowed out from time to time," he replied. "The rest of the pack are still locked up."

"Why do you go back?" asked Sally, stepping forward to join her travel companions. "Why not make a run for it, make your way back to Blake and Kiera? I assume you're one of Blake's pack."

She couldn't help thinking this guy was living the life of riley while his pack members were locked up and, judging by Kiera's reaction to being close to the lab, tortured.

Bren stopped talking and just stared at her. He didn't answer but his nose started to twitch, and Sally knew he was checking her scent.

"You're Sally aren't you," said Bren.

Sally was stunned. How was it possible he knew her

name? Blake and Kiera looked equally as confused as she felt.

"What makes you think that?" said Sally eventually.

"Your scent was all over Becky when they brought her in."

"You've seen Becky?" snapped Sally, unable to hide the desperation in her voice. "Is she alright? Where are they keeping her? Is she locked up with the pack?"

Sally grabbed Bren's shirt front with her fists.

"Have they hurt her?" she continued. She shook him. "Tell me!"

"Woah there, sweetheart," Bren replied, holding his hands in the air. "Hey, how do you make your eyes go that colour?"

"Never mind my eyes. Tell me about Becky."

The people in the crowd around them were starting to notice the little confrontation and staring.

"Let's calm down shall we," said Blake, resting his hand on Sally's fist, "and take this over to our table. We're starting to attract some attention."

Sally glanced quickly at a couple next to her then let go of Bren's shirt. Blake was right. The last thing they needed right now was somebody calling the police and end up in a cell this close to the full moon.

They moved over to the table they had commandeered earlier while Blake grabbed an extra chair for Bren.

"Well, who is this little beauty?" asked Bren when he

spotted Lucy sitting opposite.

"She's with me," said Sally, not in the mood for any of the usual Casanova antics she had experienced in the pack Blake had left her with when she was first bitten.

Bren seemed to be the kind of pack wolf who notices a new female and immediately sees her as fair game. She started to dislike him.

"Now tell me what you know about Becky."

"You really need to do something about those eyes of yours," said Bren, "people are going to start to notice."

Sally banged on the table with her fist. She was beginning to run out of patience and her wolf was beginning to stir.

"Hey, will you lot keep it down over there," said one of the guys at a nearby table. "We're trying to play dominoes over here."

The local guy was making his way towards their table with the obvious intent on confronting the visiting troublemakers. Sally knew her eyes would stir up some interest and she quickly pulled out a pair of orange tinted sunglasses from her inside jacket pocket.

"Come on, Matt," shouted another guy sat at the neighboring table. "Leave them, it's your drop."

With a huff he seemed to decide his game of dominoes was more important than the crazy girl wearing sunglasses in a pub and returned to his table.

"Will you two relax a little," said Blake. "Sally, sort out your eyes. Bren, tell her what she wants to know."

"What's with the eyes anyway?" Bren continued.

"It's just a wolfy emotional thing and none of your business," replied Sally, looking him straight in the eye. The challenge obvious and threatening. "Tell me what you know about Becky."

"They brought her in about a week ago." Bren lowered his voice. "They were supposed to be going after Kiera." He nodded in Kiera's direction. "She was more of a handful than they expected and made do with Becky. I got told they'd had to kill you. Anyway, they were about to put her in with the pack until I pointed out she was human. She had werewolf scent on her and it was clear to me it wasn't hers."

"Bren is one of our best trackers," added Blake.

"I was ordered to take her up to see the Doc," Bren continued. "On the way I asked her about the scent. She told me I'd better let her go or her friend, Sally would kick my ass. She's a feisty little thing your friend."

"I might still kick your ass."

"What have they done with her?" asked Kiera, the concern in her voice a bit of a surprise to Sally.

"I thought they'd just pay her off to keep quiet about the mistaken identity, but she kept telling them about this all powerful werewolf who would be on her way to teach them a lesson. So, they locked her in one of the suites upstairs."

"Great," said Kiera raising her hands with frustration, "that means they're expecting us. That puts a whole different spin on this, Blake. They know we're coming."

Blake shook his head.

"No, they know Sally's coming. They'll have no idea we'll be with her. This gives me an idea."

Chapter 17

Blake shuffled his chair closer to the small wooden table around which they all sat and leaned forward. The others followed suit, all eager to hear his plan. All, that is, except Sally.

"I've a feeling I'm not going to like this," she said.

"I've a feeling you're going to hate it," replied Blake. "But it gives us the opportunity to free the pack and get Becky out during the mayhem."

Blake turned to Bren.

"They're keeping Becky away from the pack I'm guessing."

It was a half question and half statement.

"Yes," said Bren, "well away. At the other end of the building altogether actually."

"That's perfect. Here's what we'll do."

Blake started to arrange beer mats, salt and pepper pots and empty glasses on the table in a kind of three dimensional map. He explained what each of the items represented before he began to explain his plan.

"Okay, Bren," he said, "Where are they keeping the pack?"

"In the basement just below, Goods In, at the back of the site." He pointed to a beer mat on Blake's left.

Blake placed a tomato ketchup sachet on top of the beer

mat. Sally supposed this was to represent the pack and it seemed fitting that the colour was blood red.

"Where've they got Becky locked up?" Blake continued.

Bren pointed to a beer mat at the other end of the table.

"Here, top floor. There's several empty offices in that area and most of the top brass have suites there."

Becky became a sachet of mayonnaise for the purposes of the planning exercise.

"Entrances?"

"Here and here." Bren pointed to the corners of each of the beer mats containing a sachet. "Getting through the fence should be easy. There's no CCTV pointing outwards but as soon as you're near the buildings you will be in full view."

"We'll have to be quick then once we get inside," said Blake. You make sure both these doors are unlocked." He looked at Bren. "Can you do that?"

"Sure."

"As they'll be watching for Sally, she can go in first to draw their attention away from the CCTV on the other door at the back of Goods In. That will give me time to get in and free the rest of the pack."

"You want me to be the bait?" Sally asked, feeling a little shocked and annoyed that she'd been so easily conned.

"No, Blake," Kiera interrupted. "They'll be all over her. She won't stand a chance."

This show of emotion was just as shocking to Sally as the last comment from Blake.

"No, they won't," replied Blake, "because Bren is going to be waiting for her just inside the door."

"Him!" said Sally, the distrust she felt written all over her face.

"Yes. Him. Bren will take you to a safe hiding place as soon as you're in. You both stay hidden and by the time they realise I'm inside, the pack will be free and the guards will come for us. That will give Bren time to show you where Becky is and get you both out and on your way towards the safety of the town in the opposite direction."

Sally went over it all in her head. It sounded like a plan that could possibly work, but a large part of it depended upon Bren, and Sally didn't trust him. Blake obviously did though and from the hug Kiera had given him earlier they were old friends too. Maybe she should give him the benefit of the doubt. She certainly couldn't get to Becky quickly without his inside knowledge. This could be one of those times where she would have to ignore her gut feeling and her inner wolf and go with the flow. She didn't like it but there was nothing else she could do, and time was running out.

"What about us?" asked Lucy. "What do me and Kiera do?"

Sally noticed Kiera start to fidget again. Blake looked at Lucy, then at Sally. Sally shook her head, telling Blake she didn't want Lucy anywhere near the place. It was going to be risky enough keeping her eye on Bren without having to look out for Lucy as well.

"You both stay in the trees on the hill above the lab," said Blake.

"But I want to help," replied Lucy. "Sally might need some backup."

Lucy looked far too keen for Sally's liking.

"You have a point, Lucy," said Blake.

Sally shot him and anxious look. What was he playing at? He knew as well as she did that Lucy wasn't the kind of werewolf that should go on a mission like this. Blake held up his hand to stop Sally voicing the obvious objection heading his way.

"You and Kiera will be posted at the fence just in case. If all goes well, you will be needed there to show the pack back to our camp in the hills and lead them to safety."

Sally felt a little more relaxed when she heard what Blake had in mind. It was a clear attempt to keep Lucy away from the action and she welcomed his idea. Kiera didn't look as comfortable. Being at the fence was still a little closer than she wanted to be. That much was clear.

"I want to help Sally," Lucy protested.

"I need you at the fence, Lucy," said Sally, trying her best in a hope that Lucy would be satisfied if the request came from her. "I won't be coming back that way and it would mean a lot to me if there was somebody there to make sure the pack got away to a safe place."

Lucy still didn't look convinced.

"Will you do that?" asked Sally, "for me."

That seemed to sway Lucy's decision, and she nodded. "Okay," she replied. "If it'll help."

Lucy shuffled back in her chair smiling and she appeared to Sally to be holding her head just a little higher than before. Being given a role in the plan was beginning to affect Lucy's confidence more than Sally would have liked. But at least she would be away from danger and be one less person for Sally to worry about.

"Okay," said Blake. "That's settled." He turned to Bren. "How about timing? Should we go in early before the workers start to arrive?"

Bren hesitated with his answer. His eyes flicked towards Sally before he answered. Sally got the impression that her presence and the news she would be with him was giving him more to worry about.

"No that's probably not the best time," he replied. "I won't know exactly where Becky is being held at that time. Leaving it later in the day will give me time to do some scouting and warn Becky, so she's ready to move as soon as Sally gets there."

Bren had negative answers for each of Blake's suggestions so they both agreed on going in after the workers had finished for the day and headed off home.

"That puts us too close to the full moon," said Sally. "I would rather have Becky out of there and away to safety before the moon forces us all to shift."

"You will still have time," replied Bren. "There will be a short period when the vampires won't be up and about so security will be at a minimum. You can be in and out before they give you any trouble."

It seemed to make sense, but Sally's inner wolf was restless and uncomfortable with the situation. Blake and Kiera both seemed to trust him, and they knew him better than she did. That didn't really make her feel any easier.

Kiera excused herself and headed off to the ladies. Sally decided to join her. She needed to get her on her own and find out more about this sudden extra member of their group, upon whom so much of the plan now depended.

Keira was already in a cubicle when Sally entered so she washed her hands and started to fix her hair. When Keira appeared she walked to the sink next to Sally.

"Do you trust him?" Sally asked.

"Who?"

"You know who. Bren."

"Of course," Kiera replied. "Don't you?"

Sally shook her head.

"There's just something that doesn't sit right."

"Like what?"

Sally turned and rested her bottom on the sink.

"Well for one thing, how come he gets to roam around the town and doesn't seem to mind going back there. To the lab I mean. It doesn't make sense that he hasn't legged it before now."

"He's just worried the pack will be punished if he doesn't return. That's all."

"You didn't go back. Did they punish the pack when you disappeared?"

"I didn't have their trust."

"Why does he? What's he giving them in return?"

Kiera didn't answer. She just washed her hands more thoroughly. Sally could tell she'd hit a nerve. Normally she would have let it drop. But there was nothing normal about the situation they were in.

"Would you have gone back if you knew they were going to punish the pack?" Sally asked.

"No. The plan was for me to get out and get back to Blake. Tell him where they were and what was happening. They all helped me out because I was close to losing it in there." Kiera stared at her reflection in the mirror. "I couldn't take anymore."

Kiera's eyes filled up with tears and Sally could smell the fear rising up inside her compatriot again. Kiera certainly had a very strong fear of the place. Sally didn't know her very well but she didn't come across as the kind of girl who would cry for very little reason.

"Being locked up doesn't agree with many people, Kiera."

"Neither does being tortured to make you shift so they can do their experiments on you."

Just at that moment the door opened, and another woman came in to use the toilet. Kiera wiped her eyes and washed her hands once again. Sally decided to do the same. The news that the pack had a plan to get Kiera out and for her to get to Blake for help was an interesting piece of information. If that was the plan, why had Bren looked so surprised to see her and why not show more excitement when the girl he had a relationship with turned up in the pub he happened to be laughing and joking in?

When the woman who had interrupted them was gone Sally turned off the tap.

"Why should I trust him?" asked Sally.

"He's a good man. Give him a chance. You may get a surprise." Kiera turned to Sally while she dried her hands with a paper towel. "I know you have your doubts, but he will get you to Becky and get you both out. It's Lucy who worries me."

"Really? Why?"

"Oh, come on, Sally. She idolizes you. She is going to get herself, and possibly you as well, into trouble because she wants to be like you. She wants to go in there with you and be a hero."

"I've tried to discourage her," said Sally. "I think she'll wait at the fence like I've asked her."

"Are you sure about that?"

Sally felt her wolf fidget showing she wasn't comfortable with what was being said. Sally agreed. She knew there was no way Lucy was staying put without her being there. If Lucy came into the lab it would be another worry that Sally could do without.

"You need to keep her at the fence and wait for the pack," said Sally.

Kiera laughed. "What makes you think she will stay with me?"

"Because she's scared of you. She'll do as you say."

Kiera moved close, almost face to face. Not a challenge but definitely a move to show the seriousness of what she was about to say.

"Sally. I can't guarantee I'd be able to stay at the fence. Never mind look out for a girl who shouldn't even have come with us."

"I don't want you in there either, Kiera."

"I wasn't meaning I would be tempted to go in and help. Being that close isn't something I would choose and I don't know how long I can stay there." Kiera turned off the tap and looked Sally in the eyes. "Be careful in there, Sally. It's a very dangerous place."

She dried her hands and walked out, leaving Sally no

clearer as to whether she should trust Bren or not.

When she got back to the table Bren had moved closer to Lucy and had the hungry look she remembered from her own experiences with a pack. Sally sat in a chair between them, a clear indication to the male werewolf that Lucy was off limits. Bren simply smiled but the menace in his expression was all too evident to Sally. Her inner wolf was now pacing and getting agitated. Controlling her wolf this close to the full moon was always difficult. The last thing Sally wanted was an unwanted shift into a wolf in the middle of a pub, so she decided it was time to go.

"I think we should get some rest," said Sally and got to her feet.

"Not a bad idea," agreed Blake. "Bren, you get back to the lab and find out anything you can about where Becky will be. Sally will meet you at the back door as agreed and we go from there. Okay?"

Bren nodded and shook Blakes hand. Sally thought she saw Kiera make a move towards Bren as if to move in for a hug. Bren didn't notice. He was too busy eying up Lucy. He looked away when he spotted Sally staring at him. Sally's eyes never left him until he was out the door and disappeared into the night.

Out of habit from working in a pub Sally gathered some of the glasses from their table and placed them on the end of the bar on her way to the door.

Stay Away

"You must be strangers round these parts I reckon." said the old man behind the bar.

"Excuse me?" asked Sally, not sure if he is talking to her or another close by.

"Nobody from this town would bring back their empties."

"Yes," replied Blake as he too returned the one glass Sally couldn't carry. "We are just passing through."

"We're camping just outside of town," Lucy added as she bounced up behind them like an excited puppy. The talk of her role in the rescue plan obviously giving her a little more confidence than Sally would have liked. Lucy pointed in the general direction of the hills.

Kiera gave her a sharp look that said, shut your mouth. Sally was also nervous about anybody round her knowing where they were. It was too late though. The barman had heard and obviously knew the area well.

"Really?" asked the barman. "You don't want to be going up there."

"Where?" asked Sally.

"Baskerville. Especially not at night."

"Baskerville?" repeated Sally with a smirk. "You've got to be kidding me."

The barman laughed. "Don't worry. It's just a nickname us locals call the research lab in Smuggler's Hollow."

"Why do you call it Baskerville?"

"It's a very secretive place, and there's strange noises up

there at night. Some people have heard howling and seen what they say is a big dog on the moor. Bigger than any normal dog mind you. A hound if you will. People around these parts have very colourful imaginations. I don't believe a word of it myself."

"Well, thanks for the advice," said Blake putting on what Sally could tell was a fake laugh. "We'll keep a look out."

The barman joined in with a fake laugh of his own then smiled and waved as they all left the pub.

"It can't be any of the pack," said Kiera, looking at Blake then at Sally once they were clear of the door. "We were always locked up."

"Apart from your double agent friend," said Sally. "He could have had the privilege to get out and run."

Kiera shook her head. "He wouldn't be that stupid."

"He's a werewolf. He has to run somewhere."

"There's no scent of werewolf anywhere round here," said Blake. "I'm sure it's only people's imaginations, like the barman said." Blake was obviously trying to stop all the talk on the subject of people hearing howling out here near the lab. Sally thought he looked nervous. That wasn't a normal look for Blake.

They began their walk back up the hill to the small camp site they'd created for themselves earlier. Sally wanted to know more about Bren. This plan of Blake's relied a great deal upon the actions of this sudden new member of the team and it made her feel uncomfortable.

Blake was bringing up the rear so Sally dropped back as the path got narrower. Blake may not want to talk about Bren, but she did.

"You both seem to know Bren pretty well," she said once she was level with Blake.

"He's an important member of the pack, my lieutenant I guess you could call him."

"So, he's the next Alpha in line then?" asked Sally.

Blake smiled and gave Sally a sideways glance.

"It doesn't work like that. There is no line of succession in a pack. The alpha has to be challenged and beaten for another werewolf to take his place."

"Do you think Bren is the type to have aspirations for the throne?"

Blake shook his head. "He's an ambitious guy but he knows better than to try and challenge me."

"You'd kick his butt?"

Blake laughed. "Yeah, something like that."

"He'd have to be a little cleverer to get the crown from your head then?"

"He'd have to get up very early to get one over on me. Don't worry, Sally. I trust him with my life, and so should you."

That did nothing to put Sally's mind at ease. If he was ambitious as Blake had said, then maybe Bren was an early riser after all and this situation was his opportunity to take his chance. Maybe it was just her general distrust of strangers, and werewolf pack members in particular, but something was giving Sally the jitters. Her wolf hadn't settled all night either so she was getting the same butterflies. They were very close to the full moon and Sally was used to the restless feeling inside around this time of the lunar cycle. It did feel a little different from usual though and Sally couldn't put her finger on exactly why. However, she was sure it had something to do with Bren.

Blake picked up the pace and was soon at the head of the line. The conversation was over. Sally said nothing else all the way back to their adopted little den.

Kiera sat on her own, fidgeting with her fingers and looking all around every so often. Sally could smell her fear still. Blake wondered off into the trees without saying a word. Only Lucy seemed not to be thinking of the dangers that lay just over the hill in the valley below.

"I'll take first watch," said Sally, as she dumped her bag in the spot she had claimed as her own.

She made her way up to the ridge where she could look across to the research lab but stayed in the cover of the bushes which lined the ridge, the vampire scent that was being blown across the fields from the complex of concrete buildings turned her stomach and she found herself fiddling with her fingers too, the same as Kiera. What was she about to face? This was a new experience. Going on a rescue mission, coming up against new supernatural creatures she didn't even consider existed, and now to fully understand what fear was had her heart beating in an irregular rhythm and her mouth was dry. What was Becky feeling? She was over there in one of those buildings, surrounded by vampires and probably scared half out of her wits. What if she had been hurt, or was weak through mistreatment and was laying there too weak to escape, relying on Sally to come to her rescue? A rescue Sally was now not totally sure she could deliver. The thought of the vampire guards also had her wolf constantly on edge, and that was making Sally even more anxious.

Sally heard footsteps approaching from behind as she sat. Excided footsteps. Sally turned her head as Lucy plonked herself down on the ground at her side.

"Are you sneaking out to rescue the pack and Becky yourself, Sally?"

"No. I'm just keeping watch."

Lucy shuffled a little closer, checked over her shoulder towards where the others were resting and whispered, "I'm sure I could help you. We could go down there together before anybody even knew we were there."

"No, Lucy," said Sally, "It's going to be a team effort tomorrow. We all have our roles to play in this."

"But I've learned a lot from you. I'm braver now and I can do things I couldn't before I met you." Lucy leaned in closer. "Look, I think I can even turn my eyes orange like you."

Sally watched as Lucy contorted her face and forced her eyes wider. They stayed dark brown.

"You don't have to be like me, Lucy. In fact, you probably shouldn't be like me. I'm not the best role model."

"You must be joking. You're amazing and so brave."

Lucy stared at Sally again, her eyes widening.

"There, I did it," said Lucy, "I can feel my eyes changing colour. Are they golden orange like yours?"

Sally felt sorry for Lucy. Maybe she shouldn't have invited her along with them but the thought of what Lucy would have been left behind to face made Sally shiver. If they could get through this then maybe Lucy could come back to Popwood with her and Becky. She would be safe there. But Lucy obviously wanted to be more like Sally by the way she was trying to impress.

"I think they may be changing a little," said Sally, the way you would talk to a youngster, trying to not hurt their feelings but not exactly tell them they had managed to get something right. She immediately regretted her dishonesty. She didn't want to encourage Lucy any more than she already had.

"I'll help you on watch," said Lucy and tucked her legs up, resting her chin on her knees and staring out towards the Lab.

Sally let her stay. It was clear she wasn't going to change Lucy's mind. It wasn't long, however, before Lucy was asleep. That helped Sally concentrate on the lab herself. She was convinced Bren was going to go straight back to the lab and tell the vampires where they could find the would-be rescuers. She was uneasy and her wolf was still pacing. All seemed to remain quiet though.

After a couple of hours, Kiera came to replace Sally on watch. She seemed edgy and nervous and Sally could tell she wasn't happy being in site of the lab. The smell of Kiera's fear betrayed the look of confidence she tried to portray.

"It's okay," said Sally. "I'm not tired. I'll stay on watch for a while longer. You get back down to the den and rest up."

Sally was tired though. She couldn't remember the last time she had slept properly. Her body felt drained with the lack of food and sleep. Being so close to the full moon was making her restless. She always had trouble sleeping during the run up to the one night each month where her body was forced to take another shape and personality.

For the next few hours, Sally concentrated on the area between her and the lab. She twitched at every sound and found herself holding her breath on more than one occasion.

Eventually the sun started to rise and the fear of the vampire guards began to subside. Soon she could see workers turning up one by one and going into the lab complex through the security turnstiles near the car park.

Sally began to wonder what had happened to society recently that so many people could work in a place that did tests on werewolves and kept an innocent girl like Becky locked up. How could they turn a blind eye to something like that? They all looked so ordinary. Just people going about their own busy lives.

Sally noticed that none of them were going anywhere near the building which Bren had told them held the pack. Maybe they didn't know everything that went on in the lab. The arguments for and against buzzed around in Sally's head in a constant battle.

One by one the others started to wake. The sun was quite high in the sky and bathed the lab complex with a warm morning light. It looked less menacing than it had through the night and the whiff of vampire had disappeared. The surrounding trees, fields and hills looked spectacular and Sally would have loved the opportunity to lay back and enjoy the view. The thought of a relaxing day in the sun disappeared with the sound of Blake's voice and she was snapped back to reality.

"I think we should get started, check out the area, plan escape routes."

Blake looked around and studied each of them.

"Kiera, you take Lucy and find a new den. This place has too much of our scent and will be easy to find later. Sally, you come with me and we'll plan our way in and out."

"I want to go with Sally," Lucy protested.

"No, you and Kiera are our backup, and I need you two

to be together and for both of you to know the location of the new den."

The two teams split up and Sally circled the lab complex with Blake. The way in was pretty obvious, a broken piece of fencing towards the rear of the complex would give Sally easy access to the door where Bren was going to be waiting. The way out was more of a challenge. The location of the building where the pack was being held would mean them all crossing an open area to get to the closest part of the fence once free.

"They would be expecting us to make straight for the fence once they realise we have freed the pack," said Blake. "Going back the way we came in is too far and will cause more problems than it solves."

"I watched the complex most of the night," said Sally. "They only have one security guard at the main gate after everybody has left."

They probably don't need any human security once the sun goes down," said Blake. "Having a few vampires around will mean they are well covered in that respect.

"Going out through the front gate may be the easiest and least expected option."

"Good idea, Sally. That's our way out then. We can have Kiera watching the front to guide the pack to the den and Lucy can cover the place we came in just in case some of us need to go that way. You can circle round and pick her up once you have Becky away. Get back to Kiera and Lucy now. I have one more thing I need to check, I'll meet you on the edge of town in an hour."

Sally made her way to the trees to find the others. It was full moon tonight and her skin was already starting to get prickly. If she was successful, then being with Becky so close to the full moon was risky. The last thing she wanted to do was rescue Becky from the lab only to deliver her to the jaws of a hungry werewolf whether it be herself or one of the pack.

Blake was late meeting up with them all. Lucy was already struggling to stay human. She sat rocking back and forward and more than once Sally had gone to give her a calming hug. Kiera was pacing and ready to go looking for Blake when he finally turned up.

He walked up to Sally first and handed her a piece of paper. On it was an address.

"I've booked Becky a room at this bed and breakfast. Whatever happens tonight make sure you get her there straight away and tell her not to leave until you collect her tomorrow."

It was getting close. This was for real now. Becky's life depended upon this ragged group, upon Sally, Blake, Kiera and even Lucy. She folded the piece of paper and put it in her pocket. If any of them failed now, somebody was going to die. She had to make sure it wasn't Becky.

Standing at the top of the hill that overlooked the lab they all watched the workforce leave, one by one. Sally could smell fear once again, Kiera's fear was now joined by her own. She hadn't been able to shake the thought of the vampire guards from her mind and the longer they remained there the more of her confidence slipped away. When the last office light went out they started down the hill and made their way towards the fence.

Chapter 18

Blake led the way on the short walk to the fence surrounding the laboratory complex. When they reached the boundary, they crept the last few yards on the ground. Sally got a strong aroma of fear coming from the complex. What on earth was happening in there for the scent to emanate that far? The buildings were over two hundred yards away. Sally's skin began to prickle again. Her own fear was combining with her inner wolf's anxiety and pushing her wolf closer to the surface.

"Okay," said Blake quietly, "Kiera, you head round to the front gate. Lucy, you take up position in those bushes behind us. If any of the pack come this way, lead them back to the new den. Okay?"

Lucy nodded.

He looked at Sally then added, "Lucy, if none of the pack come to you stay put until me or Sally come for you."

Sally didn't realise her unease was so obvious, but she was a little happier knowing Lucy would be staying where she was. Kiera took off to make her way to her allotted position.

"Are you ready, Sally?" he asked.

Sally nodded her head but felt her heart begin to race as her nerves built.

"Bren will be just inside that door there." He pointed to the small fire escape at the rear of the building directly across the grassy area in front of them. "I'll go and find the pack at the Goods In building." He nodded towards a building closer to the front gate. As soon as you and Bren get Becky out make your way to the address I gave you. Send Bren to me in case I need some help. If all goes as it should, we'll be able to slip out the front and away. You can then circle back round for Lucy."

Sally nodded again and her and Blake slipped through the fence without another word. A look back over her shoulder confirmed that Lucy had done as she was told and taken cover in the bushes a little way back from the fence. Blake turned right and headed off leaving Sally alone. This was it. This was why she was here. Becky's rescue was next once she had found Bren.

She made her way swiftly over the grass to hug the wall of the darkened building. A quick check both ways and a sniff of the air told her all was well, so she made her way along the wall to the fire escape door.

As promised, the door was open. She sniffed at the opening and could smell only Bren. There were no other scents to set the alarm bells ringing so she slipped in through the gap.

Bren was stood waiting for her. Maybe she had been wrong about him. She hadn't expected him to stick to his part of the plan but here he was, just as Blake had assured her he would be.

"Great, you made it," he said.

"Yeah, thanks for opening the door. I guess I had you all wrong. I didn't think you'd be here. I'm sorry."

"Oh, I wasn't going to miss this," he smiled.

"Now where is it we're supposed to be hiding?" asked Sally. She looked around but couldn't see anywhere obvious.

"Oh, there's no rush for that," said Bren. "There will be no vampires coming this way. They've all been sent to grab Blake as soon as he sets foot through the door at Goods In."

"And why would they have gone there, when they didn't know he was coming and should have been expecting me to rescue Becky from this side of the building?" Sally stared straight at Bren, her inner wolf now starting to take more interest in the sudden change in the situation.

"Because Becky isn't being held in this part of the building. She's in a cell above where the pack are being held, way over on the other side of the complex."

"Then why am I here?" Sally's hands rolled into fists and she started to grind her teeth and breathe more heavily through her nose.

"You're here so I can make sure you don't get in the way. I have a nice little number going here and I wasn't going to let you and Blake free the pack. That would be, how shall I put it, detrimental to my wellbeing."

"You mean the pack already see you as a traitor and will tear you apart."

"Traitor is a very strong word, Sally. I prefer, astute

businessman."

"I'll use more than strong words when I get back," said Sally with a low growl and turned towards the door.

Bren grabbed her by the arm and Sally spun round and glared.

"Let go!" Another command with an underlying growl which was meant to warn him off.

"There go those lovely eyes again, Sally. I do like it when they do that. It's so cute."

Sally pulled her arm from his grip.

"I'm going to help Blake. I suggest you not being here when I get back."

She turned to the door but once again Bren stopped her. This time he wrapped his arms tightly around her body, pinning her arms to her side.

"I'm afraid you're not going anywhere sweetheart," he said. "I promised them I would take care of you and keep you out of the way until they were ready for you. I'm afraid it's just you and me for the time being."

Sally raked the claws that had grown from her finger up his thigh, shredding the flesh and getting an animal like howl out of Bren. He let go quickly and grabbed at his leg.

"What the hell?" said Bren and looked down at Sally's hand with the werewolf claws. "How did you do that?"

Sally simply growled at him and moved closer to the door. Bren looked confused and unsure what to do next.

Suddenly he launched himself at her. Sally tried to sidestep him but there wasn't much room to manoeuvre and Bren grabbed her with his outstretched hand. His momentum and weigh advantage toppled them both to the ground and with a twist he pinned Sally to the floor.

"Neat trick," he said, "but it won't get you anywhere. I'm too big for you, little girl. You're staying put."

Sally growled again and bared her teeth. They were now elongated canines and she snapped her head forward, sinking them into his shoulder. Another animal howl of pain came from Bren. He let go of her and sat up. This gave Sally the chance to push her claws deep into his chest and with all her supernatural strength hurled him off and he hit the wall. Sally was on him in a second and once again her teeth found flesh, this time in his neck.

His face screwed up in pain and his breathing started to quicken. Sally could see his change coming. She was caught in two minds. This traitor deserved what was coming to him, but her own dislike of the violence she was capable of was urging her to help. She wasn't in the mood to help this particular werewolf, however. She got to her feet and watched as his body morphed and changed, his arms and legs cracked and bent. The body under the clothing grew larger than the clothes were meant to fit, and the thick collar of his tee-shirt started to strangle him. His leather belt didn't give under the strain of his growing waistline and it began to crush his organs inside. He began to pull at his clothes, trying frantically to get out of them. Letting him die was against Sally's nature and she moved forward again to try and help, but his change had gone too far. Bones cracked, and joints dislocated. His snout grew long and let out an unearthly howl. His tongue grew and slipped from the side of his mouth. The howl was stifled by the restricting clothing and became a rasping gurgle. There was a loud crack from deep inside the half wolf torso and the flailing limbs stopped as abruptly as the howls. He was dead. Sally felt a sadness for the loss of life but felt nothing for the person he was, which frightened her more than a little.

She turned to the door once more. She was running out of time. She had no idea if Blake had already been captured. She had to get to the other end of the campus quickly.

She had one hand on the door when she felt herself being launched across the room with a force so powerful that she hit the far wall without touching the floor. Before she could recover she was raised off the ground and pinned to the wall. Then, the dead, stale smell hit her senses. Vampire.

The vampire's cold, clammy hand closed around her throat like a tightening noose. He appeared in front of her. She could see the evil in his dark, lifeless eyes. Her inner wolf started to panic and threatened to break the surface. Sally couldn't breathe. She felt her eyes starting to bulge. She knew she couldn't shift now or she would end up having the same fate as Bren. She begged her wolf to stay down. to give her some time, but the wolf knew they didn't have much time. Blake's warning echoed around her head. *"Don't let a vampire catch you off your guard, or it's game over."*

She could feel her body weakening and everything started to fade and darken around her. Her struggles were now pitiful, and she started to lose consciousness. The vampire forced her head to one side, and she felt its cold breath on her neck.

Suddenly the vampire was gone. Sally hit the floor. She coughed and choked as she tried to get air into her lungs. Her throat burned and she gasped for breath. With a struggle she managed to get onto her hands and knees, breathless, panting, coughing and choking. Then she vomited. Her sight started to return, the coughing slowed, and she was able to take more breaths. The memory of what had just happened flashed back into her mind. Why did he drop her? Where was he? She looked up and scanned around the room. There he was, kneeling over another body. His mouth on his victim's neck. Then, the other scent then hit. A scent she recognized. Lucy.

The rage and horror Sally felt was unprecedented. A pressure inside her built like a volcano preparing to erupt. Her hands and teeth were already in the form of a werewolf and she could feel muscles building in her legs. Muscles that were swelling and thickening and storing energy ready to launch an assault up the creature kneeling over the body of one of her own.

Sally sprung forward and low to the ground with all the speed and power she could muster. Her claws dug deep into the vampire's torso at the same time as her canines sank into its neck. They rolled over and over with the force of Sally's impact, but Sally's claws and teeth held a firm grip on the vampire. She didn't notice which way up she was facing or what they were hitting as they rolled. Her focus was on the dangerous predator she had in her clutches. The strength of the creature was immense, but Sally held on, biting and slashing deeper and deeper with every strike as he tried to fight back. The vampire tried to get his fangs to any part of Sally's skin, but she could sense every movement almost before it happened and stopped him with a slash of her claws or a punch from her powerful werewolf paws. All the while her teeth remained locked into the vampire's flesh. Blake's instructions about removing the head of a vampire with the short sword she carried in her backpack flashed into her mind. Retrieving the sword from her backpack wasn't an option but she already had the tools she needed at her disposal.

Suddenly, doubt crept into her mind. She was about to kill somebody. That was something she'd never done before. Her hesitation gave the vampire the chance he needed, and Sally felt the fangs sink into her arm. Her inner wolf yelped in pain, or was it herself? Sally didn't need to know. The pain snapped her back into action. With another burst of supernatural strength and speed she slashed her claws deeply across the vampire's neck. Her other set of claws pulled its head to the side. She crunched down as hard as she could on the exposed vertebrae.

The vampire's strength disappeared, the body and head hit the floor separately. Sally collapsed onto her knees and vomited once more. The dead, musty taste in her mouth was the worst thing she had ever experienced. She coughed and spat as much of the creature's blood onto the floor before resting back on her feet. She looked down at her attacker. The vampire was lifeless on the floor and was already shriveling and withering before her eyes.

Sally spotted Lucy about twenty feet away. She was laying on her back, motionless. Running over to her, Sally knelt by her side. Lucy's eyes were open, staring at nothing. Her skin was grey and all the colour had disappeared from her lips. Sally listened to Lucy's chest, there was no heartbeat. Placing her hand on Lucy's abdomen, she closed her eyes and slipped into herself like the Neuromancer had taught her. She imagined the door into Lucy's body and a grey, featureless panel of wood appeared. There was no handle and no way to open it. She felt around the edges but there was nothing. Sally knew then Lucy had gone. Even the power of her lycanthropy wasn't going to bring her back.

Sally slipped back out of herself. Tears were rolling down her cheeks. She was growling without even knowing she had been. She had saved this girl from a pack of werewolves only to get her killed by a vampire. Why had Lucy followed her into the building? She was supposed to stay outside the fence. If she'd done as she was told she'd still be alive. But then Sally would probably have been dead. It was plain to see Lucy had saved her life. She'd let the vampire surprise her and was at his mercy. Without Lucy, Sally's mission to save Becky and the pack would have failed. Sally knew she was responsible for Lucy's death.

"Oh, Lucy. What have I done?"

Sally hugged the lifeless body and rocked Lucy like a baby. Crying and sobbing for her fallen comrade. Then she remembered Blake, and the trap Bren had said was waiting for him. Drying her eyes, she laid Lucy back down onto the floor.

"I'm sorry, Lucy. I have to leave you here."

She got to her feet and ran out of the door. Checking both ways Sally confirmed there was nobody else close by. She caught the sound of a fight going on over towards the Goods In building. Hoping she wasn't too late, she ran at full speed and headed for the sound of battle. She made no attempt to stay out of sight of the other buildings. There was no point now. They knew she was here.

Rounding the corner of Goods In, she spotted Blake fighting off two vampires with the short sword he carried. He was slashing and stabbing furiously, but the vampires hardly seemed to notice.

Sally charged forward to join the fight. Blake spotted

her coming.

"The door, Sally!" shouted Blake. "Get the door!"

Sally looked around quickly and spotted a metal door with a broken lock and chain. A large metal bar was still down in the latch, and she could hear sounds of growling and hammering from the other side.

One of the vampires fighting Blake broke off and made for the door at the same time. Sally seen him coming and put all her strength and weight behind a side kick. The vampire was lifted off the floor with the force of her kick and hit the wall. He was back on his feet quickly and came at her again. She remembered the sword but didn't have time to get it out before the vampire was on her again. She punched him in the face and it stopped him in his tracks. She followed the punch with another, then another. She spun round, bringing up her leg and catching him across the face. The power of the kick sent him to the floor which gave her enough time to get to the door. She lifted the bar holding the door closed and swung it open. A mix of wolf and human shapes spilled out. They were a sorry looking bunch. Some werewolves had already shifted into their wolf form but were skinny and weak. Those in human form were no more impressive. They looked like hungry homeless people, the disadvantaged and scruffy who Sally had seen during most of her visits to larger cities. All in all, Blake's pack weren't in good shape. The mistreatment at the hands of the research lab had knocked all the fight out of them.

There was one werewolf, still in human form, who came out first and seemed to be ready for a fight. He looked to be a little older and taller than Sally and was in slightly better shape than the older members of Blake's pack.

"Hold on, Blake," he was shouted, "I'm coming," but he was hit by another vampire who had suddenly shot out from the main building entrance.

The vampire Sally had kicked was back on his feet and was heading straight for her again. With a flurry of punches and kicks she put him back on the floor. She had just enough time to shrug off her backpack and take out the little sword. As the vampire pounced she slashed the blade across his front, quickly upwards then slashed horizontally through its neck. Three very accurate strikes and the vampire hit the ground as if its power had been turned off.

The vampire attacking the new werewolf was about to be joined by a second so Sally launched her own attack. Her claws dug in and she knocked the vampire off his feet. She dropped her sword but had no time to pick it back up before the vampire was attacking again. She slashed at him with her claws, left paw following right paw furiously. She saw an opportunity and sank her canines into his neck. She dispatched him in the same way she had the vampire who'd killed Lucy.

Looking back she saw the other werewolf throwing punch after punch at his vampire attacker. He wasn't landing many, but he didn't look like he was going to give up in a hurry either. Sally moved in and sank her claws deep into the vampire's side. That backed him up and gave her enough room to land a powerful side kick. The vampire rolled backwards and as he got to his feet Blake removed the head from the vampire's shoulders with one clean swipe of his sword.

"Thanks," said the werewolf next to her, breathless and obviously tired.

He looked straight into Sally's eyes and smiled. She felt a sudden warmth spread through her whole body. Her heart was racing, but that could have been because of the fight. She realised she was staring but snapped out of it at the sound of Blake's voice.

"Sally, meet Ben. Ben, this is Sally. A very handy little werewolf to have by your side."

"So, I see," replied Ben. "Thanks."

Sally noticed his smile again and managed to smile back but couldn't speak. She just nodded. She could feel her cheeks starting to flush and turned away, hoping neither of the werewolves noticed.

The rest of the pack were growling weakly and whimpering all around them. Those in human form were slouched against the wall or kneeling on the ground. The dead vampires were decomposing quickly where they lay. The area had a look of a war zone.

"Your mate, Bren sold us out," she said.

"So, I gathered when this lot turned up," said Blake. "I'm sorry, Sally. He will pay for that when I see him."

"Don't bother. He already has." Sally didn't elaborate. "He said Becky wasn't in that building either, it was just somewhere to keep me out of the way. She is somewhere above here, in a cell."

"I overheard the guards talking about a human on the third floor above us." said Ben, pointing at the building behind them. "Are you here for her too?"

Sally nodded.

"They said she was in a holding cell, and they were waiting for somebody to arrive."

"I guess that must be me. Okay," she said, "you two get the pack out and meet Kiera. I'll go get Becky."

"I'll come with you," said Ben.

"No," said Sally, "Help Blake get this lot out. I know her scent. She will be easy for me to find."

"Okay but be careful," said Blake and started to gather the disheveled bunch of werewolves together.

"Lucy's dead as well," added Sally, then turned and headed for the door to the main building.

Inside the door there was a small reception area. A reception desk sat across from the door and seats lined the walls. There were double doors to her left and the same to her right, presumably leading to offices. Ben had said the human he'd heard the guards talking about was on the third floor, so

Sally ignored these exits. To the right of the reception desk was a lift and a set of stairs. She decided the stairs would be a better option and less likely to draw attention. Quietly, she made her way up the first flight to the floor above. The scent of human and vampire was strong, this was obviously a busy area during both day and night activities. There was no scent she recognised, so she made her way cautiously up to the second floor. Her ears twitched. Was somebody moving around in the corridor on the second floor, or was it just the building creaking as it cooled after the heat from the sun? Sally stood motionless, listening carefully and sniffing the air. There were lots of different scents but the building had been in use all day. The scents could be from anybody and were probably at least an hour or so old. She pressed on up the third flight of stairs. The third floor was next, the floor where she suspected Becky was being held.

Double doors led off the stairwell on that floor. Gently pushing one of the doors, she opened it slightly and pressed her sensitive nose to the gap. There was a faint scent of somebody she recognised. Sally's heart started to race. Becky had been along this corridor recently, probably earlier in the afternoon.

There was that noise again. That wasn't the noise of a cooling building. It was somebody moving around on a floor somewhere beneath her. Sally couldn't tell how far below, or who it could be, but she guessed she was starting to run out of time. The door creaked a little as she slipped through and Sally winced, hoping the noise hadn't traveled too far. If it had, she'd given away her location. She needed to hurry. A few quick sniffs and she was convinced Becky was along the corridor to her left.

At first glance, the corridor could have been that of any office block, but the rooms on either side of this one weren't offices. The doors had solid locks and spy holes at head height. They looked like prison cells. Sally could smell old blood and werewolf all around as she passed. Checking the first few spy holes she could see the rooms were plain. Each contained a single bed pushed against the far wall with thick leather straps across the mattress. The windows in each of the cells had bars and the glass was frosted. She quickly checked each cell as she made her way along the corridor, all were empty. However, Becky's scent was getting stronger. Sally was getting closer.

About halfway along the corridor, on the side of the building Sally guessed was the rear, she got a strong scent. Becky's scent. She'd found her. Looking through the spy hole she saw Becky sitting on a similar small bed, fidgeting with her fingers. Sally's heart skipped a beat.

"Becky," called Sally, quietly.

"Sally?" Becky replied nervously. She got up and ran to the door. "Sally, get out. Quickly. It's a trap."

"I'm not leaving without you."

"But they know you're coming. Some werewolf told

them he'd seen you with Blake in town and you were going to attempt a rescue tonight. They know you're here, Sal. Get out before they find you."

"Just stand back from the door, Bex."

Becky backed up as Sally allowed as much of her supernatural strength to flow into her muscles as she dared. This was full moon night, and she was close to shifting into her wolf form already. She was holding off the change, but only just. Allowing too much lycanthropy power into her body now could send her over the edge and start the transformation. When she felt she had as much power in her muscles as she needed, Sally launched herself at the door, making contact with her shoulder. With a loud crash, which Sally assumed would have been heard all over the building, the door swung open. Becky stood there, shaking. staring at Sally through tear stained eyes.

"Come on, Bex," said Sally. "Let's get you out of here."

Grabbing Becky by the hand Sally made for the stairwell she had just come up. When she opened the doors a frightening scent hit Sally's senses. The vampire guards were on their way up the stairs towards them. She couldn't tell how many, but she was convinced there was more than one. She reached for her backpack and the short sword then realised it was gone. She must have left them on the floor outside the building during the fight. She looked round, searching both ways for another escape route. The corridor was long, probably the full length of the building, there was bound to be another stairwell at the opposite end.

"Back that way." Sally pointed back the way they had come and gave Becky a little shove to start her off.

They ran as fast as Becky could go. They passed the cell where Becky had been held and headed for the far end of the corridor. Once past Becky's cell the rooms changed from being simple cells. Large windows looked out onto the corridor, revealing what looked like laboratories and operating theatres. Sally got the impression secrecy of what they were doing in this place no longer mattered once you were allowed inside the building.

When they reached the other end of the corridor, they found another stairwell. Sally got the scent of more vampires drifting up from below and getting closer.

"How many vampires does this place have?" said Sally, more as a question to herself than to Becky.

"Vampires?" Becky obviously hadn't been told about the special nighttime security team. "There's really vampires?"

"I'll explain another time. We have to get going."

Looking round again, Sally spotted a glass door which looked like it was the entrance to a walkway connecting the building they were in to the one behind it. She took Becky's arm again.

"This way."

She pulled her through the door, and together they

hurried over the bridge between the two buildings.

Another long corridor led away from them. Without any other choice they ran its full length to the opposite end of the second building. There was another stairwell and they made their way quickly down to the ground floor. Sally recognised this area at once. It was a large, open floor area and had a fire door on the far side. A fire door that had been left open. To her left Sally saw the body of Bren, still bent and broken in his tangled clothing. To her right was Lucy's body. Two men in white coats were picking her up. One had her by the hands and the other had her by the feet. Together they swung Lucy back then threw her unceremoniously onto a trolley.

That was too much for Sally to take. The uncaring treatment of another human's body was inhuman. She was the monster in many eyes but these two were more monstrous than Sally would ever be. Her anger started to boil deep inside. It joined with another anger from the depths of a place where her wolf lived and rose up quickly. She growled and snarled and felt the change coming like a train. The was no time left. She couldn't hold it off any longer.

"Run, Bex" she said in a low rasping voice. "Get away from me."

Becky remained motionless, looking at the two bodies. Horror in her eyes. The realization of what had happened here appearing all over her face as utter shock.

Sally fell onto her hands and knees.

Stay Away

"Run!"

Sally's voice was now unrecognizable. It was closer to an animal growl than human speech.

Sally felt hands on her body. They tugged and pulled at her clothing, clumsily trying to help Sally out of her constraints. She looked through darkening eyes to see Becky unfastening buttons and pulling at garments, working them down Sally's thickening limbs.

"No, Bex! Get away! Run, now! Grrrrrrr…"

She kicked all four legs as the last of the human clothing was pulled away. She got up onto her paws quickly and spun round to face the closest human. She sniffed.

'This scent is familiar, friendly but frightened."

She nudged the hand that was closest with her nose. The hand was pulled away instantly. She caught other scents from behind her. She turned. Two other humans stood motionless and staring. These humans were also frightened but the scents weren't known to her. She didn't trust them. The humans shouted at each other; they were calling for help. The two strange humans backed away. She moved between them and the human with the familiar scent, feeling a need to protect.

A fourth human, dressed the same as the two in front of her, appeared from the right. The was a loud bang. Pain exploded from her hip. She spun round, frantic to get at the wound. To lick it, soothe it. There was a long, slim piece of metal sticking out of her skin. She grabbed the tassel that fanned out at its tip with her mouth and pulled it free. The taste was foul, liquid dripping from the sharp point. She spat the object onto the floor. Her sight started to blur, her legs began to tremble and gave way underneath her. Dizziness came. A dull, cold feeling moved quickly along her body from her back legs.

Suddenly she felt soft, gentle, human hands stroking her fur, caressing her head, down her neck and along her side. There was the sound of a soothing voice, a human voice, a friendly voice. The voice got quieter and more distant then faded away. Everything got darker around her. Her howl was weak and short, nothing more than a whimper. Suddenly there was only blackness.

Chapter 19

Sally woke and opened her eyes slowly. Her head was thumping and her senses whirling. She was cold. Her body ached. The scents around her were unnatural, clinical. Where was she? Her sight slowly started to return. She managed to sit up but felt a little off balance still. She was on a cold concrete floor. She looked around. The room was bare, save for a small bed to one side of her. She recognised the layout as one of the rooms she had seen when she had searched for Becky. Her clothes were folded neatly by her side. Becky's scent was all over them.

Sally knew she had shifted and must have done so right in front of Becky. Worry spread through her body making her stomach turn and her chest ache. She hoped and prayed inside that she hadn't hurt Becky. The fact Becky's scent was all over her pile of clothes suggested she was okay and had folded the clothing and laid it next to her sleeping wolf. That gave her some comfort but where had she been taken? She had bungled this rescue attempt badly. The worry turned to anger at the thought of Becky now being held captive again. Where was she? What had they done to her? Was she still alive?

She was in human form again so it must be morning, a grey light crept through a dirty small window at the top of the wall behind her.

She dressed quickly. There seemed to be only one way

in and out; the door with the little spy hole. She could hear nothing. The building was quiet. She guessed it was too early in the morning for the staff to arrive. Still, she crept over to the door as quietly as she could to look through the spy hole. As soon as her hands touched the metal door her skin started to burn and blister. The pain was horrendous. She felt as if she had just thrust her hand into a fire. She pulled them away quickly. She looked around for a sink with a tap so she could put her hands under some cold water but there was nothing. She had to stand there while the lycanthropy attacked the injured skin and wait for the pain to slowly ease. The door must have been painted with a coating that contained silver. She looked around the room and sniffed. The walls appeared to have been treated in the same way. This room was designed to hold a werewolf.

With no other exit she tried a few well-placed shoulder charges at the door but got her nowhere. The only thing Sally could do was wait for her captors to return. She sat facing the door in the middle of the room, well away from the walls. She took the opportunity to concentrate and go inside her subconscious just like the Neuromancer had taught her. She found the glowing white ball of her lycanthropy and directed it to the still burning skin of her hands to help it heal more quickly.

She came out of her meditation but kept her eyes closed. She heard footsteps approaching in the corridor outside. Sally concentrated more on the sound. Three, no four sets of footsteps. They got louder and as they reached her door they stopped. She heard the sound of the door being unlocked. She opened her eyes but stayed completely still, watching and waiting for the door to open. When it did, four men in lab coats entered the room, rather tentatively. Each man was armed with a gun, Sally could smell as tranquilliser darts they had been loaded with. She said nothing and waited for them to speak first.

"You!" shouted one of them. "Get on your feet."

"Why?" asked Sally, keeping her voice low and calm.

"You're wanted in the lab, and if you know what's good for you, you'll come along without a fuss."

"No funny business," one of the others added in a less than confident tone.

Sally had expected them to use Becky's name as a kind of leverage, but they didn't. She was sure they would bring Becky into the threats at some point though. She could feel her anger starting to build at the thought of Becky being used as some kind of bargaining chip. She had to concentrate hard to push that thought out of her mind. She needed to stay calm.

Sally got to her feet slowly. She kept her eye on the guns they all sported. She could smell the fear of the four men, and she didn't fancy scaring one of them into hitting her with another dart. The lycanthropy had forced the earlier dose from her body while she slept, and she was now back to her full strength. She wanted to keep it that way.

Two of the men slipped out of the door and the other two parted wide enough for Sally to walk between them while they kept their guns aimed somewhat shakily at Sally's torso. She walked past them and the two in the corridor stood on the left pointing down the corridor towards the labs Sally had seen the day before.

"Along that way," ordered one of them. "Second door on the right."

As she walked in the direction indicated Sally sniffed the air. There were more people around than she could see. Others had started work.

The second door on the right was past three windows showing the contents of the lab. Overhead lighting, cupboards and worktops around the walls and what looked like a dentist's chair placed in the centre of the room. Sally walked through the already open door and was directed to the chair. She sat and with nervous hands the person waiting by the chair started to strap her wrists and ankles to it.

"What's this for?" asked Sally.

"Just a precaution," replied the man who entered the room from a door in the far corner once Sally's wrists and ankles were secure.

Sally wondered if her bonds were strong enough to hold her, probably not, she considered wrenching herself free and taking out as many of the people in the room as she could. The tranquilliser guns were still trained on her though and she had no idea where Becky was. She would have to go along with this little charade for the time being.

"Why this precaution when you have your little friends with guns?" Sally replied.

"Oh, they won't be stopping," said the man. "They get a little squeamish," he added with a smile and Sally felt her wolf start to become restless inside. He turned to the men with the guns. "That's all gentlemen. You can leave us now."

With that all the others left the room and closed the door. Sally thought they looked like they were relieved to be going.

"I'm Dr. Blackford. I'll be carrying out your procedure today."

"Procedure?"

"Oh, nothing to worry about. Just a little blood test."

He pulled a small trolley over to the chair in which Sally was strapped. On the trolley was an array of syringes, all of which were on the large side, along with a selection of knives.

"You should have done this while I was tranquilised," said Sally. "It would have been easier for you."

"No no. This particular blood test cannot be done while your unconscious. It has to be while you are on the verge of transforming into your other self as it were. Timing is crucial."

"You don't seriously expect me to shift voluntarily, do you?"

"No. Quite the opposite actually. That's why I find pain to be very useful in that respect. It persuades the subject to start their preparations. You don't have to fully transform. Just bring your little wolf to the surface. I'll do the rest. Once you're at the point where your transformation starts we can extract blood, I find the muscles in the abdomen to be a perfect collection area. One of my colleagues will then extract the Lycanthropy virus from the blood. It's all very painless, for me at least." His face suddenly took on a more sinister look then he leaned in and whispered. "I do admit that we don't always get the timing right and have lost a few subjects. The last one in this very chair. Being strapped down isn't very conducive to a healthy or even survivable metamorphic transition into a wolf so it will be much easier on you if you cooperate."

"You won't be forcing me into a shift."

Dr. Blackford just smiled again. "We'll see."

Sally heard a door behind her open and the unmistakable scent of a vampire filled her nostrils. Sally felt cold, dead hands clamp onto her shoulders and hold her down like she was in a vice.

"This is Vincent," said Dr. Blackford. "My assistant. He will just be making sure you don't move too much while the needle is in. We don't want any wasted samples. Thanks to you our other test subjects all escaped last night. That makes you the only one we have left, so it's very important you play your part."

So, the pack did get free. Sally felt a little satisfaction inside hearing that news. That meant she only had to worry about Becky now.

"Didn't you get enough samples from the others while you had them? What more could I give you?"

"During my research I've discovered four different strains of Lycanthropy, each strain giving the animal slightly different levels of ability. From what I've been told about you and the things you were capable of when you murdered some of my security team last night, I believe you have a fifth strain. Your strain seems to be more powerful than any of the others so that makes you vital to my research. Now be a good girl and hold still because this is going to hurt."

She felt Dr. Blackford pull up the front of her tee-shirt exposing her stomach. He picked up the largest of the syringes.

"Now then, Sally. It is Sally, isn't it? If you would just start your transformation this can be over with in a jiffy."

"I told you. I'm not shifting."

"Don't make me hurt you," said the doctor. "I so dislike hurting pretty girls." He leaned forward and whispered in Sally's ear. "But as you were the one who caused us all those problems last night and almost ruined my life's work, I may just make an exception in your case."

Sally growled a deep throated growl and struggled to move but the grip Vincent had on her shoulder got tighter and held her firmly down in the chair.

Dr. Blackford stood back up and tutted. "You disappoint me, Sally. You leave me no option."

He picked up one of the long knives and brought it down hard and fast, stabbing Sally through the forearm, pinning her to the arm of the chair.

Sally let out a scream of pain which turned quickly into a growl. Her inner wolf howled inside and pushed towards the surface.

"No!" cried Sally. Her wolf stopped. "It's what he wants," she added underneath another low growl. Her wolf backed off, but Sally knew her hackles would be raised.

The vampire behind her moved forward and lapped at the blood flowing from her arm.

"Stop that, Vincent," said Dr Blackford in a calm voice. "We cannot afford to contaminate her blood just yet. It's far too valuable to our work. You can have your fun later."

The vampire took one last lick of Sally's skin and moved back to his position and held her down again.

"Oh, Sally. Your eyes are beautiful when they change colour like that. I think that means you're ready." And with that, Dr. Blackford moved Sally's tee-shirt to reveal her stomach once again and pushed one of the largest syringes through her skin as far as it would go.

Sally let out a loud scream come growl. She could feel herself starting to faint with the intensity of the pain. Now was not the time. She tried to block out the pain. She concentrated on her breathing. The meditation technique the Neuromancer had taught her started to work. She slipped into her subconscious. The ball of lycanthropy healing power was shaking the cabinet in which it was being kept. Beams of white light shot from it in all directions. In here Sally could feel no pain but she could sense the knife still in her arm and the needle of the syringe being moved about, the doctor trying to find just the right spot. Sally opened the cabinet door and a blanket of white light filled every corner of the chamber she was in.

She concentrated on the syringe. The lycanthropy followed her focus and blocked the needle, preventing the sample the doctor was after being drawn into the waiting tube. She heard the doctor curse faintly in the distance. The syringe was removed but soon replaced with another, then another. Each one failing to draw out any fluid.

The light in the chamber began to fade. At first Sally feared it may be that she was losing the fight but the calmness of the echoes around her told her something else. No more syringes were puncturing her skin. The distant sounds had faded. She imagined her exit door and slipped through, opening her eyes slowly. Vincent had gone. Dr. Blackford had gone. The knife remained in her arm, pinning it to the chair but the pain had eased and the blood had stopped flowing. It was a lot later in the day now than she had realised.

"What the hell are you?" a voice to her left asked.

One of the lab coated team, similar to the ones who had escorted her to this room, stood aiming a tranquiliser gun at her.

"You know what I am," answered Sally.

"I'm not so sure," he said. We've never had a werewolf resist a transformation once Dr. Blackford starts on them. You made him angry. You shouldn't have done that."

"Why not?"

"Because he'll hurt you."

Sally looked at the knife sticking through her forearm into the chair.

"And this isn't hurting me I suppose."

"There's more than one way to inflict pain on somebody." He opened the door and shouted down the corridor. "She's awake! A little more help please!"

More men entered the room and while the first kept the tranquilliser gun aimed at Sally they started to unlock the wheels on the bottom of her chair. None of them got any closer than needed, doing their best impression of keeping their distance without looking like they were. Sweat rolled down the side of the face of the closest to her, his eyes darting to and from her as she was rolled out of the room on the chair and headed further down the corridor. Sally glanced at the sweating man and he jumped and stepped away quickly. It made Sally smile knowing she was getting into their heads.

Stay Away

Sally caught Becky's scent and it got stronger the further along the corridor they went. Becky's fear was also in the air. Immense fear.

"Where are we going?" she asked.

"To your little friend's room," answered the person behind her, "the doctor has a little surprise for you."

"More like a proposition," a second voice added.

They passed by the other labs Sally had seen before and passed some closed doors. One of the doors was open and she looked in when they got level. It was more of a storeroom than a lab. The far wall was covered in glass cabinets containing shelf upon shelf of small glass bottles. There was the whirring sound of fans above each cabinet and what looked like humidity controls on the front. Maybe the samples in the glass bottles could be from other werewolves. How many others had this mad scientist tortured into shifting into their wolf form? And how many had not survived?

She was wheeled on further down the corridor until they stopped at another plain door. Becky's scent was all over the door posts, hands had grasped the wood tightly and fingernail marks scored the sides. The door was opened and Sally was rolled inside. Dr. Blackford stood there waiting, a grin on his face which wasn't the most welcoming. He was up to something, and Sally didn't like it. Becky's scent was strong. Sally looked around and what she saw made her chest feel empty. Becky was strapped to a chair, metal straps from the frame were fastened around her wrists and ankles and she was wearing what looked like a metal headband.

"You can leave us now," said Dr. Blackford and waved his hand. The men with the tranquilliser guns left the room, again they looked more than happy to do so.

Becky looked at Sally and started to cry. She pulled at her bonds, but they were solid. Then her gaze went to the knife impaled into the chair though Sally's arm and cried out in shock.

"Oh, Sally. I'm so sorry. You shouldn't have come here looking for me. This is all my fault." She pulled harder at her bonds again. The one remaining guard put his hand on Becky's shoulder and pulled her back against the back of the chair.

"Sit still!" he shouted.

Sally looked at him and gave a growl. He stepped back, his breathing not as steady as it was.

"Hey, Bex. It's okay. Don't you worry," said Sally. "Everything is going to be okay."

"It certainly is Miss Millar," Dr. Blackford interrupted. "Sally here is about to help me with a little experiment then your stay here will be over."

"Let her go," said Sally, "Then I'll consider your offer."

"She's all packed and ready to go," said Dr. Blackford. He gestured to a small rucksack next to Becky's chair. "All you have to do is start to shift, I'll get the sample I need to add to my little collection down the hall, and your little friend can be on her way." His face got suddenly more serious. "However, if you still refuse, my colleague over there near the wall will flick that switch." He grinned wickedly. "I'm not sure if you've noticed but your friend is sat in an electric chair. One flick of a switch and you can sit here and watch her fry."

Sally could feel the anger welling up inside her. The smell of fear from Becky increased and she started to shake.

"Let her go," Sally repeated with a little more threat in her voice.

"I will. All you need to do is shift."

"Don't do it, Sal," shouted Becky.

"Shut it, girl," snapped Dr. Blackford, "or I'll flick the switch myself."

A low growl filled the room.

"This is your last chance," said Sally. "Let Becky go. Now."

Dr. Blackford looked at the straps which held Sally to the chair then slowly walked over to her. He leaned a little closer. "This is your last chance my girl. Start to shift now or your friend will die."

"I'll never shift for you," snarled Sally.

"SHIFT! You stupid girl. Shift or he will flick that switch."

Dr. Blackford pointed a finger at the trembling lab technician who stood against the wall next to Becky.

Sally stared straight into Dr. Blackford's eyes. He stared back at her eyes then began to smile. "That's it," he said, "She's turning. Quick get my syringe!"

The lab technician hurried across the room and grabbed a large syringe.

Dr. Blackford turned back to Sally. "Those eyes my dear. Those golden orange eyes are beautiful but have given you away. This is exactly the right time." He took the syringe from the lab technician and aimed it at Sally's abdomen.

Sally wrenched her left arm free of the straps. Her hand had been slowly changing, growing razor sharp claws, filling with werewolf strength without the doctor noticing. He had been too engrossed in Sally's eyes and the thought he was finally going to get the sample he was after. Once her arm was free she grabbed Dr. Blackford by the throat. With one powerful thrust Sally threw Dr. Blackford across the room and he hit the wall opposite with a sickening thud. He staggered away from the wall, standing there stunned for a moment. Sally looked immediately at the lab technician who was staring wide eyed straight back at her. His mouth was open, his hands were shaking and Sally could smell his fear. He looked at the switch he had been in charge of but instead of flicking it, he grabbed one of the tranquilliser guns from a trolley close by. He didn't aim, he just raised the gun and shot it at Sally in one movement. She seen it coming and caught it in midair. The lab technician dropped the gun and ran from the room, shouting for help.

By this time the doctor had caught his breath and looked at Sally in amazement. He raised his hand to his neck, which was now streaming with blood, and his face changed from shock to anger. A rage such as Sally had not seen in anybody before built on his face. He rushed at her. His fury blinding him from the danger of the semi changed werewolf in front of him. Sally grasped the knife, which pinned her other arm to the chair. Pulling it free she threw it at Dr. Blackford with her full werewolf strength. The blade slammed into his chest sending him flying backwards against the wall once more. He fell limp to the floor.

The pain of pulling the knife from her arm caused Sally to howl and she knew her eyes would be glowing brighter than ever. Blood gushed from the now open wound and ran down her arm, pooling on the floor. She slashed the remaining straps with her now fully shifted hands and claws, and she was free. She jumped from the chair and ran over to Becky. The straps holding Becky were made of metal, but they were fastened with leather straps. These, Sally made short work of and Becky was also free.

"Sally, you need to get out of here," said Becky. "It's nearly dark and the guards in this place are vampires. They'll be awake any minute."

"Don't worry. We're getting out of here, now. Come on."

Becky grabbed the rucksack by the side of the chair and

they both headed out of the door. The corridor and the labs opposite were empty. The staff had obviously made a hasty retreat when they had heard there was a werewolf getting loose close by. Sally sniffed the air in one direction then the other.

"This way," she said, indicating left.

They headed back towards where she had been held. Sally stopped at the door to the room where she had seen all the sample bottles.

"Stay here and keep watch, Bex."

"What are you doing? We need to go."

"I think this is where they could be keeping all the samples they've taken from the other werewolves. There might even be results of experiments or something. I can't let them keep them. Keep watch. If you see anybody shout me."

Sally slipped into the room. It was full of cabinets on every wall. There must have been hundreds if not thousands of samples. Each one labeled with a name and a date. There was a full shelf of sample bottles labeled 'Kiera Chapman". No wonder Kiera hadn't wanted to come back here, she thought. Sally growled. Picking up a chair she smashed it into each of the glass cabinets, not stopping until every cabinet was wrecked. Sample bottles and test tubes shattered as they hit the floor and their contents ran all over, mixing with each other. The computer in the corner got the same treatment. If she had the time she would have burned the whole evil place to the ground.

"Sally," came Becky's voice. "Somebody's coming"

There was no more time left. She just hoped she'd done enough damage.

She left the room and led Becky along the corridor, past yet more labs and the room where she had woken earlier in the day. They made their way quickly to the stairs and down to the ground floor. The door was locked but with one kick Sally smashed it open. They found themselves in a courtyard. Fresh air filled Sally's lungs and she breathed it in deeply. The sun was going down fast. Her inner wolf was up at the surface wanting to be let out, wanting to get them to safety.

The courtyard was almost fully enclosed. The building surrounded them on all four sides in a kind of horseshoe shape leaving one small gap at the far end where they could get out. Sunlight was still shining into the courtyard through the gap but Sally knew this would be gone in a matter of minutes. There was a large, raised flowerbed in front of them so the two girls made their way around it, following the path along the side of the building. A little way along the wall the path cut diagonally across the middle and headed directly to the opening at the far end.

"Follow me," said Sally.

As she stepped onto the path she caught the scent immediately. The stale, dead stench of a vampire. The scent filled her nostrils and made her want to vomit it was so strong.

Her wolf inside growled and Sally joined her. She held up her hand for Becky to stop and stay behind. She scanned the courtyard slowing. There was nothing to be seen. She was standing in the last remaining sunlight which was quickly emptying out of the large open area in front of her. They were safe in the last of the daylight for the moment, but they had to move fast. Soon this whole courtyard would be in darkness.

"Sally!"

She spun around just as a loud crash of a window echoed round the courtyard and Becky's frightened voice cried out. The sun had gone from that side of the building and a large male Vampire had smashed the window and was leaning out holding Becky by the hair. He hissed at Sally like an angry cat and bared his fangs. His other hand reached down, grabbed Becky by her jacket and started to pull her back in through the broken window.

Sally launched herself at the vampire, her werewolf strength giving her extra speed. Her claws sank into the vampire's flesh. She pressed her feet against the wall and pulled. He was immensely strong and it took all of Sally's werewolf enhanced strength to pull him out of the window. He released Becky and landed on the floor but was up and facing Sally in an instant. Standing between him and Becky she stared straight into his eyes, the warning growl from her throat was deep and threatening but it didn't seem to worry the vampire. He simply smiled and rushed at her again. His speed was unbelievable, but Sally was ready. She kicked out as he approached and her foot hit him square in the chest. The vampire was stopped but he only staggered back a little before coming at her again. Sally caught him across the face with a righthand punch. This stopped him again but it still wasn't enough. Sally followed it with a lefthand punch then another right and another left. Her claws came out for the following round of slashes and punches. She forced him onto his back foot with the onslaught then kicked him full in the chest once again. He was sent sprawling backwards and rolled into the fading sunlight. He gave a blood curdling scream and started to burn and crumble right in front of them. The smell of burning, rotting flesh was the most acrid smell Sally had ever encountered. There was no time to waste. She pushed Becky in front of her into the sunlight and moved away from the windows.

The sun sank behind the distant hills from where Sally had first watched the lab complex and the whole courtyard was now in shadow. The stale, foul smell of vampires once again found Sally's nose and one by one they came out. Vampire after vampire stepped out of doors all around the courtyard.

"Oh my God," said Becky. "Look, Sal."

Sally followed the direction Becky's finger was pointing. Four vampires had stepped out of doors close to the only way out of the courtyard and were now cutting off their one escape route. Yet more vampires stepped out of other doors all around them. Sally estimated there to be about a dozen or more. The number was irrelevant. Sally was vastly outnumbered. They were surrounded.

Chapter 20

Sally spun around at the sound of footsteps behind them. She stepped between Becky and the approaching vampire. The other vampires made no move, they simply watched. Two girls were no great threat to them. Looking up she spotted Vincent standing in one of the upper windows, looking down upon the courtyard and smiling. He radiated confidence and authority, the vampires now in the courtyard below obviously under his command. He stood like a general surveying the battlefield before the onslaught began.

Becky started to shake with fear. Tears rolled down her cheeks. Sally showed the vampire her claws and she felt her canines growing larger. The vampire smiled and stared at her as she completed her partial shift. Suddenly, without warning, he jumped twenty feet straight up then came down onto Sally from above. She caught him in mid-air and with a slight swerve of her body helped him on his way and he landed unceremoniously in a heap on the ground. This got a laugh from the other vampires who now seemed happy to watch the show unfold.

Sally used the vampire's embarrassment in front of his peers as an opportunity to move her and Becky to a wall well away from any windows. She pushed Becky behind her and stood ready for the vampire again.

"Sally, to your left," said Becky and Sally looked to find

another vampire sneaking round to join in the fun.

He lunged at her, but Sally deflected his arm and continued the movement using the vampire's own momentum to send him sailing past. More laughter erupted from the others.

Both embarrassed vampires approached together this time. They lunged. She caught one in her claws by his neck and sank her canines into the shoulder of the other. She bit down hard and the sound of crunching bones was followed by a loud hiss and a cry of pain. She ripped out bone and flesh with her teeth then pushed him away sending him rolling backwards into some bushes. She spit out the foul tasting flesh then started to punch the other vampire repeatedly in the face while holding onto his throat in her powerful werewolf paw. He pulled and cried out trying to get away while at the same time trying to block Sally's relentless punches. She sent him falling backwards to the ground with her last punch but kept some of his throat in her claws. He shrivelled up on the floor as she watched, his head to one side and no longer connected to his body. Sally threw a lump of his throat onto the dirt next to him.

She heard a balking noise from behind her as Becky emptied the contents of her stomach onto the path. The scene was getting rather gruesome, but Sally knew it was going to get worse before it got better.

The other vampires laughs and cheers stopped. They

clearly hadn't expected her to be able to kill one of their own. There was a murmuring between them, the mood had changed. Two more vampires approached from the watching crowd. They were angry and much larger than the one lying dead and turning to ash. The one Sally had thrown into the bushes stepped out into the open, fully healed. She remembered what Blake had told her about a vampire's near immediate recovery.

Sally's wolf wanted to join in the fight but Sally wouldn't let her out. She wouldn't be able to protect Becky from herself in her wolf form. She wasn't sure how much longer she could protect Becky from the vampires in her current form either.

The two larger vampires picked up their pace and both came at her together. Sally punched and slashed and kicked with all her might. She landed blow after blow, never missing a target, slicing through flesh. Vampire blood was spraying everywhere but her attackers weren't giving up. She felt her right arm get grabbed and a set of vampire fangs sink into her flesh. The pain was unbelievable. With only one arm free, punches from the two large vampires started to rain down on her. She was helpless and wanted to go deep within herself like the Neuromancer had taught her, to get away from the pain, to fight the vampire fangs from the inside with her glowing ball of lycanthropy. To do that, however, would leave Becky at the mercy of every vampire in the courtyard. She had to fight. She pulled and wriggled but no matter how hard she tried she couldn't dislodge the vampire from her forearm or block any of the punches that were now being aimed at her face. She could feel her blood being sucked out of her arm and her veins emptying. Cuts had opened up on her face now too and she was becoming dizzy. Her strength started to fade. Even her inner wolf seemed to be staggering and whimpering. She cried out as she felt the fangs go even deeper. Her cry turned into a deafening howl, a howl full of pain and sorrow, an animal pleading for help. The sound rebounded around the courtyard, bouncing off each wall and filling the courtyard. Echoes repeated the howl which seemed to become many. The echoes didn't die. The howls kept repeating and were getting louder, or were they getting closer? The vampire feeding on her arm let go and the other two stopped punching her. Their attention drawn away by the howls ringing around the small space.

    Sally opened her eyes. The howls had turned into growls and snarls. She looked around and all the vampires were staring at the opening to the courtyard. The snarls and growls reached a climax and vampires all over the courtyard started to scurry around. Some were slipping back through the doors to the building as wolf after wolf ran into the open space. These were large wolves, they were large werewolves, a whole pack of fully shifted, completely rested and angry werewolves. As they spilled in through the opening to the courtyard, any vampire they could get their teeth into was

Stay Away

targeted by at least two werewolves. This was an organised pack.

Sally lashed out at the vampire who had been feeding on her arm. The distraction of the pack was all she needed to get her claws into his throat and pull and slash with all her strength. He shrivelled and fell back to join his friend as nothing but ash.

One dark brown werewolf looked at Sally and dashed straight at them. Becky was screaming almost hysterically. Sally once again put herself between the danger and her best friend. but the werewolf slowed. It had something in its mouth. Sally recognised the scent. Kiera dropped a small Japanese sword at Sally's feet. She growled and yapped then bounded away. Sally's inner wolf was now awake and alert.

'*Get her away from here, your friend, get her away.*'

Sally hadn't understood Kiera but her inner wolf had. She picked up the sword and turned to the cowering girl behind her.

"Are you okay, Bex?"

Becky was pale with fear but she looked up at Sally and nodded. She wiped her eyes with the back of her hand and said, "Yes, I'm okay."

Sally helped her up off the ground.

"We're making for that opening. Stay close."

They'd only gone a few metres when a vampire threw a werewolf off him and launched himself at them. Sally swung the blade. The razor sharp steel sliced through the vampire's neck with ease, and he fell dead a few feet behind them.

It was slow going but Sally cut her way through many more vampires. Each one shrivelling to nothing as their head left their body. She kept her eyes on the werewolves too but they were all busy with vampires. With every slash, cut, kick and punch Sally guided Becky closer and closer to the opening and a way out of the frenzy.

Once at the exit from the courtyard Sally looked back. Werewolves and vampires fought, bit and threw each other all over the courtyard. She couldn't tell were fur ended and fangs started.

'*Run. Get us away from here.*'

Sally wanted to help the pack. She wanted to fight and play her part, to help those who had answered her howl and come back to help her.

'*They want you to get the human out. Run, Sally. Run.*'

Her wolf was right. She had done what she had come here to do. She had freed the pack. Now it was time to save her best friend. She turned to the hills in the distance. The safest place she could think of within easy reach. As they ran Sally got slower and slower. She was weak. She'd lost a lot of blood and the vampire venom was taking hold. She felt Becky put her arm around her waist and a shoulder go under her armpit.

They set off again together but Becky soon began to

weaken. It was hard and slow going but together they helped each other get to the hole in the perimeter fence, the one Sally and Blake had come through a day earlier. Once through the fence they made their way up the hill towards the trees overlooking the laboratory complex. Sally could still hear the battle below. Hisses and snarls filled her ears. It wasn't over. She had to keep going. She had to get Becky to safety. With one big effort they dragged each other up the steepening hill and through a line of bushes. They went deeper amongst the trees, Sally following her nose and her instincts, and came across a little clearing.

"We can rest here," said Sally. "We should be safe for the moment."

She felt some comfort in the werewolf scent on the ground all around her. The flattened grass, dry, warm and soft.

"Are you okay, Sal?"

Sally nodded but she could feel the vampire venom creeping through her blood and seeping into her muscles and bones. The infection had been crawling up her arm since the first bite but now it was spreading over her chest. She started to cough. Her eyes wouldn't focus and she felt weak. The last of her strength was spent. She felt a hand on her forehead and an arm around her waist. Becky helped her lay down then curled up beside her.

"It's okay, Sal. You're safe now. Just rest a little while. I'll stay with you."

Sally heard the soft, friendly voice but it got quieter and quieter as if it was moving away and disappearing into the distance.

Sally closed her eyes and forced herself to go inside, to her safe space, to the hollow of her subconscious. The small cabinet was there. Inside, the ball of light glowed bight and pulsed with energy, fighting the intruding virus and trying to heal her wounds. It needed help. She opened the glass door and let it out. Looking around the vast cavern she could see an evil red glow getting larger, getting closer. She turned towards it and the ball of white light settled close to her shoulder. They would fight this thing together.

She walked to the burning red mass and concentrated on the darkest patch. Her lycanthropy started to shine brighter. It buzzed like and angry swarm of bees. A beam of white light shot out of the ball like a lightning strike and there was a loud clap of thunder. It struck the red mass exactly where Sally was concentrating. As the light got brighter the red glow moved further away. Sally moved slowly closer, the light ate away at the edges of the red mass, pushing it back.

The intruding venom grew darker and more menacing. Sally could sense its retaliation, but her Lycanthropy expanded in response. She focused more and could feel the stabs of light shooting out at the enemy. Pulse after pulse, faster and faster she hit it. It hissed at her and tried to fight back. It was no use. This was her domain, her safe place. With

Stay Away

a final snarl her white light grew to an almost blinding level.

When the light dimmed the red mass was gone. Sally walked back to the cabinet and her little white ball of light floated to the shelf were it stayed and hummed gently, now concentrating on her injuries. Sally looked around and willed a doorway to appear. She walked through it and woke up.

Becky was on her knees leaning over her. Tears running down her cheeks. "Sally?" she said in a quiet voice. "Oh my God Sally I thought you'd died." Becky fell on her and wrapped her arms tightly around Sally's neck.

Sally hugged her back, not wanting to leave go, happy to be in the embrace of her friend. Comfortable and warm. But then she caught the scent. It was a werewolf scent. One she didn't recognise. She knew then that the danger was far from over. Out of instinct she had brought Becky back to a safe place. A place a wolf would consider to be safe. A place where at any moment a pack of werewolves would be returning. Her strength was recovering but she was still weak. Could she have rescued her best friend from the lab only to deliver her to the mouths of a werewolf pack. With a struggle she managed to get up onto her knees and place herself between Becky and the large grey werewolf as it slipped out of cover and into the clearing.

Sally could only manage a warning growl. Her hands changed once again to paws and claws. It took all her strength to lift her arms ready to fight and stare directly into the wolf's eyes. A challenge she wasn't sure she could follow through with, but one she was going to give all she could.

The wolf just looked at her then lowered his head and moved away to the side. More wolves walked into the clearing; they were covered in vampire blood from the battle. They all did the same as the first and lowered their heads before moving away. Two more werewolves emerged from the bushes who's scent Sally did recognize. Blake and Kiera walked past her with a simple nod and joined the rest of the pack. One by one each of the werewolves nudged or nuzzled Blake as they passed. A greeting that Sally hadn't seen before in any of the packs she'd come across.

One by one, the wolves in the pack gathered round her and Becky, each of them settling down to rest from the battle and let their bodies heal and slowly shift back to their human form.

Sally could feel the love, friendship and trust radiating from the pack. They were all individuals but Sally got a sense they were more than that. A family? Maybe. Friends? Definitely. This pack wasn't like any other she'd seen. She felt suddenly accepted even though she wasn't one of them. Was this how a pack should be? Was she changing her mind about life in a pack? From the day she was bitten she had felt unwanted, an outsider, a monster. Those feelings were growing weaker somehow. All these wolves had somebody to turn to who understood what they were going through. She could turn to Becky for anything, she knew that, but Becky couldn't really understand what it felt like to be what she was.

Each werewolf closed its eyes and snuggled like a puppy would. There wasn't a piece of ground to be seen between any of them. They fit together like a perfect jigsaw puzzle. The clearing fell quiet and peaceful.

Sally's instinct told her this was a place where she could rest. Even now some of her strength was returning. Her lycanthropy working hard inside to heal her wounds. Her inner wolf was relaxed and calm.

She pulled Becky closer. This pack may have total trust in each other but they were, after all, strangers to Sally. She didn't feel the same level of trust in them when it came down to Becky's safety.

"Try to get some rest, Bex. I'll keep my eye on this lot for you."

"Can you believe it, Sal? We're sleeping in the middle of a pack of werewolves." Becky had a wide excited smile on her face. "They're not monsters. None of you are. All this," Becky motioned her hand to all the animals around her, "it's beautiful."

Sally put her finger to her lips.

"Shh. Don't be fooled, Bex. They're still werewolves. I'm not letting my guard down for a second. Not while you're here."

Becky just smiled, leaned into Sally, closed her eyes

and drifted off to sleep.

Sally wasn't long behind her. Her mood began to soften and she could sense the relaxed atmosphere of the pack. They were all in their post werewolf tranquility. They would start to shift back into their human forms soon, so she closed her eyes and let sleep come and her Lycanthropy heal her injuries.

She woke suddenly when she felt Becky move. A sideways glance told her Becky was fine. She was gently stroking the werewolf who had snuggled in next to her. Running her fingers through its fur. Kiera had taken a liking to Becky for some reason. Maybe she still felt the guilt from when Becky was kidnapped on her watch.

Becky whispered, "Her fur is almost and soft and smooth as yours, Sal."

"Just let her sleep, Bex. Best not touch her while she's resting. It could make her jump. You don't want her snapping at you by accident."

Becky moved her hand away slowly but not with any fear. She turned back to Sally and they both went back to sleep.

Sally woke early the next morning among a pile of entwined, naked humans, still sleeping. Becky was awake beside her. She had her hands over her eyes.

"I just can't imagine anything more embarrassing," she said, and Sally laughed. "I'm never going to be able to unsee this."

Sally sniggered quietly.

"Come on." She took hold of Becky's hand. "Let's me and you go for a walk while this lot wake up and get dressed.

The two girls walked away down the hill, picking up a little track which headed through a small stand of trees and along a stream.

"You did it again," said Becky.

"Did what?"

"You came and rescued me."

"Well, it's been my fault every time you've needed rescuing."

"No, it's not. You told me not to go and get my car on my own. And I knew you wouldn't want me talking to Kiera, even though she had come to apologise."

Sally just smiled. "Since when have I ever been able to tell you to do anything?"

Becky sniggered and shrugged her shoulders in agreement.

"What actually did happen," asked Sally, "when you were with Kiera?"

"It's all a bit of a blur. It happened so fast. She turned up when I was unlocking my car. She said she wanted to apologise. She'd come with me while I took my car back home then we went for a walk. We were talking one minute then Kiera just froze. She looked like she'd seen a ghost or something. She shouted run and pushed me behind her. A van screeched to a stop and four men jumped out and started fighting with Kiera."

"So, she tried to protect you?"

"Yes," replied Becky. "She was punching and kicking them and shouting at me. Run. Run." Becky paused. "I should have done as she said but, I couldn't. I was so scared. Then two more men said there's the other one and grabbed me."

Becky's voice got quieter and she looked at the floor and fidgeted with her hands.

"They just picked me up and threw me into the van. They actually threw me."

She rubbed her elbow as she recalled the scene.

"Then one of the men said we only need one, leave the other. They all jumped back into the van and Kiera jumped on the back of one of them. The van drove off with Kiera hanging out of the door holding onto him. She fell out. That was the last I saw of her."

"Did they hurt you?" asked Sally.

"They pinned me down and put a bag over my head. I felt something stick into my arm and then I just blacked out."

"Tranquilliser?" said Sally.

"Yeah' I guess so. The next thing I knew I woke up in a dark room on the floor."

"I would have been there sooner, Bex but Kiera was the only one who knew where they would have taken you, and she won't travel in a car or a train or anything. We ended up walking all the way here. I got here as fast as I could. I'm sorry you were in that awful place for so long."

"I knew you would come for me. Well I hoped anyway. I told them all they were in trouble and you would be coming to get them. I thought I was being brave, and with you being a werewolf you would walk in and threaten them like you did with Blake and Kiera that night at the Old Mill. They just laughed at me."

"Well, at least you get the last laugh."

"Yeah, you showed them."

Becky smiled but Sally didn't. She felt ashamed deep inside.

"What's up, Sal?"

Sally's eyes filled with tears.

"Hey, come on. You were amazing."

"No, Bex. I wasn't."

"What do you mean? You came and rescued me."

"And I killed somebody, Bex. Blackford. I killed him."

"He pinned you to a chair with a knife through your arm, Sal. He was evil."

Sally looked Becky in the eyes. "Maybe he was. That still doesn't give me the right to kill him. I'm no better than he is."

Becky grabbed Sally by the arms, giving her a little shake.

"Don't you say that, Sal. You're nothing like him."

"You don't know what I'm like, Bex. Not really. I'm

not even sure I know what I'm like anymore. I don't know. It's all confusing. I've hated packs since I got bitten. Last night I slept in the middle of one and I felt safe. How mixed up is that? In the space of twenty four hours I've become a murderer and a pack rat. Two things I've never been before. The monster is taking over, Bex. I can feel it."

"You're not a murderer," said Becky. "And you're not a monster, or a pack rat. You're my best friend, and that's all that matters to me."

The two girls stood and hugged for a few minutes not talking, just being there for each other.

"We best be getting back to the others," said Sally eventually. She dried her eyes and took a deep breath. "Come on, Bex. Let's get you home."

On the way back they didn't say a lot. It was Becky who finally broke the silence.

"Do you feel safe in Popwood?"

"I feel, comfortable. There's never totally safe. Last night was the safest I've ever felt."

"Are you wanting to join them?"

"No," replied Sally almost immediately. No, I don't." She sighed and ran her fingers through her hair. "But I think my inner wolf is wanting me to."

This time Becky went quiet. A thoughtful look on her face, almost disappointment.

"I'm not going to, Bex. I'm not leaving Popwood. It's

just…" she paused. "I don't know. I've never had these kinds of feelings for a pack before and I've only just met this lot. My wolf keeps saying that we belong. I think she knows more than I can understand. She's never steered me wrong before."

"Ask her," said Becky. "I'm not sure how all this inner wolf thing works but you've said you talk to her. You obviously trust her. I've only met her once, but she seems nice. I trust her too."

Hearing Becky talk like that got Sally a little worried.

"Don't, Bex. I've told you. Stay away when I'm a wolf."

"Why? You're such a beautiful wolf. You wouldn't hurt me."

"I'm not me when I'm a wolf."

"Well, whoever you are you have such lovely soft fur. It even has flecks of your blonde hair through it."

"Wait. She let you touch her?"

Becky nodded. "She was protecting me from the people in the lab."

It had never crossed her mind that her inner wolf would have a connection with Becky. Once her wolf was out she wasn't aware of anything, what her wolf had done, if she had hurt anybody. She could smell the scent of small prey animals when she shifted back but never any humans. She hoped she hadn't hurt anybody but she couldn't be sure. A picture of Kiera as a wolf dropping the sword at her feet flashed into her head. How had she got her wolf to do that, to bring her the sword? The more she thought about it the more confused she was getting.

"Come on, Bex," said Sally. "The rest of them should be almost decent by now. We should get back, and I think I need a word with Kiera too."

They made their way back to the clearing and found everybody dressed and chatting in little groups. A few stood up when they saw Sally.

"We thought you'd ran out on us, Sally," said Blake.

"Not after what you'd all done for me," replied Sally. "I couldn't just leave. Not without saying thank you."

"For what?" Kiera stepped up beside Blake.

"You came back to the lab," said Sally. "I owe you my life." She looked around at the rest of the pack. "All of you."

"We both do," added Becky.

"Blake held up his hand and shook his head.

"It was payment for services already given, Sally. Without you the pack would still be prisoners in that awful place." He motioned his head back towards the lab complex. "You owe us nothing."

Sally looked past him following his gesture. "What about the vampires?"

"Most are dead," Blake answered.

"A few got away," added Kiera, "but they've scattered and will be long gone. Or they would have burned if they couldn't find cover before morning."

Stay Away

Sally moved closer to Kiera and gave her a little hug. The surprise on Kiera's face at the show of affection was almost comical.

"You brought me the sword. While you were a wolf. Thank you."

"I knew you would need it."

"How did you do it? Control your wolf like that I mean?"

"Just a little trick you taught me," replied Kiera with a smile, gently pulling away out of Sally's embrace.

Not a hugger. Sally made a mental note.

"A trick I taught you?"

"Yes. I've started talking to my inner wolf. We've come to an understanding."

"To go back to that place though, that must've been hard for you."

"I was with the pack. It wasn't the same as being there as a prisoner."

"Still," said Sally. "I saw all the samples they took from you. It was a brave thing you did."

Kiera's smile disappeared and she looked down at the ground.

"Don't worry," said Sally reaching out and placing her hand on Kiera's shoulder. A gesture Kiera seemed to accept a little easier than a hug. "I destroyed them all, and as much of the lab and equipment as I could."

"What happened to Lucy?" Blake asked. "You said she

was dead yesterday. I searched the place, but I couldn't find any sign of a body.

Sally's smile disappeared this time. "I lost her. She followed me in and took on a vampire for me on her own. She saved my life. There was nothing I could do. I couldn't save her."

Blake went quiet, took a deep breath and looked skyward. Sally could tell losing one of the team, one of the pack, wasn't part of his plan, especially a new member.

There was a long silence until Kiera spoke.

"She's better off now. Once we took her away from her pack she was never going to survive. She was an easy target for any rogue wolf or even for somebody like Blackford."

"She was supposed to be coming with us. I should have taken more care of her," said Sally.

"Who is Lucy?" asked Becky.

"Somebody we picked up on our way to you," replied Sally. "She was being mistreated by her boyfriend. I got her away from him. She was supposed to be safe with me. I only got her killed."

Ben walked up and put his arm around Sally's shoulder.

"Hey, it's not your fault," he said.

The sudden contact with him made Sally hold her breath. Becky moved away with a smile on her face, obviously trying to give Sally and Ben a little space. Her inner wolf seemed to be comfortable with him, but Sally's human side didn't know if she agreed. Other than Becky, nobody outside of her family had ever shown her any affection. She didn't know if she liked it. Her heart began to race. The awkward moment was broken by Becky.

"Okay, so who's got a phone?" she asked.

The others just stared at her.

"Somebody must have a phone," she added and looked around the pack. "Anybody got a signal? To call a taxi?"

That seemed to lighten the atmosphere and Blake laughed.

Becky looked around. "I'm not walking back. You three may have walked all this way but I'm not a werewolf. I'm a girl who likes her comfort."

"Do you know how much a taxi would cost from here?" said Sally with a bit of a giggle.

Becky stood and thought for a while. "It's just dawned on me, I don't even know where here is. Where the hell are we anyway?"

"Devon," added Blake with a chuckle of his own.

"Oh." Becky hesitated. "Devon!"

At that the whole pack started to laugh.

"Don't worry," said Blake and put his arm around Becky's shoulders. "We can take the train."

Just then one of the pack who Sally had not seen before ran into the clearing and up to Blake.

"The police have arrived down there," he said. "We

should get going before they start looking for who ransacked the place."

"Come on everybody," shouted Blake. "Pack up, we're leaving. Those of you who're going with Kiera head back up into the hills. The rest, including you and Becky," Blake looked at Sally, "come with me. Theres a small train station on the edge of town."

"What about Lucy's body?" asked Sally.

"They would have hidden her body," said Kiera. "Got rid of it somehow. They were good at handling bodies they no longer needed."

Sally caught the scent of Kiera's fear again. She was trying to hide it but the look on the girl's face betrayed the horror of the memories.

Sally's regret about Lucy was building inside. Lucy shouldn't be just left there, but she knew Kiera was probably right. There would be no body now. No sign poor Lucy had ever existed. Dr Blackford's words came to mind when he had said that some werewolves hadn't survived once he had initiated the shift into their wolf form. Yes. They would've had plenty of practice at getting rid of unwanted bodies, hiding any evidence of the darker side of the lab's activities.

"She's right," said Blake, his alpha male side taking over. "We can't do anything for Lucy now. Okay everybody, let's move."

The pack hurried around collecting any other discarded

clothing and splitting into two groups without even discussing who should go with who. Sally saw Kiera slip away with three friends though the bushes. Blake, Ben and the rest of the pack headed out of the clearing towards the south with Blake taking the lead.

"Come on, Sally." Ben had stopped and was waiting for them. "You two go ahead with Blake. I'll bring up the rear."

With a little pressure on her arm, Ben ushered Sally forward gently.

"Come on, Bex. He's right. Let's get you home."

Chapter 21

They set off through the trees. Sally could see every member of the pack looking out for each other. There was a werewolf always to either side as well as in front and behind. Sally sensed they were protecting her as one of their own. A strange feeling for Sally but also reassuring. Her wolf seemed settled and that had always been a good marker.

The pack moved quickly. Becky was finding it hard to keep up and needed Sally to urge her on, which included dragging her up some steeper parts of the trail. Ben was always on hand too. He never let Sally out of his sight.

When they reached the outskirts of the town Blake suggested staggering their arrival at the station. A large group of bedraggled looking strangers would attract unwanted attention. Sally looked down at her jacket, it was covered in vampire blood. She took it off, turned it inside out and tied it by the arms around her waist.

"I'm thirsty and starving," said Becky. Can we nip into McDonalds at the station and get a cheeseburger and a drink or something?"

Sally was feeling a little hungry too. It had been two days now since she'd last eaten properly, and she assumed Becky hadn't been high on Dr Blackford's list of priorities either.

"Good idea, Bex"

The rest of the pack didn't want anything. They'd been out hunting the night before to build up their strength ready for the attack on the lab. Becky was appalled when she realised this meant they'd been eating live animals in the woods close to where they'd all be sleeping. She was so hungry though she refused to let it put her off a full McDonalds meal including a large portion of fries.

When they'd all arrived at the station Blake handed out train tickets to various places. Only Sally, Becky, Blake, Ben and one other male werewolf, who Blake introduced as Thomas, got tickets to the small station near Popwood. Thomas, she later found out, was Blake's Lieutenant. He was large and looked powerful.

They boarded the train and spread out to various carriages. A real military operation if ever she'd seen one. Sally's group stayed together in the rear most carriage near the dining car.

The train built up speed but not before it rolled slowly past the lab complex. A dozen sets of blue lights flashed on all sides of the building. People in white coveralls were going in and out of the main building which housed the labs Sally and Becky had seen. Sally guessed they had found Dr Blackford's body. She wondered what possible story the staff could concoct to explain away that scene.

Becky stared out of the window too. "What will they say about all the bodies?"

"Bodies?"

"Yeah. All the vampires. Kiera said they'd killed most of them."

"I don't think there'll be any bodies, other than Blackford's," said Sally quietly. "Just a few piles of ash."

The train continued, gliding smoothly on the gleaming tracks. Sally gazed dreamily out the window as the fields sailed passed. Farmers on tractors, people in their gardens enjoying the sun, children playing in streets and playgrounds, families, friends, all oblivious to the train full of werewolves rushing past on the top of a familiar embankment. She thought of how lucky they all were to be free of a world such as hers. The pack she hadn't known for more than a few hours flashed through her mind. They could almost be one of those families down there. Was she the odd one out? She'd felt very comfortable laying with them in the forest last night. Was this meant to be her family now? A werewolf family? They had certainly accepted her into their numbers without question and made a stranger welcome.

"Are you okay, Sal?" Becky asked.

Sally nodded. "Yeah, I'm fine. Just thinking things over."

"What things?"

Sally didn't want to say she'd been thinking about being in a pack again and what life would be like as part of a pack who really cared. She wasn't sure herself how she felt about it. How could her feelings about pack life change so dramatically and so quickly? Maybe she was just tired and her wolfy instincts were taking advantage of her?

"Oh nothing. Just trying to come up with an idea of how to keep you from getting yourself into so much trouble all the time." She laughed.

"Getting myself into trouble?" giggled Becky. "I thought we always did that as a team?"

Becky was right. They were a team. They had been for two wonderful years. These last few days shouldn't change that. Becky could be her little pack of one. She decided to forget about Blake's pack for a while and see how she felt when she got home.

"Yeah, we do seem to do that don't we, Bex?"

They both laughed.

"It's nice to see you two laughing," said Ben.

A deliberate attempt to join in the conversation thought Sally. He had been sat in the seat across the aisle opposite and she had felt him staring since the train set off. Every time she looked over and caught him he smiled then looked away quickly. He was a fidgeter as well. Sally could smell his nervousness.

"Oh, you should see us in Popwood, we're always laughing." Becky broke the silence when Sally didn't answer.

"I'd like that," he said.

"Like what?" replied Sally, a nervous little flutter

suddenly appearing in her voice.

"To see you in Popwood." Ben cleared his throat. "I mean, to see you two in Popwood obviously. Not just you. Not that I wouldn't like it to be just you. No, that's not what I mean either." He cleared his through once more. "I was meaning... like... a visit or something."

Ben's face started to go red as he rushed out the last few words.

"Excuse me," he said. "I need to visit the little boys room."

He disappeared quickly along the aisle. Becky looked at Sally and burst out laughing.

"Oh, dear somebody has an admirer," she said.

"What do you mean?" replied Sally.

"Come off it, Sal. He's head over heels."

This time Sally blushed.

"Don't be silly, Bex. He doesn't know me. We only met yesterday."

"Well, I'm only saying what I see," said Becky with a smile. "Want me to swap seats with him?"

Sally thumped her in the arm and Becky collapsed in another fit of giggles. Sally soon followed and they were both in tears by the time Ben returned. He sat across the aisle again and stayed quiet for the rest of the journey. Sally hadn't meant to embarrass him. She suddenly felt a little sorry for him as he sat fidgeting with his hands again and stealing the occasional sheepish glance back across towards the girls.

The train flashed by more villages, towns and farms on its way northwards. Sally relaxed more the further away the train took them from the laboratory in Dartmoor. Every now and then one of the pack would pass by on the way to the dining car and smile at Sally, pat her on the shoulder and say, 'thank you'.

They changed trains a couple of times, saying their farewells to pack members at each change. When they reached their stop, they got off and walked the last few miles along a bridleway to the sleepy little village Sally and Becky called home. As soon as Popwood came into view Sally got a warm feeling inside. That made up her mind. This is where she belonged and no pack, even one as nice as this one, was going to drag her away from it.

They walked down into the village with people shouting hello to Sally and Becky as they passed. They all gave a strange look to the three rather bedraggled looking guys tagging along with them. Sally, noticing their concern, introduced them as old friends from a newspaper she had once worked for, adding they had been camping up in the hills. This seemed to satisfy most of the inquisitive villagers.

They skirted around the village green and Becky disappeared into her house, telling the others to wait. She returned with a key to one of the holiday cottages.

"Here," she said, handing the key to Blake. "There's

some holiday lets back down the lane to the right. You're welcome to stay there. It's not booked until next month."

"Thank you, Becky," he replied. "That's very kind of you. It'll only be a few days until Kiera catches up."

"So where do you live, Sally?" asked Ben.

Everybody stared at him and he went quiet again.

Sally pointed across The Green. "Just above the shop. Over there."

Blake broke the silence. "How about we all get cleaned up and meet up in your quaint little pub over the way? I think we owe you two a proper dinner. Say about 7.30?"

Sally wasn't sure but Becky, as enthusiastic as ever now she was back in Popwood said they'd be there. Sally watched as they wandered off to look for Moon Night Cottage, which she thought seemed appropriate, before making her way to the stairs leading up to her little flat while Becky went to collect Penny from one of the neighbours who'd been dog sitting.

The first thing Sally did when she got home was stand in the shower for nearly an hour. A full week's worth of dirt and grime was washed away along with all her confusion about her feelings for the pack. She wasn't going to be one of them, but she had a feeling she'd made some unexpected friends.

At around 7.00pm there was a familiar knock on her door. She opened it and the scent of Becky mixed with that of Becky's favourite bath bombs from Lush wafted in.

"I've never enjoyed a bath so much," she said as she stepped in. "When you see Blake you make sure to tell him he owes me a phone."

Sally stood and smiled. The smile then became and snigger which turned into a laugh.

"What?" said Becky.

"You're back, and I've missed you."

"You've been with me for the last two days."

"I know. But I've missed this one. The Becky who comes in and makes me happy even when she's secretly trying to tidy up my living room."

Becky stopped fluffing up the cushion in her hand and put it back on the sofa. Then she laughed too.

"Shall we go to the Black Bull then, Bex, meet the others and see if we still have jobs."

Becky giggled. "Don't worry. Tim couldn't run that place without me and you."

They got to The Black Bull before the boys. Tim was a little miffed that they didn't jump straight behind the bar and help out. Eventually Sally felt sorry for him and started to take some orders for drinks and, with a sigh, Becky gave in and started pulling some pints for the regulars.

Sally could hear whispers about the three strangers staying in the Millar's cottage and some ridiculous rumours about them. Robbers and possible serial killers seemed to be a popular suggestion. She quashed the rumours with her usual smile and charm then joked on with the lovely people of the prettiest little village in the country. She was convinced there couldn't be another village like this one anywhere.

The boys were late and when they did finally arrive Becky put in the food orders and the girls joined them at a table near the window, away from any ears that might be trying to find out if the new story of them being on the run was true. Ben made an obvious move to sit next to Sally and Blake positioned himself in a typical alpha wolf seat so he could see the whole pub as well as a large portion of the village from the window.

The talk at their table was surprisingly normal after all they'd been through. They all told stories of holidays and fishing trips, bands they'd seen or wanted to see. while Becky kept steering the conversation towards musical theatre and London's West End. Not once did anybody mention the last week or so. For that Sally was thankful. She even enjoyed talking to Ben about where he was from. She was still a little protective about her own family and the coastal town where she grew up, but nobody seemed to push her on it. Only Blake knew where he had first bumped into her, but he seemed to sense Sally's reluctance and didn't mention it.

After last orders Sally and Becky stayed back to help Tim close up as they normally would. Ben looked a little disappointed at the news that Sally wasn't leaving with them but Thomas grabbed his arm, whispered something that made

Ben blush then pushed him out the door with a laugh.

"How long will it take Kiera to get here?" asked Becky as they walked around The Green.

"It won't take her long," Sally replied. "A couple of days maybe. Why the sudden interest in Kiera?"

"Oh nothing. I was just wondering how long the boys will be here. Did you know they're art thieves now, according to old Tom anyway," she laughed. "If they don't leave soon they'll be accused of being aliens and invading Earth the way this village gossips."

Sally woke later than usual. She looked out of her window. Popwood was going about its normal business and the smell of freshly baked pies seeped up from the shop below.

"Welcome home," said Joyce when Sally padded bare foot down into the shop. "I'm glad to hear Becky's mam is on the mend."

Joyce crept a little closer and whispered, "It's a good job Becky has a friend like you. Not many would do what you just did for her. She was in earlier and told me all about it."

Sally's heart skipped a beat. "What did I do for her?"

"Dropping everything like you did to go and visit Becky's mam with her. All that way to The Lakes when you have a job here and your news writing to do. You're a good friend to that girl and no mistake."

Sally almost laughed.

"Oh, it was nothing. Any friend would do the same."

Sally got a few bits of shopping and retreated to her flat before Joyce gave her any more shocks.

Sitting down at her desk she stared at the blank page on her pad. Should she write a new exposé story about the lab?

Her wolf stirred a little.

"*We're safe. Let it go.*"

Her wolf was right. The lab was somebody else's problem now.

"We'll stay safe too. This is our pack. Just us two," said Sally quietly.

"*Three.*"

Sally thought about what her wolf had just said, and about the third pack member. There was no reason pack members can't trust each other. The right pack members that is. People who are real friends. And who says pack members have to be supernatural? Should she make that little pack official? Her wolf nudged her gently from inside.

"You're right," she said, "let's do this".

Penny started barking as she got to the door and Becky opened it before she even knocked.

"I knew it'd be you," said Becky with a grin. "There's nobody else Penny greets so lovingly."

Sally sat on the sofa and Becky placed tea and cakes on the small table in front of them.

"You've been up early and busy I see," said Sally.

"Well, I knew you'd be here for a chat this morning. So, what's up, Sal? Is it the being in a pack problem again? You can talk to me about it. A cup of tea, a cake and a chat is always good if you've got something on your mind."

Sally shook her head.

"No. It's not that. Well, it kind of is." Sally hesitated. "It's something you told me, about my wolf when you said she protected you. Did she make no move to bite you at all?"

"No, she sniffed at my hand then stood between me and those men."

"You weren't afraid?"

"At first, when she looked at me, but not after that. She's nice. Why?"

"Something strange happened when I mentioned your name to her last night. She said, '*she's our friend*'."

Becky smiled. "That's so sweet. See, when you're a wolf you're still you, Sal. You'd never hurt me, so neither would she."

"So, you trust her?"

"Yes."

Sally closed her eyes.

"Don't hurt her, please," Sally whispered to herself.

"I won't," Becky replied.

"Sorry, Bex. I wasn't talking to you."

"Then who... Oh. I see."

Sally felt her inner wolf urging her on.

"Okay, Bex. This is going to sound crazy… I'm staying in Popwood. I'm not going to be part of Blake's pack."

Becky smiled, "That doesn't sound crazy."

"That's not the crazy part."

"No? What is?"

"You are part of my pack, the one I have here. So, you should know all of the pack."

"What do you mean?"

Sally took a moment and breathed in deeply. She hoped she was doing the right thing.

"I want you to meet her," said Sally. "Properly, my wolf I mean. I want to meet me as a wolf." Before Becky could answer she pressed on. "I know that might be scary and I wouldn't blame you if you said no. I'd understand."

"I'd love to meet her," said Becky with a huge smile. "Properly," she repeated. "How could I be scared of you, human or wolf?"

They hugged.

"We'll wait until the others have gone," said Sally. "She will need a run by then and we could slip into the south woods after work."

Becky smiled.

"I'll look forward to it."

Stay Away

For the next few days Blake and the others kept themselves to themselves and Sally didn't see them. Sally heard a distant wolf howl one night and imagined they had all gone for a run as wolves but they were far away over the other side of the valley. Nobody in the village had mentioned it the next day so Sally didn't think there was too much wrong with letting them use her territory for one night.

On the third night Sally found it hard to sleep and when she did eventually drop off she tossed and turned all night. Dream after dream invaded her sleep. There was the usual one about the night she was bitten. This time though she knew the animal attacking her. She recognised the scent as Blake and called out his name as she woke. Other dreams were about Dr Blackford. She tried not to throw the knife but each time it flew out of her hand and slammed into his chest. He would call out, "Murderer" as he fell. She woke up soaked in sweat and crying out. Eventually she got up and headed to the kitchen for a drink. The word, murderer, echoing round her head.

"She watched the sun come up over the eastern stand of trees then stared across The Green towards Becky's house. She could see the light still on in Becky's bedroom and wondered if her best friend was also having nightmares.

Around 6.00am she heard the shop below open up and the sound of the bell on the door signaling that people had already started coming for their papers and milk. She decided today was an early breakfast kind of day, so she put on some clothes and made her way down the stairs to the shop. Becky was already there talking to Joyce.

"Don't you ever sleep, Bex?"

"It's a lovely sunny day," said Becky. "Why would I be asleep?" she laughed. "Anyway, now you're here, you can help me to carry my groceries back home. Grab a bag."

Halfway across The Green Sally caught the scent.

"Kiera. She's back," she said.

After dropping off the shopping at Becky's they hurried down the village to the holiday cottages. They didn't knock. Sally just burst in. Kiera was sat on the sofa talking to Blake. She smiled when she saw Sally and Becky stumble in together.

"You got back quick," said Sally.

"I didn't want to be away from the pack too long so we more or less just kept walking."

"Any trouble?" asked Sally. "Any vampires follow you?"

"No. We saw nothing of them. If those vampires aren't dead they would have gone to ground. I doubt anybody from the lab would be looking for us now either. They were busy with the Police last I heard."

"You must be tired," said Becky.

"Yeah," Kiera nodded, "a little."

"She's going to rest here today and we are going to set off home tonight," said Blake.

"I'm fine," Kiera answered.

"You might be but the others aren't." Blake indicated the three guys who had accompanied her sprawled out on the furniture. He turned to Becky. "Thank you for letting us use the cottage. We'll tidy up before we leave and I'll send you some money for rent when we get home."

"Thanks," said Becky, "but there's no need. I still owe you for the train ticket."

Blake smiled.

"We'll call it quits then shall we?"

Becky held out her hand and Blake shook it.

"Deal," he said.

"Not quite," answered Becky. "You still owe me a phone."

"How about we all meet in The Black Bull tonight? We can have a bite to eat together before we go."

Both girls nodded. Ben's eyes lit up when Sally agreed to be there.

"It's our night off but I guess me and Becky could swing by."

As they left Sally shouted back, "By the way. The word in the village now is you're starting a cult here. It's going to play havoc with the house prices."

Everyone was there when Sally and Becky got to The Black Bull. A few of the regulars watched closely as the girls sat with the ever growing band of strangers. Ben jumped up and pulled Sally's chair out for her as she sat.

"See, he's a proper gentleman," whispered Becky.

"You do know he's a werewolf and can hear every word you say, Bex?"

Becky looked up at Ben and he smiled at her then took the seat next to Sally. In the middle of the table was a small phone sized box. Blake pushed it closer to Becky.

"With my apologies," he said.

They all chatted happily while they ate, and no mention was made about their supernatural world. Anybody eaves dropping would have simply heard tales of drunken nights, holidays and how politicians and the mainstream media had lost the plot during the Covid crisis.

When it was time for Blake and the rest to start their journey home the mood dulled a little.

"You're very welcome to come with us, Sally," said Blake. "Pack life isn't as bad as you've been led to believe."

"To be honest, I can see that now," said Sally. "If I was to become part of a pack it'd be an honour to be part of yours. But I think I'll stay here. Popwood is a nice place." She looked around. "There's some quirky characters here I admit but I guess I almost fit in." She laughed but she could feel a tightening bond with Popwood and the people who lived there.

"Well come and visit sometime."

Sally held out her arms and gave Blake a hug.

"Thank you. I will."

"Can I walk you home?"

Sally turned to see Ben standing close by. His confidence had obviously grown and he was back to the confident werewolf she'd seen fighting side by side with his alpha back at the lab. His return to normal made her smile.

"I should really make sure Becky gets home," she replied.

"I'll be okay," said Becky, "Kiera is coming to my house with me. I want their address in my little book. You go with Ben."

Ben's smile was as wide as she'd ever seen a smile get.

"Oh, okay," she said. A little nervousness creeping into her own voice.

Thay all hugged and said their goodbyes with promises to visit when they could. Becky and the others walked around The Green to the left while Sally and Ben went right towards the village shop.

"It's a nice little village you have here," said Ben as they walked.

"It has it's little peculiarities, but I like it."

"You live on your own then I guess."

"Yep. Just me." There was an awkward little silence then Sally asked, "How about you?"

"Me too."

There was another silence.

"You know you really should come and visit sometime," added Ben suddenly.

He spoke quickly as if he'd been trying to think of the best way to say it and had decided to just blurt it out in case his courage deserted him.

Sally smiled.

"We'll see," she said. "Well, this is me."

She stopped outside the shop under the streetlamp.

"I guess I'll see you later then."

"Yeah. I'll give Blake a call and arrange something."

Ben held out his hand. There was a little piece of paper in his fingers. There was something scribbled on it.

"My number. In case you want to phone me instead of Blake."

Sally took it from him, feeling a little embarrassed. Her wolf stirred but there was no concern. Her wolf was comfortable with the situation.

"Err… Your eyes are turning orange, Sally."

"Yeah sorry. They do that sometimes. Usually when I get angry."

"Oh. Are you angry now?"

"No." Sally shook her head.

There was another awkward silence then Sally stepped back.

"Well, I should go," she said. "Thank you for walking me home. Bye."

Sally turned and walked quickly up the stairs. Once she was inside her flat she leaned back against the closed door, rubbed her face with her hands and puffed out a big breath in relief. She crept to the window and peered out. Ben was still standing by the lamp post looking up. He saw her before she could step away again and waved. She waved back at him. He turned and made his way back across The Green to meet the others, looking back over his shoulder a few times. She watched him all the way across to Becky's house. Once Kiera came out they all disappeared along the side of the building and through the bushes towards the Old Mill warehouse.

Sally crawled onto her bed and lay there, staring up at the ceiling. She still had the piece of paper that Ben had given her in her hand. She looked at the number. Taking out her phone she stored the number in her contacts before putting it down on the bedside table. She stared at the ceiling once more.

"Oh, what the hell," she said to herself then sat up, picked up her phone and sent a text to the new contact.

'Hi it's Sally. This is my number just in case you need it."

Chapter 22

The weekend arrived. Sally was more nervous about this night than any other in her life. She helped Becky close up the bar after work as usual then they both left quietly through the back door. Becky shouldered her rucksack, which she had packed with a change of clothes for Sally, just in case, a blanket, a torch, a few snacks and a flask of coffee. In Becky's own words, "If I end up spending the night in the woods I want to wake up to a coffee." They made their way across the carpark then slipped into the south woods. The midsummer sun had not long set and there was still a little light from a beautiful sunset orange sky.

"You can still change your mind, Bex."

"Are you kidding? I've waited all week for this. I want to meet her, Sal."

Moving deeper into the woods they found the clearing where the barbeque party had started this whole adventure. The light from the sky seeped through the trees and gently lit the area. They stood in the middle of the open space facing each other.

"Are you ready?" asked Sally.

Becky nodded.

"While I'm shifting don't try to help. Stay away. Ignore the sound of my bones breaking, once it starts I can't stop it anyway. Once she's out stand still. Wait for her to come to you."

Becky nodded again. Sally thought her friend looked a little nervous but there was no fear there, just a little nervous excitement.

Sally started to undress, and Becky turned away. Sally appreciated the privacy. Closing her eyes she let her wolf come to the surface then fell to her knees as her body began to change. Bones cracked and broke, some grew larger and thicker, some got smaller, but they all changed shape. Fur started to push through her skin and large claws grew from her fingers and toes. Her mouth and nose enlarged, growing outwards as huge teeth and elongated canines sprouted. Sickening crunching and grinding sounds could be heard from her hips and other major joints as her whole skeleton transformed. Strong, powerful muscles formed all over her body, thickening her neck, shoulders, torso, legs and paws. She was used to the pain but she still howled because of it. Her fur grew longer. Different shades of light browns and ginger fur were then highlighted with flashes of golden blonde around her head and down her neck. Sally collapsed onto the ground then remembered no more. *Her wolf was out.*

She lay there for a moment, panting from the ferociousness of her shift from human to wolf. Opening her eyes she sniffed the air. There was a familiar scent nearby. She sat up and looked around. The human was standing perfectly still, just staring.

She sniffed again. It was the friendly human. Part of the pack now. She got to her feet and walked slowly towards the girl who lowered herself to her knees. She sniffed the offered hand then nudged it with the top of her head. She felt fingers running through her fur, fingernails scratching at that spot just behind her ear she could never quite reach. The girl was speaking softly. Gently words, reassuring and kind words. She closed her eyes and leaned against the human. The girl fell sideways. Laying down beside the human she rolled onto her side and felt an arm around her. A warm body pressed against hers and she experienced the pressure of a hug for the first time. She lay like that for a few minutes but her hunger and the instinct to run and hunt was urging her to get moving. She got up and sniffed the air. There was prey close by. The human's hand fell away as she trotted out of the clearing and into the woods. She soon found her small prey. Two rabbits tried to flee but she was too fast, too experienced. She ate one quickly. The other she picked up and took back to the clearing where the human was still waiting. She dropped the rabbit on the ground at the girl's feet then jumped up onto a large rock nearby. She watched the last of the sunset fade away then howled gently into the night air. The girl appeared beside her and she felt a hand on her back, once again fingers ran through her fur. She jumped down from the rock and walked on a few paces before looking back at her new pack member. The girl seemed to understand and followed her.

Stay Away

***

Becky couldn't believe how beautiful Sally was as a wolf. She had seen her in the lab, but out here in the forest the wolf walking beside her was simply magnificent. She had never really been the type to walk in the woods by herself. At night the blackness of the trees was too scary, but walking through them with a huge wolf by her side as a protector made her feel safe in a way she could never have imagined.

They walked on and were soon down by the river. Becky sat on a little rock and dabbled her feet in the cold water while the wolf splashed about trying to grab some fish. To Becky the wolf could have been playing, pausing occasionally to sniff the air and check the surroundings.

The night was warm but the breeze off the water had turned chilly.

"Hey!" shouted Becky and the wolf looked towards her. "Shall we head back?"

The wolf was too busy in the water and pounced onto another fish.

"Sally!" she shouted but the wolf didn't respond.

Of course, she thought, Sally wasn't the wolf's name. They were one and the same, yes, but they were two different personalities. Sally had never mentioned her wolf's name. Maybe she didn't have one. Becky's chest tightened with sadness. An animal as beautiful as this deserved a special name, but what? She thought for a while. Something wild? No. Something beautiful, something connected to Sally. She googled the name on her phone. Sally meant Princess. She couldn't use that. She searched for versions of the name and there it was, Sadie. She said it a few times out loud while watching the wolf. Yes, Sadie seemed to fit.

She whistled and the wolf looked up. Becky waved her arms and motioned her to come closer. The wolf walked out of the water towards her. She knew what was about to happen a second before it did but there was no time to prevent it. The wolf shook herself and river water sprayed in all directions. Becky got the full force of it and the sudden cold water shower took her breath away. The wolf just stared, and Becky burst into laughter.

"I think I'm going to have trouble with you," she said, ruffling the wet fur on the wolf's head with her hand.

She placed her hands either side of its head and turned its face toward her own.

"I don't know if you have a name already but I'm going to call you Sadie. Is that okay? Sadie?"

Sadie looked intently and put her head on one side.

"Sadie? Would you like that name?"

Becky couldn't tell if Sadie agreed but decided it was going to stick. She got up off the rock and brushed as much of the water off her jeans as she could.

Stay Away

"Come on, Sadie. It's time to head back."

She started to walk away from the river and Sadie followed and was soon walking by Becky's side, constantly sniffing and looking either side. Becky guessed Sadie was on guard duty.

They made their way back to the clearing. Well, it was Sadie who got them there because Becky had no idea where she was in the dark. By the time they reached Sally's pile of clothes, Sadie was dry. Becky, however, wasn't and her clothes were still cold and wet. She opened the little rucksack she'd brought and pulled out the dry clothes.

"These were for you," she said to Sadie, "once you'd changed back into Sally. But, as you soaked me, I'm going to use them."

She changed quickly and snuggled up with her back to a tree and pulled the blanket around her then poured herself a coffee from the flask. Sadie stared at her.

"Yes I always come prepared. I didn't know if you would change straight back or if we would have to sleep out here for a little while."

Becky patted the ground beside her but Sadie simply sat close by. It looked to Becky as if Sadie was on watch again, looking out into the darkness, listening and sniffing the air for any danger.

She leaned back against the tree, feeling reassured in the safety of her surroundings knowing Sadie was on guard.

Gazing at the wolf, a warm smile spread across her heart, and she whispered to Sadie telling her how beautiful she was. Though sitting in that position was slightly uncomfortable, exhaustion made it easy to ignore. Eventually, Sadie curled up nearby, and Becky slowly drifted off to sleep.

***

Sally was awake early. She sat up quickly and looked around in panic. She spotted Becky lying on the ground, slumped beside a tree, she wasn't moving. Sally's heart almost stopped. She moved slowly towards Becky, not wanting to find what she thought she'd found, not wanting to see Becky's lifeless body covered in the teeth and claw marks from a crazed werewolf monster. Tears well up in her eyes, then Becky mumbled in her sleep. She was alive.

"Oh thank, God," whispered Sally.

She dropped to her knees and breathed out long and slow, not realizing she had been holding her breath. She buried her face in her hands for a moment and then looked up to the sky.

"Thank you, thank you, thank you," she repeated.

She wasn't sure if there was anybody up there looking down on them, but if there was, she was grateful.

Finding her clothes where she'd left them she dressed quickly. The relief at seeing Becky safe and unharmed was like a huge weight being lifted from her shoulders. A quick sniff confirmed there was no human blood anyway. There was a dead rabbit a little way off but if that was the worst thing she was going to find she could live with that.

Becky shuffled about a little for a few minutes while Sally sat and watched her, smiling. Becky yawned and stretched then sat up.

"Oh, morning, Sal."

"Morning. What're you wearing? I thought those clothes were for me."

"They were, until Sadie soaked me when she got out of the river."

"Who's Sadie?" asked Sally.

"Your wolf. I figured she was too beautiful to be nameless. She seemed to like it."

"You gave my wolf a name?" said Sally slowly.

"Sure. Why not? She deserves a good name, and Sadie is a version of Sally, so it kind of fits."

Sally shook her head, smiling and trying to hide a small chuckle.

"I'm guessing you two got on well last night then."

"She was amazing, Sal." Becky's face lit up with an excited smile. "She's the most beautiful wolf I've ever seen." Becky almost did a little dance on the spot. "Okay, she grossed me out by bringing me a dead rabbit for some reason, but yeah, it went well."

"Yeah I seen it." She looked back to where the dead rabbit still lay. "She was sharing her food with a pack member. She's accepted you."

Becky told Sally everything that had happened and, being Becky, didn't leave out any details.

The sun began to break through the trees while the girls talked. It had heat in it already. They let it get a little higher in the sky and Becky repacked her rucksack then put it over her shoulder. They walked into the sunlight until they reached the road then began the walk up the hill into Popwood side by side, the best of friends, as they had been since the day they met.

For the next month Sally concentrated on life in Popwood. Things were normal again. Becky and Sadie enjoyed weekly weekend walks in the woods together. The regular runs for Sadie kept them both happy and Becky never missed an opportunity to be out in the wild with her favourite wolf. The only downside seemed to be Penny's agitation upon her return.

Epilogue

Sally woke to the sound of her phone as usual. Ben's texts hadn't slowed down over the last few weeks. It was a daily occurrence. A 'good morning' message buzzed her phone at 6.00am every day. At first she thought it was sweet. Now, she sometimes wished he would leave it until a more respectable hour. Today she was glad of it. She had some work to do. A magazine had commissioned her to write a two page spread on a burning issue for its readers, that's what they called it anyway. Commissions were hard to come by, so she accepted it with enthusiasm. By 9.00am that enthusiasm had begun to wane. She spent the morning and most of the afternoon working on the article about the difficulties of rural life and why families were being forced to move into towns and cities. Living in Popwood was wonderful but for an aspiring investigative journalist it was a little restrictive to say the least. When late afternoon arrived she needed a walk. She left through the shop but was stopped by a voice before she'd got more than ten feet.

"I've got a surprise for you," said Becky walking across The Green.

"Really? What is it?"

"If I tell you that it wouldn't be a surprise. Come on, it's in The Black Bull."

"I've got work to do, Bex. Remember, the commission?"

"Oh, you can have a break can't you?" Becky grabbed Sally's arm. "Besides, I insist."

The Black Bull was full of the usual regulars and some of the new crop of holiday makers from the cottages.

"Just through here," said Becky and pointed Sally towards the back room.

"Oh no, Bex," said Sally. "I know what you are trying to do."

"Do you?" asked Becky.

"Yes. Ben's been texting me for weeks saying how much he misses me and I knew he'd get you involved."

"Don't be silly. Get in there, Sal. There's somebody here to see you."

She pushed Sally forward through the crowd until they reached the back room. The door was closed but it usually was. The room was little used other than for late night dominoes by Old Tom and a few of his friends. Sally was a little irritated that Ben had been smuggled into The Black Bull. The fact it'd been done by Becky was the biggest disappointment. She thought her friend was better than that.

Becky stepped back and let Sally open the door herself. As soon as it cracked open she recognised the scents. Tears flooded into her eyes. She pushed the door open all the way and stood there crying.

"Mam?"

Becky nudged Sally in the back gently and steered her

further into the room. Jasmine was the first one to move, clearly unable to contain her excitement as she ran over and flung her arms around her big sister. Her mam and dad followed. They all stood in the middle of the room in a group hug. No words were needed. The tears said it all.

It was a few minutes before anybody could move or say anything. It was Sally who broke the silence.

"What are you guys doing here?"

Through the sniffles it was her mam who answered.

"One of your friends came to see us," said her mam. "She told us where you were living, and she could arrange for us to see you again."

Sally looked round at Becky.

Becky shook her head. "It wasn't me."

"Who?"

"Kiera," said Becky. "Before she left Popwood I asked her if she could find your family. It wasn't easy. You didn't really give us much to go on."

Sally's dad walked over to Becky and gave her a hug.

"Thank you," he said.

"She's my best friend," said Becky. "It was nothing. Kiera did all the work anyway."

Jasmine wasn't letting go of Sally anytime soon. She looked up at her sister. "Your friend said you'd saved the lives of her whole family."

"She's pretty awesome your sister," said Becky, ruffling

Jasmine's hair. She walked to a table near the window, picked up a package and handed it to Sally. "I got you this too."

Sally removed the wrapping paper slowly and gazed at a canvas print. On a large rock in the middle of a stand of trees stood a wolf with light brown and ginger fur highlighted by blonde flashes over its head and down its neck. Glinting in the moonlight were bright, golden orange eyes.

"I've told you many times you're a beautiful wolf. I thought you should see her."

Sally wrapped her arms tightly around Becky.

"Thanks, Bex."

THE END

Acknowledgements

Thank you to Lesley Eames for all the help and support throughout the Writing Magazine Fiction Writing Course which made this book possible.

Thank you to my youngest daughter, Katie, for believing in me from the very start of my writing journey. Thanks also to my wife, Christine and eldest daughter, Hannah for being there as a sounding board when I was making the decision to publish.

Also, thank you to Alex Davis (Author) and Rebecca Guy (Author) for your help and advice during my self-publishing troubles.

www.ingramcontent.com/pod-product-compliance
Ingram Content Group UK Ltd.
Pitfield, Milton Keynes, MK11 3LW, UK
UKHW041406010425
5259UKWH00022B/173